Charlotte L.H. Papendiek

# Court and Private Life in the Time of Queen Charlotte

Vol. 1

Charlotte L.H. Papendiek

**Court and Private Life in the Time of Queen Charlotte**
*Vol. 1*

ISBN/EAN: 9783337322793

Printed in Europe, USA, Canada, Australia, Japan

Cover: Foto ©Raphael Reischuk / pixelio.de

More available books at **www.hansebooks.com**

# COURT AND PRIVATE LIFE IN THE TIME OF QUEEN CHARLOTTE:

BEING THE JOURNALS OF MRS PAPENDIEK, ASSISTANT KEEPER OF THE WARDROBE AND READER TO HER MAJESTY. EDITED BY HER GRAND-DAUGHTER, MRS VERNON DELVES BROUGHTON

*VOLUME I.*

LONDON: RICHARD BENTLEY & SON, NEW BURLINGTON STREET, PUBLISHERS IN ORDINARY TO HER MAJESTY THE QUEEN

MDCCCLXXXVII.

# PREFACE.

THE manuscript of the memoirs which I now offer to the public came into my hands a few years ago through the death of a relation, and it seemed to me that the record of a life of one so intimately associated as was Mrs. Papendiek with the Court of George III., and of his Queen, Charlotte Sophia, could not fail to have some interest for the general reader.

The long reign of this sovereign was one full of stirring public and political incident, and of much special interest in the matter of art and science, having been prolific in men of note in all branches of artistic learning—men not only of English, but of foreign birth and lineage, many of the latter having been induced to settle in this country by the liberal encouragement given to them by the Royal patron of art.

Painting and music may be said to have been in

their zenith during this reign; and as at the present time everything appertaining to art and science and to the social life of past generations has so great and universal an attraction to readers of all classes, the fact of Mrs. Papendiek's personal acquaintance with most of the professors of those arts then in England, and with other prominent men of her day, will doubtless give to her writings an exceptional interest.

The labour of inditing the following pages was begun by Mrs. Papendiek in the year 1833 with no thought of publication, but simply, at the suggestion of her daughters, as an amusement during a long period of convalescence after serious illness. The pleasure and interest, however, that this retrospect of the events of her own times gave to herself and her immediate family, as time went on, acted as an incentive to her to continue her task, which she did at intervals during several succeeding years, finding also in the exertion necessary to such an undertaking an alleviation of the great sorrow caused by the loss of her two last surviving sons, which overwhelmed her shortly after she commenced her work.

The memoirs were still unfinished at the time of her death, early in 1839, a matter of regret to her surviving grandchildren and other relations and friends.

The narrative having been written from memory after the lapse of a considerable number of years, and quite the early part of it only from hearsay, is necessarily fragmentary. I have endeavoured as much as possible to put the facts of which she tells into chronological order; but as human recollections are always liable to error I crave indulgence on this score should any inaccuracies have crept in, not only in the matter of dates, but also in titles, names, &c., for any errors of which kind I do not hold myself responsible.

Mrs. Papendiek's descriptions, given sometimes with quaint, old-fashioned expressions, of her home at various periods and at different places, of her 'gala' days, and of the various entertainments in which she took part, I have purposely left unaltered and unabridged, as being illustrative of the very primitive style of living in the days of which she writes. Though these descriptions may possibly, on a first impression, appear somewhat trivial and at times almost childish, they would lose the ring of genuineness were they altered or modified.

The intense delight which she evinces in the few

innocent pleasures of her early life, and which she recounts at the age of seventy and more with so much naïveté, forms a curious and, to my way of thinking, a refreshing contrast to the artificial and luxurious condition of the society of our own times, even the young people of the present day being blasés and discontented if some new excitement be not constantly set before them; and the charming reality and personality of Mrs. Papendiek's writing, which would undoubtedly be lost if modernised, will, I trust, serve as apology, should apology be needed, for the simplicity and homeliness of her style.

The earnestness of her character, with the strict sense of duty which pervaded her whole life and was the ruling power of her every action, is evidenced in her story; and this quality, combined with her reverence for religion and simple trust in the goodness of an all-merciful Providence, enabled her to spend the last years of her life in pious resignation to the Divine will, and which, though passed in comparative loneliness, were rich in hope and love.

We, her grandchildren, who recollect her amiable nature and her characteristic energy and activity, can only lament that she did not live to complete the record of her well-spent life, which could not be recounted by others with half the force or fidelity of her own pen.

In their unfinished state, then, I present these reminiscences to the public, trusting in the forbearance of the intelligent and discriminating reader.

A. D. B.

KENSINGTON :
*November* 1886.

# CONTENTS

OF

## THE FIRST VOLUME.

CHAPTER I.



CHAPTER II.

## CHAPTER III.



## CHAPTER IV.



## CHAPTER V.

## CHAPTER IX.



## CHAPTER X.

## CHAPTER XI.

## CHAPTER XII.

M... MACENDIEK AND CHILD

# COURT AND PRIVATE LIFE

## IN THE

# TIME OF QUEEN CHARLOTTE

---

## CHAPTER I.

Early family history—Princess Charlotte Sophia chosen to be wife of George III.—Marriage of the King announced—Life at Mecklenburgh-Strelitz—Marriage by proxy—Journey of the Princess to England—Reception at St. James's Palace—Description of the Princess—The wedding—The King's presents—Different opinions of Mademoiselle Schwellenberg—The coronation—The Lord Mayor's Show—Visit to Mr. Barclay—Lord Bute and Pitt—Visits to the theatres—Mrs. Tunstall as housekeeper—Birth of the Prince of Wales—Installation of Knights of the Garter—Appointments in the royal nursery—Mrs. Albert arrives from Germany—Purchase of 'the Queen's house'—House-warming—Birth of the Duke of York.

It is said that our family are descendants in the direct line of the Alberts of Saxe-Teschen. It may be so; but as we at the present time derive no advantage from that honour, it matters little beyond the satisfaction of knowing that, in searching the pedigree of our ancestors, no blemish was found in the character of any members of the family.

My father, Frederick Albert, was born in the

commercial town of Frankfort on January 28, 1733. He began life in the service of the reigning Duke of Mecklenburgh-Strelitz, and in addition to the situation he held at the Court of the Duke, he farmed the land attached to his house in the suburbs, according to the custom of his country.

In the year 1761, when the Princess Charlotte Sophia, the younger of the two sisters of the reigning Duke, was summoned to be the Queen Consort of his Majesty George III., my father was chosen to accompany her to England. This he at first refused. It grieved him to leave his country and everything dear to him, to begin life a second time among strangers in a foreign land, and with no one to meet his joys or sorrows. The Princess, however, was urgent, and prevailed. She promised much, and added that he should be her constant and confidential attendant.

When King George III. succeeded to the throne of England upon the death of his grandfather, George II., it was considered right that he should seek some lady in marriage who should fulfil all the duties of her exalted position in a manner to satisfy the feelings of the country at large, and at the same time those of a Prince so ardent an admirer of the fair sex as was George III.

Such perfection was not easy to find; but when Colonel Graeme, who had been sent to the various

Courts of Germany on a mission of investigation, reported in strong terms the charms of character and the excellent qualities of mind possessed by the Princess Charlotte, it was at once decided to ask her hand in marriage for the young King.

Her father, the Duke of Mirow, was the second son of the former Duke of Mecklenburgh-Strelitz, whom he succeeded only in 1751, so her early life had been passed in the utmost simplicity, her excellent mother, a member of the ducal house of Saxe-Hilburghausen, having herself superintended the education of her two daughters, instilling every feeling of piety and reverence for religious duties into the minds of her children.[1]

---

[1] The following passage, taken from the *Memoirs of Queen Charlotte*, by John Watkins, LL.D., published in the year 1819, is interesting as showing the manner in which the Princess had been brought up, and the tone of piety which characterised her early education, and which same principles of religion she endeavoured, in after life, to instil into the minds of her own children. 'One of our old poets has observed that " a virtuous court a world to virtue draws "—an assertion which is unquestionably true to a much greater extent than is generally imagined, even by those who take the closest and most correct view of the moral effects of great examples. When the Duchess Dowager of Mecklenburgh was forming the minds of her children and attending to the manners of her household, she had no prospect of any splendid alliances for her daughters; and it is certain that she neither indulged such ideas herself nor suffered them to be encouraged in conversation. Totally free from worldly policy, she regulated the whole system of her maternal government by the principle of religious duty, in a pious conformity to the direction of Providence. Thus laying her own foundation of happiness in the deepest humility, and feeling the benefit of it in the calm tranquillity of her passions amidst many severe trials, she was anxious that those in whose welfare she was most tenderly interested should experience the same blessing.'

The King announced to his Council in July 1761, according to the usual form, his intentions respecting his marriage with this Princess, and Lord Hardwicke was despatched to Mecklenburgh to solicit her hand in his Majesty's name. He was received with every honour that the little Court was capable of showing him, and returned within a month after having completed all the necessary preliminaries, well pleased with his mission.

A few weeks only were allowed to make the necessary preparations. The Princess had learnt that my father visited intimately in the family of my mother, which consisted of herself, a brother, and her widowed mother. Her Serene Highness, who was of a disposition founded on religious and moral principle, was anxious that no thought of wrong should remain after her departure either against herself or any of her suite; and she advised my father under these circumstances to marry this young person. This he refused under the feeling that it never had been his intention, which they knew, and that now he should consider it imprudent. This determination the Princess could not reconcile to her mind. She expostulated, advised, and again prevailed. At length my father consented and was married. It appears hard that no situation could be found to take my mother in the suite to England; but that being the case, she was satisfied to remain with her family till my father could find a proper opportunity to send for her.

The *cortège* arrived that was to conduct Princess Charlotte to England: the Duchess of Ancaster, the Duchess of Hamilton, Ladies of the Bedchamber; Mrs. Tracey, Bedchamber Woman; Earl Harcourt, Proxy for the King; and General Graeme, to conduct the whole escort; Lord Anson being appointed commander of the squadron. They were magnificently received, and were entertained with the greatest splendour and pomp.

[Dr. Doran, in his ' Lives of the Queens of England of the House of Hanover,' quotes the following description of the ceremony of the marriage by proxy from Mrs. Stuart, daughter-in-law of Lord Bute, who left the following note of the early life of the Princess :

' Her Majesty described her life at Mecklenburgh as one of extreme retirement. She dressed only *en robe de chambre*, except on Sundays, on which day she put on her best gown, and after service, which was very long, took an airing in a coach and six, attended by guards and all the state she could muster. She had not " dined " at table at the period I am speaking about. One morning her eldest brother, of whom she seems to have stood in great awe, came to her room in company with the Duchess, her mother. . . . In a few minutes the folding doors flew open to the saloon, which she saw splendidly illuminated; and then appeared a table, two cushions, and everything prepared for a wedding. Her brother then gave her his hand, and, leading her in, used his favourite expression: " Allons, ne fais pas l'enfant, tu vas être Reine d'Angleterre." Mr. Drummond then advanced. They knelt down. The ceremony, whatever it was, proceeded. She was laid upon the sofa, upon which he placed his foot; and they all embraced her, calling her " la Reine."']

My father had been introduced to General Graeme on his first visit to Strelitz, and was now presented by him to the rest of the party, who were delighted with him. He was a very handsome man both in face and person; he was of elegant and fascinating manner; he had the knick-knackery of fashion about him; he spoke French well, and was very companionable. He, with the Mesdemoiselles Schwellenberg and Hagedorn, were the only attendants to the Princess from her own country.

At the end of August 1761 they set out on their route. A most dreadful storm of thunder overtook them, and the lightning fired several trees of an avenue through which they had to pass. They arrived nevertheless in safety at Cuxhaven, and embarked on board the yachts, in the midst of every heartfelt and dutiful attention, shown to the Princess both by high and low, male and female, for she was generally and greatly beloved.

They were nine days at sea and in the greatest danger, the voyage being usually accomplished in about three days. The Princess, however, did not lose her gaiety through all this trying time, nor did she suffer from sea-sickness, but sang to her harpsichord, leaving the door of her cabin open, so as to encourage her companions in their misery.

Instead of going on to land at Greenwich, where everything was prepared for the reception of the Princess, Lord Anson thought it better to make for the nearest port, and ran into Harwich, where they remained at anchor for the night. This was on Sunday, the 6th of September, and landing the next morning they travelled to Lord Abercorn's at Witham, in Essex, where they rested, and the following day continued their journey towards London. At Romford, after being conducted by Mr. Dutton to his residence, where an elegant *déjeuner* was provided, the Princess, with her suite, entered their travelling equipages, and proceeded on their route. They entered London by the suburb of Mile End, and passing through Whitechapel, which could not have given the strangers a very promising idea of the beauty or grandeur of the metropolis, or the Princess a very exalted notion of the people over whom she had come to reign (for that was at that time, as it is now, one of the most squalid and dirty quarters of London), they continued along the New Road to Hyde Park, which they crossed, and thence down Constitution Hill to St. James's Palace, where the King then resided. His Majesty, surrounded by his brothers, received his bride at the small private garden gate, in the Friary, and led her through the garden, up the flight of steps to the Palace.

It is said that at the moment of her reception she was on the point of kneeling to the very far from handsome old Duke of Grafton, as the crimson cushion that was placed for her seemed to point that way, when the King stepped forward and embraced her. How great the reaction to her overwrought feelings must have been is easy to imagine, and the pale face and trembling lips of which one hears and reads must have greatly brightened up when she found herself in the arms of one so handsome, so elegant, and so fascinating as was our gracious King, George III., at that time.

General Graeme, in his lively report of the Princess's most amiable qualities, spoke only moderately of her personal beauty. Yet it would seem that the King was somewhat struck with disappointment on first beholding her. The perilous travel she had undergone, the loss of her mother, who died just at this time, the quitting a happy home, never to return to it, had naturally faded the cheerful bloom of a youthful countenance, not to mention the anxiety her Royal Highness must have felt in coming among strangers on so trying an occasion.

She was certainly not a beauty, but her countenance was very expressive and showed extreme intelligence; not tall, but of a slight, rather pretty figure ; her eyes bright and sparkling with good humour and vivacity; her mouth large, but filled with white and even teeth ; and her hair really beautiful. On the journey, the ladies who were with her were very anxious that she should dress it more in the English fashion, and curl it. She, however, would not hear of it, but preferred her own style of *toupet*, as it was called, saying that she thought it looked as well as that of any of the ladies sent to fetch her, and adding: 'If the King should desire me to wear a periwig I will do it ; but till he expresses a wish upon the subject, my hair shall remain as it is.'

[Walpole says of her that 'she looked sensible, cheerful, and remarkably genteel;' but Croker's opinion of her charms is, though amusing, certainly not flattering. 'Queen Charlotte,' he says, 'had always been, if not ugly, at least ordinary, but in her later years her want of personal charms became, of course, less observable, and it used to be said that she was grown better looking. I one day said something to this effect to Colonel Disbrowe, her Chamberlain. "Yes," replied he, "I do think the *bloom* of her ugliness is going off."' Dr. Doran also observes that, 'Northcote subsequently declared that Queen Charlotte's plainness was not a vulgar, but an elegant plainness. The artist saw another grace in her. As he looked at Reynolds's portrait of her, fan in hand, Northcote, remembering the sitting, exclaimed, "Lord, how she held that fan!"'—ED.]

In the Palace the Princess Dowager of Wales, the King's mother, and his sisters met Princess Charlotte. After the usual ceremonies of introduction they conducted their *protégée* to her apartments, where her elegant and magnificent trousseau was displayed. The assistant dressers were now brought forward— Miss Laverocke, an Englishwoman, and Miss Pascal, a German. The latter had been with the King's mother, on which account our Queen never liked her, looking upon her as a spy upon her actions. She was, however, a cheerful, clever person, executing her business with diligence and punctuality, and appearing to disregard any opinion that might be formed of her.

In the apartment termed wardrobe, the different people appointed to make the wedding attire were in readiness to fit on the essential parts of it, under the superintendence of her Grace of Ancaster, the then Mistress of the Robes. This very necessary trouble to the bride being ended, the travelling party took leave of their charge to repair to their respective homes in order to prepare for their attendance at the wedding in the evening. The parting was equally painful to all, for they had mutually endeared themselves to each other during their long and dangerous journey.

Dinner was now served ; the party at table consisting only of the family, the four pages to the Princess being in attendance. In the course of the day she recruited, and resumed her cheerfulness, and that peculiar sweetness of manner which she possessed, and which combined with her interesting and expressive countenance now seemed to touch the heart of the King ; and when they separated to dress for the wedding he assured his family that he already felt a great affection for her.

At about ten o'clock the procession entered the Royal Chapel, the Princess being led to the altar by the Duke of York and Prince William. The Archbishop of Canterbury performed the ceremony, the bride being given away by the Duke of Cumberland. Ten bridesmaids attended her, who carried her train, which was of purple velvet, lined with ermine, the rest of her dress being of white satin and silver gauze.

[Horace Walpole says : 'The Queen was in white and silver ; an endless mantle of violet-coloured velvet, lined with ermine, and attempted to be fastened on her shoulder by a bunch of large pearls, dragged itself and almost the rest of her clothes half-way down her waist. On her head was a beautiful little tiara of diamonds; a diamond necklace, and a stomacher of diamonds, worth threescore thousand pounds, which she is to wear at the Coronation, too.'—ED.]

The bridesmaids were: the Ladies Sarah Lennox, Caroline Russell, Caroline Montagu, Harriot Bentinck, Anne Hamilton, Essex Kerr, Elizabeth Keppel, Louisa Greville, Elizabeth Harcourt, and Susan Fox-Strangways, who were all dressed in Court robes of white and silver.

The King's particular present to his bride was a pair of bracelets, consisting of six rows of picked pearls as large as a full pea; the clasps—one his picture, the other his hair and cypher, both set round with diamonds; necklace with diamond cross; earrings, and the additional ornaments of the fashion of the day. Also a diamond hoop ring of a size not to stand higher than the wedding ring, to which it was to serve as a guard. On that finger the Queen never allowed herself to wear any other in addition, although fashion at times almost demanded it.

The likeness of the King in miniature, done exquisitely beautiful for the coin, by our valued friend, Jeremiah Meyer, was set as a ring, and given also to her Majesty to wear on the little finger of the right hand on this auspicious day.

Finding that my father was to be placed in the chapel close in sight of the Queen, Mademoiselle Schwellenberg desired that herself and Mademoiselle Hagedorn might also have accommodation, which was immediately granted, and they were placed next in inferior rank to the maids of honour.

The ceremony of the marriage being ended, and the State attendants of the Queen having all been introduced to her in public, their Majesties now returned to the apartments, on their way to the grand supper which had been prepared for all the wedding company. This the bridal Queen, from excessive fatigue, requested that she might be excused from attending. The King consented willingly, but led her to the table, as it were, to welcome the guests, and then back to her dressing-room, to be disencumbered of the brilliant parts of her dress, while a supper was prepared in a private room for the King and Queen alone, on whom my father was now desired to attend. This opportunity introduced him to the King in the most favourable manner; and his Majesty, who was always sincere in his friendships, never swerved from the attachment he at once formed for my father, confirming it after his death by his liberal allowance to my mother.

We now view the royal couple as a married

pair—the one mindful of every delicate respect and attention, every hour becoming more affectionately attached to his Queen, who, on her part, was punctually strict in every duty, neglectful not of the least trifle that could convey to the King her strong feeling of gratitude towards him, with increasing love for his peculiar kindness to her under many considerations.

Among the various public duties of receiving congratulations, addresses, holding drawing-rooms, &c., they failed not to form such domestic arrangements as would give comfort to themselves and their household.

Mademoiselle Schwellenberg, who had been with the Queen from her infancy, and who was a shrewd, ambitious woman, now assumed to herself a new character—that of female mentor to the Queen. She was to be styled Madame, as a distinction from her companion; her apartments were to join those of the Queen, and no one was to be admitted to her Majesty's presence without first having been introduced to Madame. The Queen at the time of her marriage was only seventeen, and with some princesses this line of conduct might have been highly proper, but with our Queen totally unnecessary. She was a young woman of strong understanding, superior judgment, sound principle, and of considerable experience. Her temper was quick and rather warm, but softened by an excellent heart, and a benevolent and kind disposition. She was pious and devout in religion, and alive to every moral and social duty; charitable without bounds, and her charities were directed in a way to convey the good she intended to individuals, of whatever rank they might be, totally disregarding any trouble it was necessary to take to achieve the desired end.

In Lord Chesterfield's correspondence the follow - ing passage occurs, showing the opinion that he, with many others, had formed of Queen Charlotte's good qualities: 'You seem not to know the character of the Queen; here it is: she is a good woman, a good wife, a tender mother, and an unmeddling queen. The King loves her as a woman, but, I verily believe, has never spoke one word to her about politics.'

By some unaccountable forbearance, the inter- ference of Madame Schwellenberg was never done away with, though many ladies expostulated with the Queen upon her presumption. Her prevention of the intrusion of visitors may in some instances have saved the Queen much trouble, but in others it had the effect of disturbing, if not of destroying, friend- ship, and with the Duchess of Ancaster, who was high- minded, it was quite an unnecessary interference.

By imperceptible degrees, Madame brought her- self to the head of the wardrobe department, to the regulation of the persons therein employed, and to the regulation also of the expenditure, as far as was to be defrayed by the Queen's private allowance. She certainly kept up from first to last a becoming dignity in the system, but the discipline was severe, and the power she usurped to herself was unjust towards the companion with whom she had embarked, who was a placid, amiable, ladylike woman. Madame Schwellenberg no longer dressed the Queen, but stood by while others performed the task, sometimes of difficulty, which her presence did not ameliorate. My father was a silent observer of what was going on, and greatly regretted it, fearing the consequences. It is natural that with this feeling he did not cultivate any compatriotic friendship for her. Mr. Nicolay, a German, from the Princess Dowager's establishment, and one of the four appointed pages to the Queen, a clever and excellent man, was regarded by Madame as a gentleman to be preferred; while a little jealousy, amid much caprice, no doubt lurked in her mind towards my father. She must have had great influence over the mind of the Queen, for the four sons of Mr. Nicolay were amply provided for through the intercession of Madame, while the favour asked by my father, that my brother should be placed at the Charter House, was persistently denied him.

What my father expected did occur within a few years. The strides of Madame were too great. The

King desired that she should be dismissed, and return to Germany upon an allowance suitable to her position in that country. Finding that this intention made the Queen uneasy, not so much from sorrow at parting with her, as from regret that so unpleasant a circumstance should have happened, the King revoked his determination, upon these conditions, that she should not resist his commands, nor influence the Queen's mind upon any subject, that she should share the labours of her place equally with her companion, and infringe upon no regulations unconnected with her immediate appointment. This remonstrance, given by the King in the presence of his mother, hurt the Queen very sensibly; and I fear that at times through life the overbearing disposition of this woman did disturb the harmony of the circle, although the check given did, in some measure, put her on her guard.[1]

[1] Dr. John Watkins in his *Memoirs of Queen Charlotte* says of Madame Schwellenberg that 'she was a well-educated and highly accomplished woman, extremely courteous in her manner, much respected by all the domestics of the royal household, and devotedly attached to the illustrious family with whom she lived, who, in their turn, entertained for her the sincerest affection. Madame Schwellenberg had been, however, most cruelly and wantonly held up to public ridicule by a profligate wit, whose delight lay in ribaldry, as a woman of a sordid disposition, than which nothing could be more opposite to her real character, for she was ever ready to oblige all who applied to her for assistance; and though, like her royal mistress, she chose to do good by stealth, her charities were very extensive.'

This opinion of the character of Madame Schwellenberg does not quite coincide with that of Mrs. Papendiek, or of her father. Mr. Albert, whose views are, however, corroborated by Miss Burney, who was

We will now retrace our steps, and say that the next public ceremony after the wedding, on September 8, 1761, was the coronation, on the 22nd of the same month. The Queen was far from well, with a nervous pain in her face and teeth ; and she wished my father to be placed so that she could see him, which was done. Seats were also provided in the Abbey for her Majesty's German dressers.

No particular private anecdote is attached to the spectacle, which was magnificent. The Princess Dowager, with her sons and daughters, and the suitable State attendants appeared first in procession, distinct from that of the young King and Queen, who were attended by the beauties of the Court of both sexes.

The church service was imposing. The sermon

intimately associated with her for many years of her life. In the *Diary and Letters of Madame D'Arblay*, her colleague, Madame Schwellenberg, is constantly mentioned as being of a disagreeable nature, and as being difficult to live with. One passage which I will quote shows clearly the terms upon which they lived together : 'Mrs. Schwellenberg was very ill. She declined making tea, and put it into the hands of the General. I had always kept back from that office, as well as from presiding at the table, that I might keep the more quiet, and be permitted to sit silent ; which, at first, was a repose quite necessary to my depressed spirits, and which, as they grew better, I found equally necessary to keep off the foul hands of Jealousy and Rivality in my colleague, who, apparently, never wishes to hear my voice but when we are *tête-à-tête*, and then never is in good humour when it is at rest. I could not, however, see this feminine occupation in masculine hands, and not, for shame, propose taking it upon myself. The General (Budé) readily relinquished it, and I was fain to come forth and do the honours.'

was by Archbishop Secker; the music by what we now call the old masters, though the modern of that day, Dr. Arne and Dr. Boyce, not to omit the inimitable Handel.

When their Majesties took the Holy Communion, after the ceremony of the coronation, the King, just before going up to the table, whispered to the Archbishop to inquire if he should not divest himself of his crown. Being surprised at the question, and not knowing what was the custom upon such an occasion, he, in turn, whispered the question to Bishop Pearce, one of those dignitaries who were taking part in the service, but he was equally at a loss as to what answer to give. The King therefore decided the matter for himself, and laid aside the crown, feeling that humility best became such an act of devotion.

The next public exhibition was that of the Lord Mayor's Show, followed by a dinner and a ball, to which the King and Queen were invited, and went. The Queen went to see the show pass, to the house of the great Quaker firm, Barclay & Co. Madame Schwellenberg and my father accompanied the Queen, her other.ladies having to go in procession to the Guildhall.

When their Majesties arrived at Temple Bar the usual form of opening the gates to Royalty was gone through ; and at the east end of St. Paul's Churchyard they received an address, read by the head scholar of Christ's Hospital School.

The young Queen made herself most popular at Mr. Barclay's, accepting the attentions of his daughters and grandchildren with the most amiable condescension, he having done all in his power to receive his royal guests in a fitting manner, and to show the honour and respect in which he held them.

[An amusing account of this visit is given by Dr. Doran, who says: 'Robert Barclay, the only surviving son of the author of the same name, who wrote the celebrated "Apology for the Quakers," was an octogenarian, who had entertained in the same house two Georges before he had given welcome to the third George and his Queen Charlotte. The hearty old man, without abandoning Quaker simplicity, went a little beyond it in order to do honour to the young Queen, and he hung his balcony and rooms with a brilliant crimson damask, that must have scattered blushes on all who stood near—particularly on the cheeks of the crowds of " Friends " who had assembled within the house to do honour to their Sovereigns. How the King—and he was at the time a very handsome young monarch—fluttered all the female Friends present, and set their tuckers in agitation, may be guessed from the fact that he kissed them all round, and right happy were they to be so greeted. The Queen smiled with dignity, her consort laughed and clapped his hands, and when they had passed into another room, the King's young brothers followed the example, and in a minute had all the young Quakeresses in their arms—nothing loth. Those were unceremonious days, and " a kiss all round " was a pleasant solemnity, which was undergone with alacrity even by a Quakeress.

'In the apartment to which the King and Queen had retired the latter was waited on by a youthful granddaughter of Mr. Barclay, who kissed the royal hand with much grace, but would not kneel to do so, a resolute observance of consistent principle which made the young Queen smile. Later in the day, when Mr. Barclay's daughters served the Queen with tea, they handed it to the ladies-in-waiting, who presented it kneeling to their Sovereign—a form which Rachel and Rebecca would never have submitted to. From the windows of this house, which was exactly opposite Bow Church, the Queen and consort witnessed the Lord Mayor's procession pass on its way to Westminster, and had the patience to wait for its return.'—ED.]

The Princess of Wales, the King's mother, was also a guest at Barclay's, and watched the procession with her son and daughter-in-law, and after the show had passed, and returned again, the State carriages arrived to take up the royal party. The Queen sat in a State coach with the King, the Duchesses of Ancaster and Hamilton occupying the back seat.

The King had his eyes opened upon this occasion to the unpopularity of Lord Bute, and to the measures that had led to the resignation of Pitt (shortly afterwards created Earl of Chatham), which took place almost immediately after his Majesty's accession; for while the populace received him almost with indifference, and Lord Bute with hisses and execrations, Pitt made almost a triumphal entry into the City.

[Lord Macaulay, in his essay on the Earl of Chatham, describes this incident in the following words : 'Soon after his (Pitt's) resignation came the Lord Mayor's Day. The King and the Royal Family dined at Guildhall. Pitt was one of the guests. The young Sovereign, seated by his bride in his State coach, received a remarkable lesson. He was scarcely noticed. All eyes were fixed on the fallen minister ; all acclamations directed to him. The streets, the balconies, the chimney tops, burst into a roar of delight as his chariot passed by. The ladies waved their handkerchiefs from the windows. The common people clung to the wheels, shook hands with the footmen, and even kissed the horses. Cries of " No Bute !" " No Newcastle Salmon !" were mingled with the shouts of " Pitt for ever !" When Pitt entered Guildhall, he was welcomed by loud huzzas and clapping of hands, in which the very magistrates of the City joined. Lord Bute, in the meantime, was hooted and pelted through Cheapside, and would, it was thought, have been in some danger, if he had not taken the precaution of surrounding his carriage with a strong bodyguard of boxers. Many persons blamed the conduct of Pitt on this occasion as disrespectful to the King. Indeed, Pitt himself owned that he had done wrong. He was led into this error, as he was afterwards led into more serious errors, by the influence of his turbulent and mischievous brother-in-law, Temple.'—ED.]

On alighting, the Lord Mayor and Lady Mayoress received their illustrious visitors. The whole affair was well conducted, to the entire approbation of the royal party and of the public, and no accident happened.

My father was the acting attendant upon the Queen at the dinner. Her amiable and interesting behaviour, first at Barclay's and secondly at the Guildhall, endeared her to everyone present.

The Queen announced her intention of attending the theatre once a week, but their Majesties, later on, greatly increased this number of visits. They attended Drury Lane Theatre first on November 26, when the Queen was requested to choose the piece to be performed. She selected, 'Rule a Wife, and have a Wife.' Not long after they visited Covent Garden in State, when the King, with a sense of humour, bespoke in return, 'The Merry Wives of Windsor.'

No other public days occurred of any note. The Drawing-room on New Year's Day was very fully attended, and on January 18, 1762, when the first of her Majesty's birthdays was kept, the court was crowded to excess, and the magnificence indescribable.

It now became necessary, among other arrangements, to make some settlement on my father, and it was found difficult to place him. It was, however, decided that his stipend should be the same as that of the pages, with rooms in St. James's Palace for himself and his attendant, and also at the Lodge at Richmond, that he might always remain near the Queen.

A few new appointments were made by the Queen, especially among her lady attendants, and all soon settled down quietly and satisfactorily.

['When some persons expressed surprise,' says Dr. Doran, 'at the Queen having named Lady Northumberland one of the ladies of her bedchamber, Lady Townshend said, " Quite right. The Queen knows no English ; Lady Northumberland will teach her the vulgar tongue!"'—ED.]

My father now began to think about my mother coming over to join him, but on inquiry he found that her approaching confinement would make it difficult to manage before that event took place, and afterwards it would be too late in the season. In those days the accommodation for passengers on board the packets was very different to the convenience of the present time, added to which we were at war. The Queen also was in the same condition, and my father knew full well that, whenever the event should happen he would be required not to leave his attendance even for a moment.

This state of things being fully explained to my mother, she was satisfied to remain, as it were, a second time with her family, and to enjoy for a little longer the pleasures of a home to which, having once left, she would probably never return.

During the summer she gave birth to a little boy, whom the King desired should be named George; the usual gifts being transmitted, and many kindnesses shown.

After the King's birthday on June 4, upon which occasion the Queen appeared in the greatest splendour, the family removed for a few weeks to Richmond.

There Mrs. Tunstall was housekeeper, and her husband had the care and direction of the grounds and outbuildings connected with her appointment. They were people of property; both of them suited to their employments, and more than usually loyal.

The Queen at once felt the comfort of Mrs. Tunstall's judicious regulations; and so fond did her Majesty become of her amiable housekeeper, that she was frequently called to the Queen's workroom to assist in works of fancy, and to relate her method of managing the royal establishment, according to English customs. Her Majesty desired Madame Schwellenberg to make no alterations whatever in the existing arrangements, which did not conduce to friendship between those ladies.

Mrs. Tunstall's house was open to all belonging to the household. Miss Hagedorn was at home there, and my father was welcomed with hospitable feeling that soon ripened into a friendship which ended only at death.

Betty Snoswell was the Queen's housemaid at the age of nineteen, and so admirably were all things ordered that this young creature never either neglected or made a mistake in her business. She was in the same capacity through life, and attended at the Queen's death. His Majesty George IV. then pensioned her at 100*l.* a year with apartments. The other female servants were: housemaids, three; laundrymaids, two, and a helper; eight guineas a year, and 25*l.* a year for each to Mrs. Tunstall for their board and washing. In the course of time these wages were raised to ten guineas; but no alteration was ever made in the arrangements, as the Queen's expressions of approbation at Mrs. Tunstall's *ménage* remained the same as at first.

The family now left this happy retreat for St. James's, where, on August 12, 1762, the Queen gave birth to her first child, the Prince of Wales. On the same day the immense riches taken in a Spanish galleon passed by St. James's to the Bank. All was joy, merriment, and gladness in London.

On September 13 the Queen attended the Chapel Royal to offer the usual thanksgiving of women after childbirth. The ceremony of christening his Royal Highness the Prince of Wales, which took place at St. James's Palace, was attended with every circumstance of splendour. The cradle upon which the infant lay was covered with a magnificent drapery of Brussels lace; the attire of her Majesty, as well as of the guests and attendants, was also of great magnificence, and the whole scene was most interesting.

On the 21st of the same month the installation as Knights of the Garter of Prince William, afterwards Duke of Gloucester, and of the Earl of Bute took place at Windsor. Being the first of these ceremonies after the accession of George III. unusual pomp was displayed upon the occasion.

My father associated with Messrs. Nicolay and Chapman, and found it agreeable to visit their families. They, as well as Messrs. White and Weybrow, were pages, and waited two together every alternate fortnight.

Mrs. Chapman, the wife of the second named, was now appointed nurse, to conduct the nursery, and to see that all under her were vigilant and faithful. She was a fine active woman, and it may be truly said that while she lived, about twelve years, everything was well done, with an affection supported by truth and sincerity. Her daughter, Miss Chapman, was appointed sempstress to the young Prince, which appointment was continued to the succeeding eight children. Their frocks were of cambric, the tucks and hems being hem-stitched with Valenciennes lace tuckers and cuffs for the evening; plain for the morning. This place was no sinecure.

In the spring of 1763 Mr. Nicolay, from a feeling of friendship for my father, offered to send his nephew to Strelitz to bring my mother and her baby over. They travelled, with the addition of her brother, to Hamburg, when, after seeing the little party safe on board, he returned to his mother; but after her death, which occurred about six years later, he settled in London for the remainder of his life, which, however, was but of short duration.

The voyage was favourable. They landed at Gravesend, and proceeded to St. James's, where my father then was. Their Majesties, with their usual kindness, saw her and her boy. He, poor little fellow, was then taken to his nurse, my mother being left with the Queen to relate everything, even the most trifling anecdote, that had occurred since her Majesty had left her happy home.

About this time their Majesties removed to the house at the top of St. James's Park, which had been purchased from the Duke of Buckingham and settled upon the Queen for her jointure residence. An additional wing on the garden side had been added; extensive and convenient offices; and, on the Pimlico side, a most elegant building for a library, with rooms for attendants, for rebinding books, &c. Buckingham House was a red-brick mansion, and very much more handsome than the present Buckingham Palace, which was built by George IV. about 1826. He first applied to Parliament for a grant of money to repair the house; but Nash, the architect, began by making so many alterations that at last it became necessary to entirely reconstruct it. The fine collection of books and pictures made by King George III. was removed by his son when the house was demolished, the former being made over as a grant to the nation, and the greater number of the latter being sent to Hampton Court Palace. All public days, without exception, were to be held at St. James's as usual; and this new abode, termed 'the Queen's house,' was to be in future the London residence for their Majesties and their children. June 4 being cele-

brated publicly as the King's birthday, the 6th was
proposed for the Queen to give the house-warming,
when a most elegant entertainment was planned—a
concert, a ball, the gardens to be illuminated, sup-
pers, bands of music, the whole of a magnificent
description, under the direction, principally, of Mr.
Kuffe, a German, and general invitations to the
nobility were to be issued.

The rooms allotted to my father at St. James's,
though convenient for him and his servant, were by
no means calculated to accommodate a family, nor
were any provided for him at the Queen's house.
Consequently it was thought better to lodge my
mother where she would be comfortable, as my father
could but seldom be with her, and where she would
have the opportunity of making herself acquainted
with the customs of this country, and of learning to
converse in its language. My mother, her little boy,
and nurse were therefore placed with the Queen's
milliner, Miss Downs, who had a house in Maddox
Street, Hanover Square. She was the daughter of a
man on the estate of Lord William Bolby in the
North, an active, clever person, much in favour with
the Queen.

My father, after June 6, went down with the
Royal Family to Richmond, and returned with them
to the Queen's house for her Majesty's confinement,
which took place on August 16, when the second son

was born, the Duke of York. After that, they returned to Richmond until November. My mother in the meantime was on a visit to Mr. and Mrs. Petch, an agreeable and worthy family, Mr. Petch being on the King's establishment.

## CHAPTER II.



AT the meeting of Parliament in January 1765, the King announced his royal assent to the ill-starred marriage between his sister, Princess Caroline Matilda, and the Prince Royal of Denmark ; but, both being minors, the marriage did not take place till two years later.

About this time the very distressing state of the Spitalfields weavers was brought before the notice of the Queen, and she, with her usual kind-heartedness and charitable sentiments, at once laid aside all foreign silks, and not only herself wore gowns of English manufacture, but requested the ladies of her

Court to do the same. This gave no small amount of dissatisfaction among a few, who prided themselves upon their French costumes, but the greater number of her ladies were glad to follow her Majesty's example.

And now came the Queen's first serious trouble. In this year, 1765, the King was attacked with alarming illness. The close attendance of the Princess Dowager at first appeared to proceed from the amiable motive of keeping the Queen from the knowledge of the full extent of his dreadful malady, as well as from the affection the Princess bore towards her son ; but when the Duke of Cumberland, the King's uncle, began to express that he thought himself the most entitled to be at the helm of affairs during the incapacity of the King, the tactics of the Princess, with those of Lord Bute and his party, became apparent. Power was what they desired, and, the more effectually to obtain it, they did not scruple to endeavour to undermine the affection of the King for his Queen.

It was not known beyond the Palace that his Majesty was mentally afflicted, but our poor Queen found this out only too soon for her peace of mind, for notwithstanding the Princess Dowager's endeavours to keep her from her proper place at her husband's side, she would not be wholly excluded, both inclination and her strong sense of duty prompting her to assert herself in this emergency.

It was, however, her Majesty's wish, as well as that of others around the King, to prevent the public from discovering the nature of his illness, and as long as it was possible his Majesty appeared upon all State occasions. It was thought that he looked pale, but no idea of the real truth was then discovered, and the general fear was that he showed a tendency towards consumption.

The Princess Dowager was not liked by one faction in the country, but she was upheld and admired by the opposite party. The Tories and Whigs were at this time very strongly opposed to each other, and in those days party feeling in politics ran quite as high, if not more so than at the present time.

[Lord Macaulay, in his essay on the Earl of Chatham, speaks in the following terms of the Princess of Wales:

'The detractors of the Princess Dowager of Wales affirmed that she had kept her children from commerce with society, in order that she might hold an undivided empire over their minds. She gave a very different explanation of her conduct. She would gladly, she said, see her sons and daughters mix in the world if they could do so without risk to their morals. But the profligacy of the people of quality alarmed her. The young men were all rakes; the young women made love, instead of waiting till it was made to them. She could not bear to expose those whom she loved best to the contaminating influence of such society. The moral advantages of the system of education which formed the Duke of York, the Duke of Cumberland, and the Queen of Denmark, may perhaps be questioned. George III. was indeed no libertine; but he brought to the throne a mind only half opened, and was for some time entirely under the influence of his mother and of his Groom of the Stole, John Stuart, Earl of Bute.'

What he says later on about Fox and the Princess Mother is interesting and may be quoted here: ' He (Fox) was, on personal grounds, most obnoxious to the Princess Mother. For he had, immediately after her husband's death, advised the late King to take the education of her son, the Heir Apparent, entirely out of her hands. He had recently given, if possible, still deeper offence; for he had indulged, not without some ground, the ambitious hope that his beautiful sister-in-law, the Lady Sarah Lennox, might be Queen of England. It had been observed that the King at one time rode every morning by the grounds of Holland House, and that on such occasions, Lady Sarah, dressed like a shepherdess at a masquerade, was making hay close to the road, which was then separated by no wall from the lawn. On account of the part which Fox had taken in this sin-

gular love affair, he was the only member of the
Privy Council who was not summoned to the meeting
at which his Majesty announced his intended marriage
with the Princess of Mecklenburgh-Strelitz.'—ED.]

Madame Schwellenberg, being at this time under
no restraint, had assumed a powerful ascendency over
the mind of the Queen, who was seriously ill from
trouble and anxiety; and did her best to persuade
her to show her resentment at the interference of the
Princess, having gleaned intelligence of how things
were going on.   My father, however, entreated her
Majesty to consult no one, but to act upon her own
superior judgment, and to show no spark of resentment.   The Queen, without answering my father,
must in part have listened to his precept, for on his
recovery the King returned to the Queen more
than ever impressed with her good sense, and, if
possible, more fond.   The Princess Dowager meanwhile made her own keen observations.   Towards the
Queen she was more distant and cool in her affection;
but, to vent her spleen on sure ground, she accused
Madame Schwellenberg of having acted a wrong
part; whereupon the reprimand was given by the
King to which I have already alluded.

The illness of his Majesty was not upon this occasion of long duration, and immediately after, his
recovery he went down to the House of Parliament
to urge the question of a Regency being appointed

in case of anything happening to him before his son should come of age. A long and violent debate ensued upon this question, one party wishing to exclude the Queen from taking any share in the guardianship of her son, the Heir Apparent, and the other desiring that the name of the Princess Dowager should be altogether omitted. Eventually both names were inserted, and the Bill was passed through both Houses.

My mother remained with Miss Downs in Maddox Street, and there, on the 2nd of July, 1765, I was born, being immediately sent from home to be nursed, according to the custom of that day.

On the 21st of August in the same year the present King, William IV. (I am writing in 1833), was born, and such an interest was kept up between us, that once a month, at least, we were brought together for comparison of improvement. The Queen, Princess Louisa, and Prince Henry, the late Duke of Cumberland, brother and sister of the King, were my sponsors. I was christened, by the names of Charlotte Louisa Henrietta, at St. George's, Hanover Square. The Prince was christened William Henry.

Nothing particular occurred until I was brought home ; which being about the time when the Royal Family removed to Richmond for the summer, my father took a house in Hill Street. A painful adieu was taken of Miss Downs, who had in every respect treated my mother with kindness and feeling, and a lasting friendship was maintained between us all. Now my father began to experience the cares of a family. His finances failed him, and he spoke to the Queen, who settled. I must observe with some reluctance, that she would pay for his country house, and for one in London the following winter, when my father should decide upon one. The young man who had come to England with my father as his servant, at this time returned to Germany, and, being well recommended by him, soon obtained a good situation there.

At Richmond, my mother was very happy. She was always welcome at the Tunstalls', and kindly received at Nicolay's, who had a house and large garden in the vineyard; also at Petch's, where she had previously visited for six weeks. On Michaelmas Day in this year, 1766, the Princess Royal was born at the Queen's House in London. My father was in attendance there during the time, but returned with the family to Richmond for the remainder of the season.

The Queen now appointed the daughter of Mrs. Griffiths, formerly nurse to the Duke of York, semp-stress to the Princesses, with apartments. Her sons were also provided for—two in the army, and the third as surgeon to the Queen's household.

To return to ourselves; new difficulties arose. The house which my father had engaged, in a street near St. James's, was neat, compact, and convenient; but how was the furniture to be obtained? The Queen could not again be applied to. My mother had brought with her, according to the custom of her country, quantities of linen of every description; a large double bedstead, with green silk hangings, eider-down quilt, and every other part of the bedding complete, and of the best materials; a child's bedstead, equally the same; and a travelling couch. These were removed from Richmond with other portable articles, some few purchased, and others hired for the season; my father starting with the determination of not incurring debt. He was fortunate through life to escape the misery, I should almost call it crime, of it.

This year passed without anything remarkable to relate.

On November 2, 1767, the Queen was confined with the late Duke of Kent; so that the Royal Family moved early to London for the season. My mother also expected an addition to her family during the winter months; and as I had the whooping cough, my parents were advised to leave me with a neighbour, who had been useful to our family, and was a kind woman, a widow Smith, with two daughters and a son. I was very happy with them, and remained there until all was in its usual routine at home. The new baby was again a boy, and was

christened George Edward.  Just before we were to
leave London for the summer, his nurse brought him
to pass the day.  He appeared well, but inclined to
sleep; and while they were preparing to go home in
the evening, he was seized with convulsions. Aid was
immediately called in, but before midnight the poor
little fellow was a corpse. I neither saw him die nor
after he was struck ; yet his death so unnerved me,
that I was afraid of the dark and of my own shadow.
Nothing could divert me from this feeling of dread.
Sweetmeats and toys had no pleasure for me; I was
whipped with a rod, that only added terror, and to
be allowed to sit quietly in one spot was the only
thing that seemed to make me easy.  The servant
engaged to wait upon my mother, to take care of
me, and to give me air and exercise, had no preten-
sions to beauty, and was of an age when one might
expect steadiness ;  but this creature would constantly,
when she took me to the park (the usual walk for
children), place me in the house where they sold milk,
or in a sentry-box, until her frolics were ended.
Then, after a short walk, she would return home
with me, no doubt being raised in the minds of my
parents of the rectitude of her conduct.  They were
advised, on account of this dullness which had taken
possession of me, to send me to day school, which
was done on our going to Richmond without difficulty, for it was then the custom, and eligible places

were easily found. This change had the desired effect. I soon became the lively child I had been before ; ran on a half-holiday first to the old Maid-of-honour shop for my bun, then to papa at the Richmond Lodge, into the royal nursery for a little play with Prince William under the eye of dear nurse Chapman, and on whole holidays, home to dine first, and then for the play as above described. When otherwise than good I am sure it was not overlooked, for my father, through fondness, was strict, and my mother severe.

Early in the season we returned to town for the Queen's confinement with Princess Augusta, which took place on November 8, 1768.

During my summer gaieties, I had told to some one or other about our servant, and her immoral conduct having been inquired into and proved, she was very properly discharged.

When the Queen had recovered, it was settled that Prince Ernest, her Majesty's brother, Prince William, and myself should be inoculated. I was taken to the Queen's house, there held by my father on one chair, the Prince by his nurse on another, their Majesties being present. It was first performed on Prince Ernest, then on myself, then on Prince William, after this manner: two punctures in the arm near to each other were made with the point of a lancet, through which a thread was drawn several times under the skin, and this on both arms. The operation was performed by Surgeon Blomfield, and was one of smarting pain, for we both cried. I was taken home in a sedan, kept warm, and in a few days had a convulsion, fever, and the pustules inflamed. On one arm they rose and dried off regularly. Prince William had pustules besides those on the arms, no convulsion, and was less ill, which was attributed to the female constitution being more delicate. On Prince Ernest it took no effect whatever. On our ultimate recovery all was considered right, and that we were secure from further fear of disease.

In this year, 1769, we remained late in the season at Richmond, as his Majesty was greatly occupied in digesting plans with Sir William Chambers for a new palace at Richmond, the lodge now occupied being was too small for the increasing family. The model of the elegant design fixed upon can now be seen by the public in the apartments at Hampton Court. A part of the Richmond gardens already formed was marked out as a private garden round the palace; the site of which was to have been near the Richmond end, opposite to Sion House, with an uninterrupted view of the river up and down, of the hill, the Cholmondeley Walk, and part of the green. It was begun. To make it complete for the prospect I have endeavoured to point out, and for other purposes of elegance and convenience, a small piece of ground was necessary that was not in the royal manor, and therefore must be purchased from the authorities of the town. This they refused. The building nevertheless went on as far as the ground floor, but was then stopped, and their Majesties determined to remove to Kew. The Princess Dowager continued in her widowhood to occupy the house that is now standing under the title of New Palace, and the one opposite to it, which was pulled down at the beginning of 1800. But when her three sons had their own establishments, the fourth being dead, as well as Princess Louisa, and her other two daughters married, the one to Prince Ferdinand of Brunswick, the other to the King of Denmark, her Royal Highness gave up the elegant house, and by far the more desirable of the two, the one now down, and fixed herself in the one now standing. This took place in 1770 or 1771, I cannot recollect which, and here she remained until her death on February 9, 1772.[1] This event caused

[1] The following account of the death of the Princess Dowager is taken from Walpole's *Journal of George III.*:—

'February 8, 1772, died Augusta Princess Dowager of Wales, the King's mother, aged fifty-two, of an abscess in the throat. . . . For the last three months her sufferings had been dreadful and menacing her life, yet her fortitude was invincible, and she kept up to the last moment that disguise and reserve which predominated so strongly in her character. She not only would not acknowledge her danger to her children, servants, and physicians, but went out in her coach. On Thursday, the 6th, her approaching end was evident, and on Friday the King forbade his Levée on that account. It was his custom to visit the Princess, with the Queen, every Saturday evening from six to eight. They now went at that hour on the Friday. Hearing they were come, the Princess rose,

great unhappiness to the King, who was affectionately attached to his mother, and the misfortunes of Queen Caroline, which began about the same time, added greatly to his Majesty's distress.

In the autumn of 1769, a serious incident was committed by me. I passed the afternoon with Augusta Fetch, who had a new set of toy plates and dishes of a size exceeding the usual children's services. These so dazzled me that I secreted one of the largest dishes and brought it home unperceived, in short regularly stole it. The following day my father, seeing it, said, 'You must have been a good girl to have had so fine a dish given to you yesterday by Mrs. Petch.' I hung my head, and shame struck me. My father, seeing that something was wrong, then said, 'Put on your bonnet; we will go to Mrs. Petch's with the dish.' I durst not refuse. We arrived; my father said in my presence, 'My child took away this dish without your knowledge; she

dressed herself, and attempted to walk to meet them, but was so weak and unable that the Princess of Brunswick ran out and called in the King and Queen. She pressed them to stay till ten, and when that hour came signed to them to retire as usual. They stayed, however, in her palace, and she went to bed. . . . At 6.30 next morning her attendants found her dead.

'13th.—The Princess of Wales was buried. The populace huzzaed for joy and treated her memory with much disrespect.

'February 1.—The jewels, plate, and trinkets of the late Princess Dowager of Wales were sold by public auction at Christie's in Pall Mall. They were inconsiderable, and it seemed very mean to expose them in that manner, especially as the amount was to be divided amongst her own children.'

must herself entreat pardon.' I recollect fully falling down on my knees and saying my usual prayers, and giving back the stolen property, which in future no persuasion could induce me to play with or even look at. When we left the Petch's for home on that unhappy day, I would not be kissed, saying I was too naughty. The chastisement my father gave me, saying little, but that with point, made me convict myself. I went 'to school as usual, but begged not to go to my dear holiday making, feeling as if everyone knew of my disgrace. Oh, I am thankful to my dear father for never suffering wrong to pass unnoticed or unpunished.

On May 22, 1770, the Queen was confined with Princess Elizabeth, and in the course of the same year my mother also had a little girl, who was christened after herself, Sophia Dorothea.

In 1771, on June 5, Prince Ernest, the Duke of Cumberland, was born. The Queen attended the Drawing-room on that day, and the ball in the evening at St. James's; and before morning his Royal Highness surprised everyone.

We were passing the summer still at Richmond, and Mr. Petch, who had been ailing for some time, died. My father, being never absent from the Queen, had officiated for Petch; and the King, who from the first had liked him very much, now appointed him to succeed his sincere friend, Petch, and gave

him the same apartments that he had occupied at
St. James's. Sir William Chambers, who with almost
every other attendant at the palace was partial to
my father, repaired these apartments for him, and
made them as ornamental and convenient as the
nature of them would permit. They were furnished
by the Chamberlain's Office, and every usual per-
quisite supplied—linen, coals, candles, turnery; and
wine on particular days specified. A carriage or
sedan-chair were always in readiness for the attendants of the person.

On coming to London in 1771, we went to our
new residence, where on December 18 my brother
George was born, being so christened by the King's
desire, my father begging to add his own name,
Frederick. This little baby went off to be nursed
as usual, and when my mother was about again,
little Sophia came home; and a fine sweet girl she
was.

The Queen, upon the advancement of my father,
deducted her allowance for the house in town. He
was anxious about Petch's widow and children, and in
addition to the King's pension offered them the use
of our residences as we vacated them. This accommodation she gladly accepted for about three years,
after which time, her son having finished his school
education, she removed into the country. We heard
of their safe arrival and then lost sight of them;

for the post in those days did not add to the revenue as in these.

In the summer of 1772 we were to be settled at Kew, of which place I must now give an account (being still a resident there at this time, 1833), and also of its inhabitants, as we were a community and associated together as friends and dependants.

The road ran up the middle of the green between the royal houses, there being no wall across it ; and at the end stood a house in the gardens. The portals of the gates are still standing. Between the gate to the water side from the palace and the ferry was a house, also in the gardens, appropriated to Lady Charlotte Finch, the royal governess, and her family. By the ferry steps was still another house, occupied by the clerk of the works, Mr. Kirby, the father of Mrs. Trimmer, the celebrated writer on education.

These houses were now fenced off, as the King and Queen were resident at Kew, a gate being left into the gardens from each as a convenience to the occupants when in attendance. The sub-governess, Mrs. Coultsworth, and the English teacher, Miss Planta, were lodged in the Queen's house, the latter also having apartments in St. James's. The Tunstalls' house was the same as that now used by the house-keeper, but kept up with an elegant neatness that made a palace in miniature. She continued in the same favour, and made the usual arrangements for the general comfort. The convenience of the Queen was increased by her being able to go into the royal children's apartments without passing through the open passages. Mrs. Tunstall had one daughter spared to her out of sixteen, her only son also having died in infancy. This daughter, Sally, as she was usually called, was now near twenty ; and as her parents never left their home, they determined to let her mix with her friends, which she could now do almost under their eyes. This the Queen advised Mrs. Tunstall not to do, for poor Sally was weak and silly, and had never seemed to profit by the instructions of her parents. Dress was her passion at that time ; I mean such as was beyond her station in life. Card-playing was then resorted to as the amusement of the evenings, she becoming a proficient in the hope of gain. Mischief quickly followed, for amongst . the most sincere friends, individuals unavoidably mix who soon know how to gain any point they are bent upon. Then poor Sally bought shares in the lottery, dabbled in speculations, and getting into difficulties she flew to her father for assistance, which fortunately for her extricated her for a time ; but her parents regretted not having followed the Queen's most excellent advice.

The house Mrs. Gwyn now occupies was given to Dr. Hurd, Bishop of Worcester, a preceptor of the

Prince of Wales and the Duke of York, one of the most amiable and able men of the day.

The house that was given to us had been originally fitted up by the King, for his mother, the Princess Dowager of Wales, and was termed the Garden Retreat. The public, however, termed it a retreat to carry on her political schemes with Lord Bute and his party. The walls of the drawing room in this house are decorated with prints pasted on the paper, collected and arranged by this fond son, with a print of Lord Bute in his robes of State over the fireplace. The cottage in Richmond Gardens is similarly decorated, as is also a room in Sion House, that being a fashion of the day. The barracks were situated as at present, the stables also, over which were the neat apartments of Mr. and Mrs. Montagu. He was riding-master to the Princes, and riding-attendant to the King; and every morning, summer and winter, he had to be in the riding-house in readiness for his Majesty. These good people never had any family, and Mrs. Montagu devoted her whole time to her husband, taking breakfast with him every morning at half-past four o'clock. There was a house for the stable people, now pulled down, where the road leads to the Botanic Gardens. The houses of the Dukes of Cambridge and Cumberland were appropriated to Sir John Pringle, the physician to the Person, and to Cæsar and Pennell Hawkins, the surgeons to the same; for the Queen would have two of them always on the spot to watch the constitutions of the royal children, to eradicate, if possible, or at least to keep under, the dreadful disease, scrofula, inherited from the King. She herself saw them bathed at six every morning, attended the schoolroom of her daughters, was present at their dinner, and directed their attire, whenever these arrangements did not interfere with public duties, or any plans or wishes of the King, whom she neither contradicted nor kept waiting a moment, I may almost say, under any circumstances.

The minister's house was next to that of the Duke of Cambridge, now pulled down. Shaw's house and the one adjoining, which then communicated, were occupied by dear and valued Dr. Majendie, who, although a Swiss, taught her Majesty English. He had been in this country from his birth, and had not even a foreign accent. He assisted in the clerical duties of the place, read to the aged, instructed the young, and, to sum up his character, if perfection can exist, he reached it. A wife, one daughter, and two sons—one in the army and one in the Church—composed this family. The small cottage next was fitted up with great rural neatness for Mrs. Pohl, late Miss Downs, who had made her husband's acquaintance through his visiting my father and mother in Maddox Street, he being a German. He possessed very superior abilities, was agreeable, fascinating, and most persevering, and married without much thought of the future. But unfortunately he never got on after his employer, the Hanoverian Minister, died, though Count Bruhl and other foreigners of distinction tried to serve him. They took the adjoining house in Maddox Street, to let, as well as the lodgings formerly occupied by my mother. Mrs. Pohl still held the same post at Court; and to further her business, as well as to give country air to her two children, this cottage at Kew was taken. The shops between this cottage and the gate were the same in those days as at present. In Richmond Lane Mr. Englehardt, the miniature painter, lived, and also his brother. The Queen's flower garden was up the lane, opposite to the engine gate; the cottage of her gardener, Mr. Green, adjoining. In this bijou of a garden were orange trees, nursed by poor Green, that would in a very short time have yielded fruit as fine as our ripened China orange, if he could have had assistance to rebuild the hothouses to a proper size; but retrenchment to a fearful degree had already begun, and, as this was a private garden of the Queen's, the Board of Works would not undertake it. The Queen could not, so the fine trees were dwarfed, and Green nearly broke his heart. He offered to pay half the expense, or to give 250*l.*, but this could not be suffered. The corner house, now the Duke of

Cambridge's dairy, was the private property of Mr. Haverfield, the King's gardener. It was a good house, according to the feeling of that day. It had beautiful garden ground, and fields at the back, a large yard with stabling, and every attendant office. His eldest son, John, assisted him in the Richmond garden; his second son, Thomas, in the Kew garden. A footpath to Richmond Green divided the two gardens, which were more extensive than at present, and highly cultivated with a luxuriance of flowers, shady walks, and a variety of temples, fancy buildings, &c. These young gentlemen ultimately succeeded to these appointments. Their younger brother was a clergyman. A Colonel West lived in Goddard House, with a family of nine daughters and a son, whom the Duke of Montague, while governour to the Prince of Wales and the Duke of York, made page of honour to the King, saying there was a spark of relationship. The timber yard of Warren, the king's carpenter, stood where two new houses now are. The farmhouse, now Hollis's, was Mr. Clewly's, who supplied the inhabitants with milk, butter, eggs, pork, and bacon. She, becoming a widow, married a Mr. Frame, whose son, by a former marriage, lived upon housebreaking and footpad robberies. Upon his father becoming an inhabitant of Kew, the question was inquired into, when he said: ' I always take care to act so as to escape justice. Blows and murders belong not to my gang, and if I am allowed to take my beer on the Green, and sit with my neighbours, without being insulted, I shall take care that no harm happen here. I am well aware of the bearings of the place.' We all spoke with him as a friend when we met; and of my father he asked for any trifle he wanted, and never was refused. Truly a curious state of things!

At the corner of the bridge on the Surrey side, a large inn was built, which is called the 'King's Arms,' now Sowter's. A little way on was a ladies' school, and next 'The Rose and Crown,' now precisely the same as in those days. Then Mrs. Schnell's, which at that time my father took from Mrs. Englehardt for three years; a cottage next; then stabling; a little farther on Dr. Newton's, the Bishop of Bristol; next Finlay's of the Princess Dowager's establishment; and then (now Hobbs's) my uncle Louis Albert's house. He came to this country unexpectedly about a year after my mother, and lived with my parents until the Queen gave him the vacancy that fortunately happened . . . [A part of the old manuscript being here torn away, the title of the appointment is lost, but it was, I think, something about the persons of the Princesses, probably that of page.—Ed.]

Most of the other houses at Kew remain (1833) now as they were at the time of which I am speaking, but the inhabitants are all changed; many of our old friends have passed away; others we have lost sight of.

In the latter part of the year 1772, my mother had a very serious illness, and was, for some time, in the greatest danger. On her recovery in 1773, it was thought advisable that I should be sent to school. My father consulted Mrs. Montagu, who recommended dear and ever memorable Streatham. Mrs. Wadsworth, a friend of Mrs. Montagu's, had a daughter there, precisely my own age, and placed under circumstances of trouble. Mrs. Wadsworth was left a widow at an early age, beautiful in the extreme, with a son and daughter. Her husband had been purveyor of every requisite for the King's mews, both in town and country. A business like this Mrs. Wadsworth was determined to carry on, having a faithful foreman, in the hope of handing it over to her son when he should be of age, unimpaired if not increased in value.

To Streatham, then, my father took me in the spring of 1773, on a Wednesday, stupefied and amazed. The next day, while in the parlour with my kind governess, I saw papa coming down the path leading to the house. He came to see if I were tolerably reconciled; and to bring me a pair of white leather shoes with stone buckles for dancing, which I was to begin that afternoon with Mons. Villeneuve, by way of amusement. They pressed my father to stay and dine, but he refused, saying he could but seldom dine in company, as he was obliged to walk up and down to coax the food into his stomach ; so that during the best part of his life he suffered from the malady of which he died. I did not see him go away, and my tears still fall when I think of this visit of paternal love. My father was very dear to me.

This excellent school was kept by Miss Eveleigh, originally by the three sisters, one of whom married Mr. Kay, in the law, the other Mr. Fry. Each of the sisters had a boy and a girl, and both becoming widows they rejoined the school, the young ladies being of course brought up in it, the young gentlemen going one to Eton and the other to Westminster. Mrs. Fry dying soon after her return to her happy home, Miss Fry clung to her Aunt Eveleigh with an affection rarely met with. The two sisters and the niece were of sur- prising height, fine women, and most pleasing, with intelligent countenances, if not exactly handsome. They were remarkably well bred, well informed, of benign dispositions, and liberal in all their dealings. Miss Fry was always in the schoolroom, and very often Miss Eveleigh. There were two English and one French teacher, and an assistant to each of these ; about eighty scholars ; and the best masters in every department—Mr. Knyvett for music and singing, a well-known musician ; Mr. Mirlan, also known, for Latin and English ; and every kind of needlework, both useful and ornamental, was taught in the school-room, embroidery in coloured silks being taught in the first line of perfection by that angelic soul Miss Fry. Among the young people that were at school with me, I recollect the Miss Sainsburys; Miss Ann Arbuthnot, aunt of my youngest daughter's husband;[1] Miss Blount, for whom George Meyer died; the daughter of Colonel Matthews, who signalised himself in the war of those days; Miss Chaworth, the illegitimate daughter of Mr. Chaworth, who was killed in a duel by Lord Byron; and many others of note. Miss Kay superintended in one room the music, drawing, and geography, the latter taught inimitably clear by Mr. Povoleri, who was also for Italian, a language at that time rarely studied, and only to enable a person to read the words of an Italian song. Miss Kay was a good musician, and on Sunday evenings classes went up to the drawing-room, where there was a church organ, to sing the hymns of the Magdalenes, the Asylum, and others, with anthems and psalms. Mrs. Kay conducted the domestic part, gardens, fields, dairy, brewery, stabling, &c., as well as the house. A carriage was kept, and a coachman and footman, the latter only to attend to the door and the rooms for company. The other servants

---

[1] My father, the late Mr. George Arbuthnot, of the Treasury, who was married to my mother, Augusta Amelia Adolphina Papendiek, on April 26, 1838.—Ed.

were, two for the ladies and linen, two housemaids, two to wait upon the schoolroom and scholars, a cook and kitchenmaid, the linen being washed by three women in the village. Mrs. James had the care of the stores and linen. She had her own room and two others adjoining, where all the linen was looked over; and each young lady who was old enough came to take her own to repair it and place it where allotted on the Saturdays. When stores were given out the young people of a certain age were called to assist, and by this means an insight into the mysteries of housekeeping was obtained; and useful as well as ornamental instruction was always going on, to the employment of the mind in pleasing variety. The danger of intimacies among the girls, too, was much lessened, an evil to be guarded against when possible, as it leads first to the marvellous, secondly to falsehood, and lastly to a great waste of time. In the village there was a charity school, superintended closely by our dear ladies, two of the girls being always in our house either training for servitude or learning needlework and the useful kinds of millinery and embroidery. Before each of the holidays at Christmas and. midsummer we had a gala, with permission to invite any young friends where we might have visited during the half-year. The refreshments were mince pies and tartlets, plum porridge, now but little known, the etceteras of almonds and raisins and so on, with large cakes, all home-made ; negus and the old-fashioned punch. A certain number of the elder scholars had to see all prepared, to assist in the decorations, and to be as it were at the head of the entertainment, the governesses all attending.

In the summer our gala took place in the garden, on which occasions our leading treat was syllabub, fruit, &c., on the same plan. After our great day came that for the charity girls, at which we also had to attend. During the length of years that this distinguished establishment was carried on, no changes took place, unless to introduce anything that could lead to improvement, which was scarcely possible.

When the French emigrated in shoals to this country at the time of the Revolution, the nature of education was changed. It became the fashion for people to have governesses in their homes instead of sending their daughters to schools, which had been supported to accommodate every rank in society. Miss Eveleigh's, or rather at that time Mrs. Kay's school, decreased with the rest, and although the same well-digested regulations were adhered to, they were compressed to a smaller scale, but with the same liberal feeling. Even in this excellent school, girls sometimes entered who were incorrigible, and who were sooner or later expelled. In the charity school, too, this happened still more frequently. One instance of crime that occurred was terrible. A girl in a quarrel killed another by pressing on her chest and stomach till she died. The survivor, on account of her youth, was not hanged but imprisoned. She never recovered her cheerfulness, and appeared to be a sincere penitent, dying of consumption under twenty.

My next visit was from papa and mamma together. They came to tell me that my sweet pretty little sister had died of the small-pox, and that my uncle's baby had also died in the measles. The medicine had been wrongly directed, and the baby had died in a few hours from convulsions. It was feared that in my poor sister's case something was wrong too, for she was recovering and fell back unexpectedly, but this could never be proved.

At that time, and for many years after, the families of those about the Court had the benefit of medical advice gratis, as well as those directly holding the appointments.

My parents came also to tell me that my father was going abroad for a few weeks with the Duchess of Northumberland, who wished to see the course of the Rhine, hoping to dissipate by travel her sorrow for the loss of her only daughter, Lady Elizabeth Percy. My father was himself but in indifferent health, which gave rise to the Queen's proposal that she should take him with her. She gladly acquiesced, and they departed with the secretary, Mr. Selby, the

Duchess' woman, her dresser, and chambermaid, also her groom-of-the-chambers, with his assistant footmen and outriders, and a suite of four carriages. Often of an evening the first three were called upon by the Duchess to make up a pool at quadrille, and in journeying to come into her carriage. She was a noble, fine-spirited woman, and she was amiable in the extreme. In passing through Frankfort my father was blessed in again seeing his father, who was in good health; and on being introduced to the Duchess by her desire, she exclaimed, ' I am delighted to bring your worthy and admirable son to see you ; and I am glad, as he must be happy, to find you looking so well and handsome at your time of life.' The following winter, poor man, he fell, from the frost, and broke his leg, which killed him before the long suffering necessary to the recovery of a broken limb. The mother was already dead before my father came to England. During his absence in 1773, my mother removed to Kew, with the assistance of Mr. and Mrs. Pohl. My brother now came home from nurse, and I from Streatham for the holidays, Miss Wadsworth being on a visit to Mrs. Montagu for the first fortnight.

I was always rather impatient with anything that kept me from the royal nursery, but my father being absent and many changes having taken place in the household, I could not go quite so frequently as usual. The Prince of Wales and the Duke of York were removed with their governour and sub-governours to the opposite house, late Princess Dowager's, now called the Prince of Wales's house, the three Miss Ducks being appointed housekeepers for their joint lives. Their family had been dependents in the household of Caroline, Queen of George II. Their apartments were in the side wing. They were by no means prepossessing, but clever, sensible women, and in the absence of the Royal Family entered into society with a friendly though rather constrained politeness. The Princes William and Edward were removed from the nursery and placed in the apartments before occupied by their elder brothers, and a page, Mr. G. Magnolley, was appointed to attend them. Mrs. Coultsworth resigned from age, and Miss Goldsworthy, sister of the King's first equerry, was received in her stead; a lady of private fortune, and of general endowments that in every respect qualified her for the situation of sub-governess. The nurse, our dear friend Mrs. Chapman, could no longer retain her place from inability to fulfil the arduous duties of it, as an addition was yearly sent in to be fostered in the nursery. Mrs. Cheveley, who had suckled the Duke of Cumberland, had contrived to blind the just discernment of the Queen, and obtained this post of trust. No one could have been more unfit for it, as gain and favour were her idols. Every

judicious arrangement hitherto followed for the benefit and happiness of the nursery and the royal children, and for the comfort of the different attendants
employed therein, was now broken into.  Confusion,
want of confidence and of respect, ensued.  It was
fortunate that those who had the laborious duties
to perform were faithful, and carried on their part
of the work with equal diligence.  Mrs. Cheveley,
on re-entering the royal household, brought with
her a sister, Miss Nevin, to be dresser to the Princesses; a person ill-bred, ill-looking, ill-natured, puffed
with pride and arrogance, the only redeeming point
in her character being that she retired more within
herself than her sister, and therefore only those who
had business with her were so fully subjected to her
revolting manner.

[Miss Burney appears to hold a different opinion
about this good lady, Mrs. Cheveley.  She says:
'Mrs. Cheveley is rather handsome, and of a showy
appearance, and a woman of exceeding good sense,
whose admirable management of the young Princess
has secured her affection without spoiling her.  She
always treats her with respect, even when reproving
her, yet gives way to none of her humours where it
is better they should be conquered.  Fewer humours,
indeed, I never in any child saw; and I give the
greatest credit to Mrs. Cheveley for forbearing to
indulge them.'—Ed.]

# CHAPTER III.

Birth of the Duke of Cambridge—Appointment of Miss Margaret Planta
—Quartett parties—Measles at school—Serious illness of Charlotte
Albert—Terrible storm—Visit to Brighton—Fashions for children's
dresses—Charlotte Albert seized with the small-pox—Birth of the
Princess Mary—Daily arrangements of the Royal Family—Education
at Streatham—Anecdote of Bach—History of Dr. Dodd—Break in
the diary—Zoffany—His painting at Florence—Mrs. Zoffany—Story
of her life.

AT the beginning of 1774 I returned to school as
usual. On February 24 in that year, Adolphus
Frederick, Duke of Cambridge, was born, and for his
Royal Highness's christening I was allowed to come
home for a few days. It was then permitted for
spectators to be present on all public days at St.
James's, and many who could not obtain tickets of
admission went in Court dresses, which franked them
through the rooms as far as the *entrée*.

For those who were in course of time to be presented, this permission was a great advantage, for it
gave them an insight into Court ceremonies, and an
ease of carriage under the peculiar dress essential for
all those who attended them at that date—the large
hoop, long lappets, heavy plumes, &c.

When this christening was over, and we were looking at the State couch on which the Queen had sat, and at the cradle in which the young Prince Adolphus Frederick had rested during the ceremony, who should accost us but Miss Margaret Planta, in a Court dress, attending as governess to the Miss Lyttletons, who were there to see the ceremony in the same attire, having not yet attained the age to be presented! Very shortly after that evening, Miss Planta, who held the situation of English teacher in the royal household, died of an accidental illness, and her sister Peggy, as she was generally called, succeeded to the appointment. Her manner was more brilliant than that of her sister; her disposition more flexible, and her whole deportment more suited to a Court; yet I should say a decided loss was sustained in the death of the former. No doubt but that Miss Peggy was equally well informed, yet as the instructive part of the education of the Princesses devolved upon the English teacher, the quiet, patient, plodding, persevering disposition of the late Miss Planta was more adapted to that arduous business. Miss Peggy Planta was, however, well received, and much approved, and the schoolroom now was one of gaiety and cheerfulness. The masters were: for French, Mons Giffadière; for drawing, Mons. Denoyer; for writing, Mr. Roberts, a relation of Mrs. Trimmer's; and for music, our dear and valued friend, Johann

Christian Bach.[1] He also gave lessons to the Queen; and of evenings, by appointment, he attended the King's accompaniment to the pianoforte by the flute. He had a house at Richmond, where my father visited him, and cultivated a lasting friendship.

These practices led to private quartett parties twice a week, assisted by Abel, the celebrated viol-di-gamba player; Cramer, the violinist; and Fisher, the oboe player.

Our old house—at least the drawing-room half of it—was given to Lady Effingham, then a widow, with every attending kindness; the rest to Prince Ernest, whenever his Serene Highness should visit England.

On my return to school after the Prince's christening, I fell ill, with many others, of the measles, but we had them favourably. Miss Dixon was one of the sufferers, and her father being a physician, and visiting her often, we certainly had the best advice. My father came constantly to see me, and was the bearer of many little amusing things to please us all, being admitted to our drawing-room when we were in a convalescent state. I remained at Streatham till the midsummer recess, and then went home well; but very shortly after was attacked with inflammation of the eyes, which increased in an alarming degree. Everything usual was tried, all to

---

[1] Johann Christian Bach was the second son of Johann Sebastian Bach, the famous composer.

no effect. Leeches were then resorted to, three on each temple, which, being applied in the morning continued to bleed profusely for twelve hours. To stop it at bedtime, a cobweb was recommended, and it was a subject of merriment with the King that in old Mrs. Albert's house such a thing could not be found. I then went on a visit to Streatham—Misses Eveleigh and Fry coming to fetch me in their coach. Young Wallace, the only son of Mr. Wallace in the law, who lived in the last house by the river, in the best part of Norfolk Street. Strand, accompanied them on horseback. The father was a particular friend of the Frys, and young Fry was to be articled to him. He was therefore to receive his education at Westminster, where young Wallace was, that they might form an early friendship, and that the quiet, thoughtful, and persevering disposition of Mr. Fry, who was rather the older, might draw toward him that of young Wallace, who was exactly the reverse.

On our way, in the middle of Wandsworth Common, the coachman begged that Mr. Wallace might get into the carriage and have his horse tied to run by the others, for it began to lighten very severely, and he wished to push on. This was acceded to, but we did not reach Streatham till ten o'clock, having been greatly retarded by the storm, which burst over us in all its fury. You can imagine how we were received, for the storm had now assumed a fearful height. It continued through the night with unabated violence. The church steeple was struck, and fell with a frightful crash, and damaged the roof. Our house stood alone. There were conductors round it, and, thank God, nothing happened to us, but many accidents occurred in the surrounding neighbourhood. The family were up all night, and assembled in the room where I lay to prayers. It was noon the following day before the storm cleared off; it had lasted without intermission for sixteen hours. A hobby groom was sent from Kew to say that the Royal Family and our own were safe and well, and that no particular accident had happened. This was at the beginning of August. At first I revived a little, but in a few days the inflammation came on again, and my father fetched me back. An issue in the left arm was then resorted to, but was of no avail, and lastly the seaside was proposed and determined on. An old servant, who had left us to be married, consented to take me, and on the last day of August my father set off with us in a chaise. We changed horses at Epsom, the second stage being to Horsham, where we dined. A bit of chicken I relished. At Steyning we changed again, and after the usual accidents of harness breaking, first one wheel coming off and then another, we reached the 'Old Ship' at Brighton about eight o'clock. Mrs. Muttlebury, who had wet-nursed the Princess Royal, was there to meet us, arranged everything for the night, and took my father home to sup with her. Her husband was in the customs, and they had a beautiful house on the West Cliff, over the subterraneous arches where the goods were landed.

On the following morning, in walking to this kind friend's dwelling, I exclaimed, 'Why is the sea green. a different colour from the river?' My father was in ecstasy, as since the last relapse I had not discerned anything beyond light and darkness. We took a lodging in West Street near the beach, two small rooms and the use of the parlour, which had a brick floor, for meals, at half a guinea a week. Medical advice was that I should take sea water on the beach every alternate day, beginning with less than half a pint, before breakfast ; and bathing, as I was not alarmed at it and even liked it, was to be used three times in seven days. I remained six weeks, when my father fetched me back, finding me quite recovered. He brought Mrs. Muttlebury a piece of plate from the Queen for her motherly attention to me, as her Majesty could not spare my father to be with me, and my mother was never willing to leave home. Besides, she had with her now my brother, who was a sweet, interesting, lively little fellow, and delighted to have me for a play-fellow till after the Christmas holidays. I was taken to see the Queen in my camlet cloak and bonnet, given to me by Mrs. Muttlebury for warmth and for damp mornings, for I was invariably to take a run. These were so approved, that Mrs. Pohl had to provide the same for the royal children, who were old enough to take exercise by walking. The outdoor equipment in those days, when pelisses and great-coats of woollen were not worn by girls, was a black cloak of a silk called ' mode,' stiff, and glossy, wadded, with hood, armholes with a sleeve to the wrist from them, a small muff, and a Quaker-shaped bonnet, all of the same material. These I had taken new with me to Brighton, in addition to my green silk bonnet, and pelisse, new for the summer, but which I had little worn.

The suffering I underwent from the inflammation was more acute than I can describe. My head was much swollen, my nose and mouth greatly enlarged, and the pain of taking food made me entreat to be excused. My perfect recovery was, therefore, miraculous. I went almost daily to the royal nursery, that the medical man might pay every attention to keep me well, and my dear little brother generally accompanied me. We left Kew in November, and nothing of note occurred. I returned to Streatham in February, with this recommendation, not to fatigue the sight, nor to let me be confined in one position long at a time. Every injunction was acceded to, and many marked kindnesses added. I remained perfectly well, was at home a few days at Easter, and for the midsummer holidays as usual. We often passed a day with the Chapmans, who had a house on Ealing Common. The Captain, Frederick Chapman, used to fetch us in his cabriolet, and bring us back in the evening. There my mother would go with us, as to old friends, but she never would enter into society without my father.

On September 22 in that year, 1775, my father came to Streatham to fetch me to be at home for a fortnight, where on arrival I found, to my great surprise, a little sister, born on the 19th. She was christened Sophia, and then went off to be nursed on the opposite side of the water. I cannot tell who were the sponsors. On our family going to town in November, my brother fell ill of the small-pox. He had them full and of course severely, but without any dangerous symptoms. At that season without the help of open-air exercise, he was left weak and out of health; but another catastrophe was to follow, which alarmed them all.

Blomfield, who had inoculated the two Princes and myself, as I have before explained, was questioned as to the probability of danger of infection, particularly to me, who would come home at Christmas from the fresh air of the country; but he would not listen to fears or doubts. Consequently I arrived.

The moment I entered the house I expressed my distress at the smell, and the following day I felt ill. Mons. Villeneuve, our dancing master, called to plan the dress and attendance for his benefit ball, when my mother told him that I had come home stupid, heavy, and anything but improved; and did not agree to my going to it. The following day Dr. Turton and Mr. Devaynes saw me. I was very ill. They gave me James's powders, which afforded no relief. They were puzzled; but in the night of Sunday appeared the small-pox in full force. I was worse than my dear little brother, and for six weeks at least suffered the martyrdom of that dreadful disease. I had my good Brighton nurse, but no one could give me any comfort or alleviate pain. I could only be lifted by four people, one at each corner of the sheet, to have my bed made; for not a pin's point could be placed between the pustules. Then all my beauty was gone, which before my father was flattered by. I was lost to all the fond hopes in which he had indulged.

Then Blomfield assured the Queen that we had been inoculated from different subjects, and that all would be safe with the Princes. It has been so, but her Majesty's confidence in Blomfield was shaken. My father was terribly distressed, for the small-pox had been very fatal in our family; and my sister at five or six months old was considered of an age too tender for inoculation as performed in those days. However, he determined upon it, and settled with Mr. Dundas, the apothecary to the Queen's household at Richmond, to take an early opportunity to do it. It was done, but had to be repeated before taking effect. She is now fifty-seven, and I hope safe from the disease; and we may affirm that in her case it did succeed.

In this spring of 1776, on April 25, the Queen was confined with Princess Mary, which gave holidays to some and close attendance to others.

During this summer, I visited our kind friends Mr. and Mrs. White at Egham, and they showed me all the lovely spots in the neighbourhood, including Windsor. That place, both as regards the houses near the Castle, and the town itself, was much the same at that time as it is at present, and I recollect no particular changes to recount, though many of the residences have, since that time, been considerably added to and beautified. They then, generally speaking, consisted of three stories, the upper one being garrets. The Home Park was then open to the public. There were four entrance gates, besides steps and sling gates from the east and north-east corners of the terrace, so that you might with ease get into any part of this sweet park. There were two keepers, each of whom had a house, garden, &c. The beauties of the Castle, Cathedral, and Round Tower were in those days enchanting ; and the natural beauties of the surrounding scenery, the forest, and Long Walk must always remain. Lady Mary Churchill was housekeeper.

On our return to town from this sweet country, which made an impression upon me never to be effaced, I remained with Mrs. White a few days at St. James's, for the purpose of going with them to see the King robed at the House of Lords. We followed into the House with the procession, but being dazzled with the show, and behind the Throne, I can say nothing of the King's speech. Full of gratitude and gratification, I rejoined my mother and brother at Kew, who rejoiced in again having his playfellow.

Here we shall find a few changes. The Princes William and Edward were placed in the house, now the Duke of Cambridge's, with Mons. de Bruyère, their governor, the Rev. John Fisher, afterwards Bishop of Salisbury, and Mr. Farhill, preceptors. Another page was also appointed, Mons. Müller, a Swiss. A gate from the garden took them privately to Kew House. The Princes Ernest and Augustus were removed to the house at the top of the Green. A page was appointed, Mr. Powell, and a dresser, Miss Sorel, for their ages still kept them in the nursery, where Mr. Compton was page, recommended by Lady Charlotte Finch ; we may almost say appointed, for since the introduction of Mrs.

Cheveley, her ladyship had assumed more power to herself. Miss Dacre, related to the Effingham family, had held the post of dresser, to see that the royal children were properly attended to in that particular, either in their airings or at home, and when they made their appearance before their Majesties. Every morning they were expected at the breakfast, which was at nine o'clock, from the eldest to the youngest, whom the wet nurse herself took in. Here the medical man saw them, and invariably directed the meals for the day, including those of the wet-nurse. Mrs. Cheveley, no doubt, while in the nursery before, had observed the growing attachment between Mr. Compton and Miss Dacre, and therefore introduced her sister, Miss Nevin, to succeed. This so disgusted Miss Dacre that she resigned sooner than she had intended, and married Mr. Compton under disadvantageous circumstances. The change was too great. She pined, and gave birth to a stillborn daughter.

Lady Effingham's eldest daughter, Lady Betty Howard, having married Dr. Courtenay, Bishop of Exeter, her ladyship now left Kew as a home, Prince Ernest having done the same before this time, and Pennell Hawkins was removed into their house, with his family. His daughter was married to the Rev. Dr. Mott, whose son afterwards had the appointment of preceptor to Princess Charlotte. I may here mention that more sentiment having been observed in the written exercises given to the Princess than was considered justifiable, he was superseded.

Prince Ernest had wished to marry the great heiress of the North, Miss Bowes, whose fortune exceeded that of the heiress of the South, Miss Tilney Long ; but the King objecting to his being united to a subject, his Royal Highness left England, and never returned. Most certainly such a fortune in Germany would have made him a Prince indeed ; but as he was a younger brother, it might have disturbed the harmony of the house of Mecklenburgh-Strelitz, of which the reigning Duke was not married.

In this summer, 1776, several houses on the Green were sold ; and my father bought the one at the corner for 400*l.* The Queen, who was Lady of the Manor, excused him from paying the 20*l.* which was usual as a fee for copyhold. Mrs. Newton, and her granddaughter, Miss Pullen, became tenants of the house which we had occupied from our first coming to Kew.

On my return to Streatham I was to take up my education with rather more diligence. Needlework, both useful and ornamental, except muslin work, I was tolerably fair in, indeed, in all that I learnt, throwing a veil over French. In music and singing I took a start, for the quartett party, who took up their quarters at the King's Arms Inn, practised at our house, to which Bach had sent a small pianoforte for that purpose. To this my brother and I used to sit and listen for hours, and no doubt our ear for music was insensibly formed from this advantageous opportunity.

The Nicolays had given up their abode in Richmond, and settled in their excellent apartments at St. James's, on the death of their only daughter, from scrofula. She was a fine, clever girl, about twelve. Her mother determined from that time to retire from society, and never to change the then fashion of her dress, and to wear it of the most common material.

As the attendance of Cramer, the violinist, could not always be depended upon, from the multiplicity of his engagements, and as, on the same account, he could not accept a regular appointment, it was then given to Mr. Nicolay, who was a very tolerable performer, having been a scholar of Dubourg's. Wiedemann, the King's master or instructor for the flute, used also to attend occasionally; but after Wendling had been once heard among them no one else would do, until his scholar, Mr. Papendiek, appeared. I will here relate an anecdote of Bach's wonderful powers while in his zenith. He still kept up his agreeable establishment at Richmond, and on Wednesdays Abel usually came down to a *tête-à-tête* dinner, to look over their productions for the morrow; as it was settled by these two that they should at the practices on Thursdays alternately produce something new, either of their own composition or adapted by them. On one occasion Bach had totally forgotten that it was his turn, so after dinner he sat down and wrote an enchanting first movement of a quintett in three flats. He sent off for two copyists, who wrote down the parts from score over his shoulders, while he wrote the harmony, after having composed the melody. This quintett is ranked among the best of his compositions, and the melody is sweetly soothing. In that day three movements formed a piece of music, and about half an hour or a little more was the space of time required for the performance of it.

At Michaelmas, I came home to be equipped for winter, and found that my brother went to day school at Mrs. Newton's. The little boys assembled in one room, Miss Pullen attending in another to the young ladies. She was a cheerful, well-bred young woman, and lived among our neighbours and friends, while Mrs. Newton remained at home in care of the whole.

The sale of these houses made a stir at Kew. Many of the smaller ones were pulled down; others were repaired and beautified; and several new ones were built in Richmond Lane, and those called Gloucester Row, to accommodate a class of assistants that increased in proportion as did the Royal Family.

Kew now became quite gay, the public being admitted to the Richmond Gardens on Sundays, and to Kew Gardens on Thursdays. The Green on these days was covered with carriages, more than 800*l.* being often taken at the bridge on Sundays. Their Majesties were to be seen at the windows speaking to their friends, and the royal children amusing themselves in their own gardens. Parties came up by water, too, with bands of music, to the ait opposite the Prince of Wales's house. The whole was a scene of enchantment and delight; Royalty living amongst their subjects to give pleasure and to do good.

The Christmas holidays brought us together again, and this year in good health.

On the Queen's birthday, January 18, 1777, my brother was to appear in a new dress. He was to be ' breeched,' the term used in those days, and literally so it was. A pair of breeches with a buckle at the knee; a coat with a falling shirt collar hanging over; a waistcoat with pockets long over the thigh; and a cocked hat, round ones not being known; was the costume.

In February, this dear little fellow was to go to school at Hampstead. The house and garden grounds were good, and Mr. Dressler a plodding, persevering teacher. His wife, also a German, was a generous, kind-hearted, active woman. His mother and two daughters composed the family, with an English and a French assistant. My brother attached himself to the youngest daughter, a girl about my age or rather older, and the little fellow soon reconciled himself to his second home. His abilities for the classics were soon discovered by this excellent master, and he was encouraged in the schoolroom, besides being fondled by the females. On Sundays, after the second service, a dinner was prepared for friends in general. The boys were around you in the garden or schoolroom without the least restraint, and it was a general holiday, quite after German fashion. The other days of the week were wholly devoted to business, but never longer than two hours at a sitting, which brought freshness to the work in hand. My father was fortunate in his choice of schools, for this establishment was also, it may be said, without fault. Dear, excellent, worthy people, doing their duty in all respects from principle. On my return to Streatham, I began geography. The manner in which Povoleri communicated his instruction, and the amiability of his whole demeanour, rather made one fly to him than walk in with a pile of books in solemnity to meet him. For the benefit of the Italian, his visits, twice a week, were for the entire day, and Mrs. Povoleri joined us at dinner. I never learnt Italian, but Povoleri used to hear me read over the words of my vocal music.

Early in the spring, the forgery and apprehension of Dr. Dodd, one of the popular preachers of the day, took place.  The young man on whom the bill for 4,000*l.* was drawn was the nephew of the renowned Lord Chesterfield, who wrote the ' Letters to his Son,' 'The Principles of Politeness,' &c., and he afterwards succeeded to the title, as the son to whom Lord Chesterfield addressed the letters was illegitimate.

This nephew, Mr. Stanhope, was a pupil of Dr. Dodd, among others, and while the establishment was carried on at West Ham all went right, but on the doctor's removal to town his ambitious views overcame his reason.  These plunged him into difficulties, which brought him to his ever-to-be-lamented end. He built the chapel in Charlotte Street, Pimlico, with the expectation of the Heir Apparent being brought there to hear him preach ; which, in his opinion, could not fail to procure for him an appointment as preceptor to some of the Princes.  Dr. Dodd undoubtedly was great, superiorly so, in the pulpit, but his disposition was known, and his project entirely failed.  When he preached, the pews were overcrowded, and there was not even standing room left in the church.  The organ was a fine one, built for the chapel, and one of the first that had the swell, or crescendo stop, added.  The children were taught to sing the hymns so prettily, with curtains drawn before the organ gallery, and the whole service was conducted with so much piety and sublimity, that, at the age I then was, eleven, the impression of the duties of religion was so rooted in my mind, that I hope I have lived to increase my veneration for devout exercise, rather than to efface it. Dr. Dodd in his duty was almost unequalled. He greatly improved the funds of the 'Magdalen Charity' by his preaching and attention to the interests of the institution. His disposition was benign, and he spared no pains to increase the welfare of all who crossed his path. The charity for 'Small Debtors' was also by his exertions greatly augmented. Our family always attended Divine service at this Charlotte Street Chapel, where the King and Queen had successive rows of seats for their attendants in the galleries, as well as several pews in the middle aisle. Dr. Dodd was handsome in the extreme, and possessed every personal attraction that could add to the beauty of the service; an harmonious voice, a heart of passion, and the power of showing that he felt his subject deeply. His fate must be deplored. He had no companion to respect, having married incautiously and unadvisedly, and his great abilities knew no check. Out of the House of God, this man lost all power over himself. Humility let us worship, and never lose sight of, depending not upon our own strength or intentions of well-doing. We are indeed weak and know so little! We see the fall of a student in divinity, who appeared to cherish religion as his joy, and may well fear for ourselves. Our instructors commented to us upon this extraordinary circumstance, and many useful lessons were read and expatiated upon.

[At this point there are unfortunately some pages of Mrs. Papendiek's MS. missing; and where we are again able to take up the thread of her narrative, we find her discoursing upon the painter Johann Zoffany, who, as is well known, came over to England about 1764, from Frankfort-on-the-Main, where he was born in 1735. After studying in Italy, he first settled at Coblentz; but being induced to try his fortunes in this country, he was so well received, and so pleased with the life and appreciation of art here, that he settled himself permanently, and was afterwards naturalised as an Englishman.

The picture that Mrs. Papendick describes was the great work executed by Zoffany, by command of King George III. (to whom he was introduced shortly after his arrival), of the ' Tribune ' in the Uffizi Gallery at Florence.—Ed.]

To proceed. The great art that Mr. Zoffany possessed was the grouping of small whole-length figures, and the excellence of the likenesses he took in any style and in any size. When the proposal was made to him to go abroad, he was in the receipt of a good income, and was classed as one of the first, if not the first, in his line. He was to be paid for

his journey to Florence and back, and was to be
allowed 300*l.* a year while painting the ' Tribune ' of
the Gallery.   This picture, when completed, was
placed in a room at Kew House, and the Royal
Academicians were desired by the King to come
down and make their report upon it.   They were
unanimous in their opinion of its superlative excellence.   The beauties of every master were so well
preserved in the copy of the pictures, that the igno-
rant many could almost point out the name of each
artist.   In the foreground is the beautiful Titian
Venus, held by the man who is supposed to be fixing
it for Zoffany to copy, while he himself is seen in
the Gallery listening, as it were, to the observations
of the spectators.   Every countenance is lighted up
with animation ; but the number that he has so won-
derfully grouped, I am ashamed to own, I have
forgotten.   Sir Horace Mann, our Ambassador at
Florence at the time, is conspicuous, as well as many
other Englishmen who were there, and were well
known among their countrymen.   The *cognoscenti*,
in addition to the professors, were agreed that an
allowance of 1,000*l.* a year for life would not more
than pay him for his vast labour, and that less than
700*l.* could not be offered.   Alas, poor Zoffany !   The
moment the question of money was raised, all sorts
of objections were made to the work ; as to the
different persons introduced, that could not interest

the King, and might even be unpleasant to his Majesty to look at; that he had deviated from the order given to him, simply to copy the 'Tribune;' that he had painted portraits of the Imperial Family of Vienna, and others, thereby having lengthened his stay, and retarded the business upon which he left England, and so forth. To these charges he answered—first, the impossibility of daily attendance at the Gallery, as the public could only be kept from it at certain times, and that by favour; that its being built of stone, and very cold, rendered a too close application dangerous, and as it was, Mr. Zoffany had once been brought home with loss of power from intense study, that state of inanition being afterwards considered as the first seizure of paralysis, which some years later carried him to his grave. To the objection made to his having painted certain portraits, he answered that the Emperor of Germany, Joseph II., was accidentally passing through Florence at the time, on his way to the family of Tuscany, his relations, and being delighted with Zoffany's performances, he himself sat for his portrait, and ordered all the members of his family to do the same. These pictures, however, were done in the intervals of his great work, with which they did not in any degree interfere. Zoffany was well rewarded by the Emperor Joseph, and was made a Baron of the Holy Roman Empire. The Emperor, moreover, strongly urged his coming to Vienna, but Zoffany refused on the ground of his commission for the King of England. On account of his having accepted these rewards from the Emperor, Zoffany proposed dropping the 300*l.* a year that was promised to him, but requested payment of his expenses to Florence and back. On this point, another difficulty was started, namely that the agreement had been made with him as a single man; that he had since married, and that therefore his expenses had been increased. What in the end Zoffany received, I cannot assert, but I am certain that it was under 1,000*l.* The picture was put out of sight, and it was not till it was exhibited in the collection of George IV. that it was again even recollected. His old friends stuck by him, and he was made a Royal Academician and Visitor immediately.

He took a house in Strand-of-the-Green, and one in town at the corner of Albemarle and Stafford Streets. Dear Mrs. Zoffany was the friend of my youthful days; it was always a holiday to go to see her. She was a perfect beauty, good-natured, kind, and very charitable. She was not of equal rank with her husband, and when she married him, at fourteen years of age, having had no education, her mind was not formed. During the seven years they spent in Italy, however, she did receive some instruction, and spoke the language perfectly. Their eldest child was a boy, who died from an accident at sixteen months old. This calamity nearly lost poor Zoffany his life; indeed, he never thoroughly overcame it.

At the time of which I am writing, I was too young to understand the position in life of Mrs. Zoffany, which was not wholly respected, but I subsequently learnt all the particulars of her story, which, though it began sadly, ended in perfect happiness as far as her husband was concerned. As it is full of interest and incident, I will here briefly relate what in later years I heard from her own lips.

Mr. Zoffany, talented as he was, and always in the best society, yet in his leisure hours prowled around for victims of self-gratification. He found out the humble dwelling of Mrs. Zoffany's parents, and the beauty of their daughter he determined to possess. Very soon after he made her acquaintance came the order for him to proceed to Italy, to copy the Florentine Gallery, and as this poor child, who was at that time only fourteen years old, already bore the mark of criminality, she hastened to the vessel in which he was to sail, and got on board before Mr. Zoffany and the other passengers arrived. During the voyage she discovered herself to him, and he resolved, on landing, to place her where she would be educated, and taken care of during her confinement. A boy was the child born.

Immediately after this event, Mr. Zoffany made inquiries about his wife, to whom he had been married some time, and who had returned to her native place in Germany on account of the unhappy manner in which she dragged on her existence in England, for he was far from kind to her; and finding that she had died a few months before, he married the object of his admiration, who had become a mother at fifteen.

Her heart was devoted to doing the best she could to render herself worthy of her husband. She made rapid progress in learning Italian, and also in reading and writing her own language, and in that polish of manner so essential to the position of a lady. She was a good mother to her boy though still so young, and her beauty, good dressing, and a natural elegance of appearance, combined with the feeling of happiness which shone in her countenance, soon fitted her for any society, and she and her husband were taken up in the most hospitable and flattering manner by the Tuscan family, the Duke being related to Joseph II., Emperor of Germany.

The boy being now more than a year old, it was advised that he should be weaned, and the governess or head nurse of the Royal Family was to have him, with his maid, under her care. Poor little fellow, all was going on well, when on one sad day he was in his go-cart, and running to the door, where this lady was speaking to some one, he fell down a whole flight of stairs. No bones were broken, but the head much bruised. Those who remember Mrs. Zoffany will suppose that she ran frantic to the spot, but fortunately so conducted herself as not to offend. The baby sucked again, and knew his mother, which augured favourably, but at the end of three weeks he died of abscess at the back of the head.

Mr. Zoffany was not to be comforted, and, as I before observed, he never wholly got over this terrible calamity. However, he was encouraged to go on with his work in the Gallery, and though this interest, in a measure, distracted him from his own private sorrow, it had an evil effect in another way—for it was at this time that, in order to drown his thoughts, he overworked himself, which brought on the first attack of paralysis, when he lost the use of his limbs, and for some time his senses.

Their eldest daughter, Theresa, late Mrs. Doxatt, was born some little time after, and before they quitted Florence, Cecilia, late Mrs. Horn, was also born.

On their return to England we made their acquaintance. I was then fourteen, and the impression she made upon me caused me to think all she did and said perfection. Before she was introduced to his friends, Zoffany should have married her according to the Protestant religion and our law.

The neglect of this laid the foundation for the supposition that she was not his wife. She could not be expected to know much about these ceremonies, and he never thought about them from a religious point of view. He was aware of the good conduct of his spouse, and took care that his friends held her in respect, but it was cruel to leave her fair fame under a cloud that could have been so easily removed.

Mrs. Zoffany's father died soon after the flight of his poor child ; but the widowed mother was settled comfortably by Zoffany in a little home of her own, not very far from his house at Strand-of-the Green.

Greatly were my parents blamed for allowing the affectionate intercourse between Mrs. Zoffany and myself. I can only say that industry, care, and a spirit to do right were the examples I met with, and a kind and warm heart ready and anxious to return every sentiment of friendship.

Notwithstanding the doubt about her marriage in the minds of .. few, she was very generally admired and beloved, and was able to introduce her two daughters after a time into good society.

While Zoffany was living at Strand-of-the-Green, he painted his famous picture of ' The Last Supper ' for St. George's Chapel at Windsor, which was repaired and beautified during the reign of George III. The picture has remained, and may still be seen in its old position.

# CHAPTER IV.

Marriage of Miss Kamus with Sir John Day—Alterations at Windsor
Castle—The elder Princes reside there—First flaw in the harmony
of the royal household—Royal entertainments and amusements—
Mrs. Papendiek introduced to the Thrales—Meets Dr. Johnson—
Marriage of Miss Eveleigh—School entertainment—Mrs. Papendiek
leaves school—Great regret—New Year gaieties—Music lessons—
Terrific hurricane—Prince William enters the Navy—Mrs. Trimmer—
Bach's troubles—First introduction of pianofortes—Illness of Miss
Fry—Death of Mrs. Sainsbury—Agreeable and artistic society—
Singers—Dancers and actors—Return to Streatham—Dancing lessons
—Dr. Johnson and Miss Burney—Sir Joshua Reynolds—Angelica
Kauffmann — Gainsborough — Anecdotes — Ball at Sir Abraham
Pitcher's—Minuet de la Cour.

ANOTHER Princess being brought into the nursery,
Prince Adolphus joined his elder brothers.

The eldest daughter of Mr. Kamus, one of the
senior pages to the King, about this time was married
to Sir John Day.  On its being notified, according to
the usual form, that Lady Day would be presented
at the next Drawing-room, the Queen objected to it
on account of the position her father held in the
household; but when, shortly after, Sir John Day
was appointed Governor of one of our East India
settlements, the right of presentation could no longer
be disputed.  Lady Day and Miss Tunstall had been

intimate friends from their infancy, and the great desire of her ladyship now was that her brother William, who was also a page at Court, should marry Sally Tunstall, and join her in India, where, through her husband's influence, she hoped soon to be able to obtain a good situation for him. No objection on the part of the lady was raised, but the gentleman could not be prevailed upon. He had formed an attachment for Miss Goldsworthy, and proposed to her; but upon the Queen saying that in the event of her marriage she must quit her situation, the idea was given up.

The Prince of Wales having now, 1778, attained his sixteenth year, it was taken into consideration how his leisure hours from study could be more amused. It was known to their Majesties that among the several preceptors, both reverend and noble, a diversity of opinion upon this question existed, and it was necessary, in consequence, to make some changes. Much do I lament to add that some of those about the young Princes swerved from principle, and introduced improper company when their Majesties supposed them to be at rest, and after the divines had closed their day with prayer.

It was now determined to examine the accommodation of Windsor Castle, which, from the beauty of its situation, the space in its parks and the surrounding country for field sports, and its general magnitude, was considered a most desirable spot for the residence of the elder Princes. The south side of the Castle was occupied by Lord Walsingham's family, the Waldegraves, and others; and the tower at the south-west corner by Colonel Egerton and his family. The King, with his well-known consideration, would not have them disturbed; but the lower range of rooms at the east side, opening on an inclosed terrace walk, was chosen for the two Princes, and allotted to them with a chosen few of their attendants. Among these, unfortunately, were Colonels Lake and Hulse, the very men who should have been avoided. The house of Lord Talbot, opposite the Castle, was accepted, upon his offer of resignation, for the Royal Family, and Sir William Chambers came down to make the necessary alterations. A building was thrown out at the back for the King's and Queen's apartments, and a new wing towards the Home Park was added for the offices. The corner house on the hill to the right was to be for Mr. Montagu, who was to come down for the riding, the third house being set apart for the clerk of the works, Mr. Tilderley, with apartments in it for Sir William Chambers. When this was all arranged, their Majesties would occasionally go down to Windsor, through this summer, from Monday to Wednesday, to expedite the works, and to make further arrangements. The King purchased the

Duke of St. Albans' house, at the back of which there was a range of rooms looking into the garden of the house now known as Windsor Lodge and the garden adjoining it. The front of this house was in St. Albans' Street, in which were also situated the King's stables. On the furniture of the Duke's house being sold, Martin, of the Castle Inn, bought the bedstead, with its hangings and the bedding, which had been Nell Gwynne's, and which to this day is in the same inn.

The people of Richmond, on hearing of the preparations that were going on at Windsor, now came forward to offer the land that had before been refused, even to entreaty; but it was too late. That portion of the mansion that had been built was now to be taken down, and the part of the Richmond gardens that had been inclosed was turned into farming land. From this period I think we may date the first flaw in the harmony of those regulations hitherto so successfully followed by the Royal Family. The concentration of the whole was disturbed, and different interests succeeded.

To say that the Princes had not been sufficiently in company, or early enough introduced, is, in my opinion, erroneous. From their infancy they had been taken to St. James's regularly on Thursdays, when the company at the Drawing-rooms had also paid their compliments to the royal children, the

Prince of Wales and the Duke of York being always in a room distinct from the others. From the age of ten they always attended the evening parties from eight till ten o'clock.

These parties were held on Tuesdays and Thursdays, when between two and three hundred were invited to cards and music. The concert consisted of the private band, with the addition of other talented performers. Among these were Stanley for the organ; Cramer, the King's former master; and the Cervettos, father and son, violinists; with Crosdil, Parke, and others, besides the Miss Linleys, and other singers of the day. Their Majesties attended the theatre once a week, and on the remaining evenings there was company more or less.

In the country at Kew, after their early dinner at four o'clock, the King and Queen would usually have their family around them, at full liberty, and enjoying themselves with their attendants, and often visitors suited to their different ages. There were birthday entertainments, dances, fireworks, arranged by Mr. Powel, and a constant variety of amusements adapted to their several tastes, to diversify the usual routine, the elder Princes and Princesses attending the small evening parties of the Queen at Kew, upon the same plan as when in London.

Mixing in company no doubt enlarges the ideas of the young, gives ease to their manner, and is of advantage to them generally, taking it for granted that those who introduce them take every precaution in the choice of their companions; but it lends little aid to the formation of the mind. That, however, should be done principally in the hours of recreation, when the tutor or attendant should discover, by imperceptible means, the inclinations and tastes of each pupil, directing their pastimes into such channels as may tend to divert evil propensities, and give encouragement to rational pleasures and pursuits. This is the great secret and difficulty of education, and makes it necessary that we should exercise great judgment in our selection of those to whose care we entrust the development of our children's minds. The young are naturally very impressionable, and with judicious training they may be led to amend the follies of youth, and, by God's grace, continue in the path of righteousness.

To return to my own narrative. After a pleasant holiday, my brother and I returned to our respective schools. In this half-year, 1778, I was introduced to the neighbouring families; amongst others, to the Thrales, on Streatham Common, where Dr. Johnson and Miss Burney usually resided, and where the late Duke of Bedford might constantly be met. Being in delicate health, he was brought up at Streatham by private tuition, in a house at the corner of the road leading to Norwood, then part of the estate belonging to the Duke's family, but which has recently been sold. Opposite were some detached houses, in which lived Sir Abraham and Lady Pitcher, with five daughters, the Whitelocks, the Chapmans, and the Groves, whose two daughters were at our school. So intimate were we with the Pitchers, that a gate was opened between our respective gardens that brought us to each other in a few minutes.

In the autumn, an occurrence took place that made an impression on us all. Miss Vaughan was to leave school to be introduced at the ball on the evening of the Lord Mayor's Day, by dancing a minuet, in imitation of the evenings of the King's and Queen's birthdays at St. James's, when the young nobility were introduced in the same manner. Her mother, Mrs. Vaughan, arrived at Streatham, not, as we expected, to fetch her for this event, but on a very different mission. It was to tell her daughter that Mr. Vaughan, who was a wholesale haberdasher, had failed, and so lamentable was their condition that they were no longer at home, but in the house of a friend. Miss Vaughan, with the presence of mind of a good heart and of a strong family affection, said, ' I thank you, dear mother, for my liberal education, which I shall hope now to turn to account for your comfort.' She was then told that an offer had been made by the Ishams to take her to Paris to keep up their children's English, but she preferred taking an engagement as a regular governess. She had always been assiduous, and very eager to improve, but she had no taste for the ornamental. She learnt music, but it could never interest anyone to listen to the extreme accuracy of her performance, with a coldness and seeming want of mind that was unaccountable. For drawing and needle-work she had more feeling, but books particularly took hold of her attention. She had an excellent understanding, and a good disposition; but as she never associated with her companions in the usual pursuits of the young, nor in any way cultivated a friendly intercourse, she was not generally beloved. She was at this time seventeen, and was highly respected, and looked up to as a superior being, and in her trouble was greatly commiserated. The carriage took Mrs. and Miss Vaughan to town, and brought back the second daughter, Rebecca, who was then in delicate health, which the present anxiety naturally increased. She remained with us at Streatham as long as she could derive benefit from the fresh air and kind care of the family; but very soon after her return home, we heard of her death in decline. Mrs. Kay then took the youngest daughter, Josepha, who from her shining abilities soon became of every use in the school. She was lively and social among us, but being very capricious she was not a universal favourite, but **was** much beloved by some and dreaded by others.

Another event of a very different character now happened at our school. Miss Sainsbury, whom I have before mentioned, had been married for some time to Mr. Langford, of the firm of auctioneers in the Piazza, Covent Garden, and on a fine golden morning in October Mrs. Langford called in her father's carriage from Morden to take Miss Eveleigh, Mrs. Kay, and her sister to town to see the King robed, as Parliament was opened on that day. We wondered first at the early start, and then at the elegance of the dresses, and still more when Mrs. Kay and Miss Sainsbury returned alone ; but as for some time before this Miss Eveleigh had been but little with us, this did not excite any suspicion. Judge, then, of our surprise when, two days afterwards, Mr. Sainsbury conducted her into our schoolroom as his bride ! So well had the courtship been managed, that not even the gossips of the village had any idea of what was going on. Miss Eveleigh was forty-two years of age at the time she left her happy home, where everyone loved, respected, and adored her.

Two immense wedding cakes were brought in, covered with favours, the bells of the church were rung, and the greatest joy prevailed, for a wedding is always a source of pleasure when the preliminaries are conducted with caution and propriety.

After a few moments' reflection, we requested their company to partake of our humble endeavours to entertain them, and the following Tuesday was proposed. Our invitations were to the families near us, whose names I have before mentioned, as well as to as many of our young friends as we could offer accommodation to in the house, for in those days people did not care to drive any distance at night on account of the highway and footpad robberies, which were of daily, or rather nightly, occurrence. Brixton Hill, now an inhabited suburb, was then a noted place for danger, as well as St. George's Fields, and Kennington Common, on which a house, called 'The Horns,' was supposed to be the rendezvous of the depredators.

Our schoolroom was spacious, and we decorated it, for this auspicious occasion, very tastefully with laurestina and mountain ash, interspersed with ribbons, and it was lighted with wax candles, as lamps were not then in use for rooms, and gas was quite unknown, it not being used to light the streets of London even, till the year 1814. The forms were covered with green baize, and the whole, for the convenience of the dancers and the comfort of the company, most properly put in order. We were divided into parties, one to receive the company, another to superintend the going, a third to conduct the dance, another the music, another the supper, and the sixth to direct the handing of refreshments, which included tea, a luxury in those days. New dresses we were compelled to dispense with, there being no time to procure them. Every guest and every inmate of the house had cake and a favour, and the whole entertainment was a complete success. The fragments were so considerable that they made an evening for our dependants in the village, the charity school being particularly attended to. To this institution Mr. Sainsbury gave a handsome sum of money, and all was joy. Our gates were illuminated, as well as several others through which the bride had to pass on her way from Morden, with the design of proving to her how greatly she was beloved for her sweet angelic nature throughout the whole neighbourhood. We received our guests in the drawing-room, in which was the organ, with choruses, and then we would have them all down to see the dancing. Dr. Johnson's own easy chair was placed by the fire, in which I think I see him now, dear old friend! He told us all to talk to him, as that was what he liked, and his kind benevolent heart made him a favourite with us all. In return for our welcome, we were to go, six at a time, which constituted a coach full, to dine at Morden, on the Sundays when the Sainsburys were at home; but only one set went this year, as it was late in the season, and I was not of the number, as for this first

occasion we cast lots.    I was, however, lucky enough
to be present at all the other entertainments that
were given in honour of the bride, by the Thrales,
the Groves', and others in the neighbourhood.    For
these occasions we had wedding dresses—garments,
I hope I may call them, as we were sincere in our
feelings.    I was a girl who put heart and feeling into
everything I undertook, and my nickname was
' Albert here, Albert there, Albert everywhere.'

Alas! this happy half-year ended, and we went
home for the Christmas holidays.    My father had
been, during the summer months of this year, 1778,
to Portsmouth, to see the English fleet when it returned after the engagement between Keppel and
D'Orvilliers off Ushant, and to visit the camps of Cox
Heath and Warley Common with their Majesties.
On this account, he had not taken me home, as usual ;
and now it was settled that I was to leave school, to
my intense regret.

Dear parent, I thank thee for what thou hast done,
but it was imperfect.    A little longer, and I might
have arrived nearer to the point you intended in
your desire to see me well educated.    As it was, I
found myself at home without the means of proceeding with what had been so desirably begun in that
ever to be respected mansion of all that was good
and amiable.    My mother was a careful, industrious
woman, and praiseworthy in all that she did for our

convenience, support, and the requisites of life; but unfortunately she never changed from the customs of her country to those of the one where all her dearest interests should now have been engrafted. Her three children were looking towards her for a home to be made congenial to their feelings. We had all been brought up to make use of time, and to endeavour to cultivate such abilities as had been given to us, by study. My mother, however, with her German ideas, kept us up to every perfection of domesticity, carefully teaching us every principle of it, and thought it loss of time when she saw us differently employed. Only one sitting-room was allowed to be used, which will speak for itself as to the impossibility of doing anything that required thought.

After the usual gaieties of New Year's Day, the birthday of the Queen, and a few evenings spent with our friends, my brother returned to Hampstead, and I found myself alone, totally at a loss what plan to pursue. I begged of my father to allow me a music master, which he did, and Bach recommended Mr. Benser, himself sometimes hearing me play his sonatas, and the third set of concertos, and playing with me a duet, also of his composition, then much in vogue. I observed to him that Mr. Benser did not communicate his art with that engaging interest I was accustomed to with dear old Knyvett; when he answered, ' Poor child, you have entered upon life early, and with heart and enthusiasm ; I pity thee, as it will be soon checked.'

It was the regulation that the move to Kew should usually take place about the middle of May, and that the Royal Family and attendants should return to town for one week to include the King's birthday on June 4. This day was always passed in gaiety and enjoyment. We were with the family while dressing at St. James's, saw the company at the Drawing-room, and had the pleasure of meeting our friends and acquaintances.

I must not forget to mention a terrific hurricane which passed over the metropolis at the commencement of this year, 1779. The wind blew violently from the north-west, and took off the upper corner of the 'Queen's House.' This was the room next to the one in which the Princes Ernest, Augustus, and Adolphus slept, which was over the bedroom of their Majesties. The King was up, and with his children in a moment. The ceiling was falling fast, and had already broken the bedstead of the elder Prince, but they were soon placed in safety with their attendant, Mrs. Long, and no harm happened to them. Nineteen trees were torn up in St. James's Park, and serious damage was done in other parts of London. The hearth was thrown up in the drawing-room of our apartments, the windows of our kitchen were beaten in, and but for the perseverance of my mother in nailing up boards, and pertinaciously keeping all doors shut to preclude the possibility of draught, we should have suffered much more than we did. Earlier in the day the storm had passed over some districts outside London. In a lane near Roehampton every tree was torn up for about two miles, with many other visitations. This was at noon. At night, Hammersmith Church was struck, and much more damage was done. In my uncle's house at Kew, a large glass, fixed to the wall, was thrown down, and the sensation of dread was universal as long as this frightful storm lasted.

On June 14, my playfellow, his Royal Highness Prince William, who was to be in the Navy, joined the 'Prince George' at Portsmouth, under Admiral Digby. He went through the different stages, cabin boy, midshipman, &c., but, at the end of the season, he was to be raised to the rank of post captain. The Reverend Henry Majendie, youngest son of Dr. Majendie, was appointed the Prince's preceptor on board, and was to proceed with him to any station to which the ship might be ordered. Naval instruction he went through minutely, and his present Majesty was always looked upon as an able seaman.

The Queen was now anxious for the Princesses' improvement in the German language, and appointed the German chaplain, Mr. Schroeder, their master. The days that he came down to Kew for this purpose, he remained with us, which gave me the opportunity of reading English with him, and we went through the ‘Spectator,’ the ‘Guardian,’ and the ‘Idler.’ Mr. Roberts also taught me to write, which introduced me to the Trimmers, whose relation he was, and with whom he resided.

[Mrs. Trimmer was the daughter of the Kirby who was President of the ‘Society of Artists’ of Great Britain, out of which grew the Royal Academy. Of this man, Gainsborough was not only a great admirer, but a sincere friend, and it was his last desire to be buried beside him. Their tombs, therefore, adjoin one another in Kew Churchyard, where they may to this day be seen.—ED.]

Morning visits in this exemplary family could not be admitted, for Mrs. Trimmer was employed in writing her excellent works on education, while the eldest daughter, acting as bookkeeper, was in the accounting-room, and the second daughter, Sarah, was instructing her younger brothers and sisters in the schoolroom. Mr. Ernst, one of the King's pages, proposed marriage to the eldest daughter, Charlotte Trimmer, but it was not consented to, much to the annoyance of the young people. Sarah became governess to the daughters of the late Duchess of Devonshire, and was held in high estimation by that family. She had been offered the post of sub-governess to Princess Charlotte,

but she refused it when she found that she was to
be restricted in the mode of communicating instructions. Miss Gale, who was also a most fit person
to hold that appointment, had resigned it for the
same reason.

Mrs. Haverfield occasionally took me to our
mutual friends' houses in the evening, but I lost
much of the pleasures of society by my mother keeping herself so persistently out of it.

Their Majesties, during this summer, went down
to Windsor every Friday till Wednesday, and Kew
Gardens were opened to the public on Mondays,
when the Royal Family were absent. The Drawing-
room now was held once a fortnight on Thursdays,
instead of weekly, as heretofore. The quartett
party, too, only met once a fortnight. Bach gave up
his house at Richmond partly on this account, and
partly on account of a serious robbery which he
suffered from his housekeeper. He was in the
habit of giving her money every month to pay his
bills, which she brought to him receipted, having,
however, appropriated the money. On its being
rumoured that he was going to leave Richmond,
the tradespeople became clamorous, and the truth
came out. The woman absconded, and Bach was
left to pay a second time between eleven and twelve
hundred pounds. This shook him, and other
troubles followed.

The oratorio performances, in which he was engaged as one of the proprietors, in a great measure failed. He had composed for the occasion, and played between the acts, his second concerto. A modern piece was usual, but as it was to be heard on the organ, it was ill chosen, for, though beautiful in itself, it did not accord with the sacred performance, and Bach being no organ player the whole thing rather tended to detract from the success of the evening. About this time pianofortes were first introduced into this country. They had been in use for some little time in Germany, and were considered a very successful invention. Those instruments now known as 'small pianofortes' were the first that made their appearance in England, and those of a square shape shortly followed, upright ones not being known till much later.

I went, by invitation, for a month to Streatham with my cousin Charlotte, when she returned there after the Christ.nas holidays. Very different was the scene to meet me to that which closed my last happy half-year. Miss Fry was seized with rheumatic fever, which confined her to her room for six weeks, and when recovering exerted herself to gain an additional mile daily in her drives, in the cherished hope that she might reach Mrs. Sainsbury's at Morden—a hope, alas! never to be realised. The latter had given birth to a daughter, and under the affectionate care of

Noverre, being a Frenchman, professed himself *en-chanté*. He was also particularly pleased with my manner of giving and withdrawing the hand. In the minuet de la Cour I was renowned for my finish of the different movements, the jump being accomplished without brusqueness. In those days, dancing was considered quite an important part of the education, and the grace shown in the various movements was very different to the rough style of the present day, proving at a glance if a young lady were refined and had received an elegant education.

My former friends received me gladly, but I found some changes among them. Miss Chapman was on the point of marriage with Lord Turnour, who soon after, through the death of his father, became Earl of Winterton; Miss Whitelock was married to the Reverend Mr. Meyrick, Rector of Morden; and the eldest of the Pitchers was married to Captain Boyce.

The Thrales and dear old Dr. Johnson were pleased to have me back again amongst them. He, the Doctor, said he liked me because I was frank and open-hearted, and glad to be corrected. He, poor man, was very untidy, but we did not love or respect him the less for that, and Mrs. Thrale, with her kind disposition, always endeavoured to hide from the world as much as possible his deficiencies in dress, &c. His wigs were a constant source of trouble, for they were not only dirty and unkempt, but generally burnt away in the front, for, being very nearsighted, he often put his head into the candle when poring over his books. Whenever he was staying with the Thrales, therefore, the butler used to waylay him as he passed in to dinner, and pull off the wig on his head, replacing it with a new one. This was of almost daily occurrence. An amusing story of Hannah More and Dr. Johnson, which I have heard, I will relate here. She was most desirous to have an interview with him, and at last obtained a promise that he would receive her at his house in town. Thither, then, she repaired with a friend, and was shown into his library to await his convenience, where, seeing a big leathern chair, she cast herself into it, saying, 'This is doubtless the great man's chair! I will try to gain from it a few sparks of his genius.' On his entering the room, she told him what she had done, when in his quiet, dry manner, he answered, 'Unfortunately, I never sit in that chair. I should be afraid of its gloomy inspirations.' About this time, Miss Burney's first publication made its appearance, under the title of ' Evelina,' and Dr. Johnson introduced it to us, saying that a novel of a new character had been put into his hand, in which each of the persons introduced spoke in his or her own line, and that the moral was unobjectionable. He would, therefore, have it read, and Miss Burney, as usual, was deputed to do so. As she pro-

ceeded, Mrs. Thrale kept saying that the turn of
the sentences and the general tone were familiar to
her ear, and that she must find out the author. Many
surmises were started, and at last Miss Burney, finding that the book met with approbation among her
friends, acknowledged herself to be the authoress.
Dr. Johnson obtained for her increased payment,
and she then produced her 'Cecilia,' which I believe
to be considered equally good.

At the Thrales I often met Sir Joshua Reynolds,
who visited there. He was knighted at the time that
he was made the first President of the Royal Academy
in 1768, when the exhibitions were held in a large
room at Dalton's print shop in Pall Mall. He painted
a portrait of Dr. Johnson for Mr. Thrale's picture
gallery, and several others of renowned men of the
day; among them, one of Goldsmith, for whom
he entertained a sincere affection. He was a great
admirer of the pretty and graceful Angelica Kauffmann, one of the original thirty-six members of the
Royal Academy, a young Italian artiste, who was
brought over to England by her patrons, the English
Ambassador and his wife, and shortly afterwards introduced to Sir Joshua. There were rumours that
he intended to propose marriage to her; but though
she certainly attracted him, this idea never came
to anything. When Gainsborough first settled in
London, Reynolds called upon him, and though there

was at first a strong feeling of rivalry between these two great painters, they eventually became firm friends. They adopted totally different styles, Gainsborough being especially renowned for his effects of colouring, for which he is as much famed in his landscapes as in his portraits, while Sir Joshua showed his great talent in the drawing and general arrangement of his figures, as well as in his delicacy of colouring, the charming adaptation of costume, and the gracefulness of his draperies, which are more especially noticeable in his female portraits. He was undoubtedly our greatest English portrait painter, though closely rivalled by Gainsborough, and followed by Sir Thomas Lawrence, who became in his turn the greatest portrait painter of his day, and on the death of Sir Joshua Reynolds in 1792 he was appointed painter to the King.[1]

[1] 'These illustrious rivals fully admitted each other's excellence. "D——n him, how various he is!" exclaimed Gainsborough as he passed before the pictures of Reynolds in one of the exhibitions. "I cannot think how he produces his effects," said Reynolds while examining a portrait by Gainsborough. These were greater praises, considering from whom they came, than volumes of encomium from ordinary critics.' From *The Life and Times of Sir J. Reynolds* by C. R. Leslie and Tom Taylor.

In the same work may be found the following description of the lovely and famed portrait of Georgiana, Duchess of Devonshire:

'It was this beautiful young duchess who set the fashion of the feather headdresses, now a mark for all the witlings of the time. Sir Joshua has painted her in her new-fashioned plumes, in the full-length portrait now at Spencer House. The picture was at this time (1775) in progress, and was exhibited the next year. But, with his usual moderation, he has lowered the bewitching Duchess's feathers.'

Among other friends I must mention Mrs. Grove, with whom I passed many a happy day. She taught me to make caps and to assist myself in many articles of millinery, in which work I became quite an adept, so that when I saw any little thing I liked, I could imitate it. At the Pitchers' we did a great deal of fancy work in trifles, such as purses, plaited ribbon, watch chains, ribbon work, and so on. With them I went to the Croydon Assembly, as our ladies were still in mourning. Sir Abraham Pitcher, during his mayoralty, rebuilt his house at Streatham, and furnished it elegantly. On opening it, a ball was given, and here I was to shine. Noverre ordered my white kid shoes from the opera-shoe maker. He also would have the sleeve of my gown made to his order, that my arm might be observed ; and the train was to be thrown back, so that it might not impede my 'beautiful' steps ! Peggy, the eldest unmarried daughter, opened the ball with Captain Boyce. Then followed her sister, Penelope, and then your humble servant. After supper, I commenced with the minuet de la Cour, and several couples joined in the gavotte. It was a very enjoyable entertainment, and all the best families of the neighbourhood were there.

In the spring I was one of the scholars who attended Noverre's benefit ball, at the Hanover Square Rooms. I was among the first minuet dancers, but second in the cotillion. My dress, therefore. was white, another set wore pink, and the third light blue. I made Bach come to see us dance, as they were his rooms, and so delighted was he that it gave me a lift in his affection.

Mr. Kay passed his Easter holidays at Streatham, Mr. Fry being still with us, and time passed gaily. Mr. Kay was always quaint, clever, and eminently calculated for the law; but, strange to say, though he possessed superior abilities, he became so diffident, or timid, I scarcely know what to term it, that instead of signalising himself at the Bar, as his good mother fondly hoped he would, he became prothonotary, and marrying a lady with money, he has passed his life almost in privacy. This time that I speak of was the last we ever met. Though we visited in the same families, and have even to this very year, 1833, exchanged letters, chance has never brought us together again. The affection I ever bore towards him, as the relative of those I sincerely loved, while living, and shall, as long as I am blessed with recollection, respect and venerate in memory, is not in the least diminished by time or the want of opportunity to renew.

# CHAPTER V.

First introduction to Mr. Papendiek—Leaving school for good—The
Gordon Riots—The royal children sent to Kew—A party for Vaux-
hall—Attack by highwaymen—Visit to Newgate—The Fleet—
Covent Garden Theatre--Lecture on Heads—Domestic arrangements
at Windsor—Birth of Prince Alfred—Daily routine—Apollo of the
Day—Bach's distress—Schroeder—Crosdill—Bach's benefit—Mrs.
Abingdon—Comedy—Gaieties at Kew—Fashion in dress—Mr. Papen-
diek—He proposes marriage.

NOTHING occurred further during this happy half-
year (I am writing of 1780) worth recording, except the visit of Mr. Papendiek at the end of it,
when he accompanied my mother to fetch me home.
Mrs. Kay seemed equally struck with myself at his
appearance, and, observing something like embarrassment in my manner, she cautioned me, before leaving
her roof, against the difficulties into which I might
be led.

Oh, I cannot describe my sensations when the great
doors closed upon us. My senses seemed darkened,
and I knew not how to regain my cheerfulness.

And now, new and sad scenes opened to my
view. London was in confusion. The Association,
headed by Lord George Gordon, had presented a

petition to Parliament against some act of concession to the Roman Catholics, and the riots, which afterwards proved so alarming, had already begun. Placards with ' No Popery ' were posted in all the streets ; the Bishops were very roughly handled, having their wigs turned on their heads as they alighted from their carriages at the door of the House of Lords ; and many members of Parliament were jostled and annoyed. Every night the rioters encamped themselves in St. George's Fields. Mr. Meyer, who was always eager for information, and my father, who endeavoured to obtain any information which might be useful to his patroness, went together among these men. For a day or two they could not liberate themselves, but they succeeded in gaining the intelligence that June 4 would be held secure, and that the pageantry would be suffered to proceed as usual, unmolested ; but that day over, extremities would be resorted to.

It was a fine day, but with a strong cold east wind. After the Drawing-room was over, the royal children, except the two elder Princes, were removed to Kew, and we also went. The appearance of the streets was desolate. The dust was rising in clouds, and scarcely a soul was to be seen. Terror was depicted upon the countenances of the few who were moving, and altogether it was an evening to create an impression of wretchedness.

Princess Mary, afterwards Duchess of Gloucester, was at Kew ill, with an abscess in the arm, and undergoing excruciating pain. The elder Princes came down on the 5th, but their Majesties remained in London. The King was almost constantly engaged with his Ministers, but as a recreation he rode every morning from four till seven o'clock, when he often came down to see his children, on whom he fondly doted. When walking on the bridge with our neighbours on the Wednesday evening during these riots (I think it was the 11th of the same month) we saw fires from eleven different places in London. The military, under the Commander-in-Chief, Lord Amherst, had orders to act whenever required, and that, at length, restored order. Newgate and other prisons were burnt, and the prisoners set free, and among other acts to be deplored was the destruction of the renowned Lord Mansfield's manuscripts and the spoliation of his house. Many of the houses of Roman Catholics were marked for destruction, and some of the Ambassadors' chapels, as well as the large Langdale Distillery, were totally destroyed.

Camps for the soldiers were formed in Hyde Park, in the Green Park, and round the Court in St. James's Park, so that the orderlies were moving under the King's eye, and no order issued without his knowledge. It was thought at the time that his vigilance saved the metropolis from further harm.

The Lord Mayor, Kennett, received a reprimand from the City for his inactivity, and it was agitated to remove him from the civic chair, and elect another to finish his term of mayoralty; but as this poor inefficient man was strong in politics for the Government, secret influence protected him.

All being again quiet, and something like order restored, everybody was, as it were, set at liberty, and while the King and Council were at work, the populace were at play—ourselves among the number, for we formed a party first for Vauxhall, and secondly for passing a day in London to visit the scenes of horror that had occurred in the short space of a few days.

The party from Kew for Vauxhall consisted of my mother, myself, Mr. Papendick, and Mr. and Mrs. Brown, and we proceeded to Mr. Stillingfleet's, in Stafford Row, Pimlico, where it was arranged that my father and some other friends should meet us. After a most elegant tea, given in tents on their lawn, we proceeded to Vauxhall, with which, I believe, we were all equally enchanted, although in these days we are so genteel that we should not admit it to have been even bearable. I heard the famous Vernon sing, and Mrs. Weichsel, a German, originally a scholar of Bach's. We supped, and went through the whole of the amusements, including the Cascade, an object of attraction at that period.    After this agreeable evening's entertainment, we parted, each to return to our respective homes.   Our Kew party returned through Clapham, Barnes, &c., by the advice of the coachman, who said it was shorter than the road by which we had come up.   The man was a stranger to us, but he was employed by Shrubsole, the liveryman at Richmond, with whom my father had dealt for years, and who had all the business of the Court, so we had no doubt but that all was right.   However, on turning from Barnes Terrace to the beginning of Mortlake Lane, I saw three men run up from the waterside. One went to the horses' heads, while one came to each side of the carriage, opened the doors, and demanded our money.   Mr. Papendiek gave his purse, which he said contained but little, as we were just returned from Vauxhall, and he had nothing more to give, upon which the fellow made him get out of the carriage to be searched. He found nothing upon him but a clasp knife, which opened with a spring, and after examining it by the glimmering daylight, and finding that he could not shut it, he returned it with an oath, saying to his companion, 'Clear your gentleman, we will not disturb the ladies,' and so it ended.   The coachman was anxious to pursue the men, but I strongly opposed having the horses left, added to which I was sure that the man on Mr. Papendiek's side was a desperate subject.  He had a horse-pistol, and from his manner of fixing the lock I was confident that it was loaded.  I had obtained some knowledge of pistol firing from the quartett party, who with my father constantly amused themselves with taking aim at a target, at which practice I was allowed to be present.  We suspected the coachman of complicity in the affair; but as his master assured us that he was free from blame, we desired that no further notice should be taken of it.

When we ordered the carriage for our second expedition, the same coachman requested to be allowed to drive us, in order to establish his character for honesty.

Our party was the same as the former one.  We started early in the morning, walked round the different camps, and then drove to Mr. Clay's, in King Street, Covent Garden, where my father met us, and where we were most hospitably received by the family, which consisted of father and son and three daughters.  The eldest daughter was particularly amiable and interesting, and was shortly to be married to Mr. King.  The son, young Clay, was a delicate, agreeable, gentlemanly man.  His father was anxious to settle us together, and no objection could be made on either side as to age or any other impediment; but not immediately bringing matters to bear, but waiting to give opportunity to the individuals themselves to find out how their inclinations tended towards each other, the moment could not be recovered, and the matter dropped.

After some refreshment, we set out, and first viewed Newgate, the walls of which were uninjured. The Debtors' Court was not either hurt by the fire, nor were the debtors liberated. At one side were the three rooms lately occupied by Dr. Dodd, which carried great interest with them. They were neatly furnished by Mrs. Rudd, who had been the mistress of one of the brothers Perreaux, who were hanged for forgery, a year or so before Dr. Dodd.

The wife of one of the Perreaux herself presented a petition to the Queen for the life of her husband, having obtained access to one of the rooms through which her Majesty had to pass on her way to hold a Drawing-room. The Queen was greatly upset by the circumstance, and not only interceded with the King urgently for the life of this man and his brother, but also for that of Dr. Dodd, it seeming to her kind heart such a terrible thing that anyone should be hanged, and much more so a divine, and one so eminent as Dr. Dodd.

The King, however, could not reconcile it to his conscience to reprieve either of these offenders, although it cost him pain to refuse any request of the Queen's; in addition to the distress he invariably felt, even to considerable emotion, when it was necessary that he should sign a death-warrant.

Mrs. Rudd was acquitted, and left these rooms just as she had used them. As the dress called the 'Polonaise' jacket and coat is still seen at fancy assemblies, I must mention that this extravagant and unfeeling woman set that fashion while she was in this very place. Oh, how differently did the divine fill up the remaining measure of his time! There was his little inkstand upon a small table at which he constantly wrote, his chair, the table where he ate— I kissed them all. Nothing had been used since he was called to leave all earthly scenes. His memory I must ever revere, for early did he lead me to love religion, from the impressive manner in which he delivered his discourses and read the Liturgy of our Church.

From Newgate we went to the Fleet, and through Holborn to the Langdales', where, from intoxication, many of the rioters were burnt or drowned in the liquors. We also viewed the walls of Lord Mansfield's house, where in the ruins of the interior must have been his writings, which were so wantonly consumed. Many other scenes of devastation we observed on our way back, which were truly deplorable. We dined sumptuously in King Street, and in the evening went to Covent Garden to hear Lee Lewis's lecture on Heads. Many characters were introduced descriptive of the times, the prologue was remarkable and extremely well written, and the whole lecture very interesting. Lee Lewis was one of our principal comic actors of Covent Garden Theatre; and as the proprietor, Mr. Harris, was particularly loyal, all allusions that were made to the late unhappy affairs were given in terms favourable to the Government.

We were met, on leaving the theatre, by a body of men, formed into a company of that district, young Clay and his friend King being at the head. Every parish had its company to patrol the streets, leaving their homes well guarded and lighted with additional lamps. This precaution, like many others, appeared to have been resorted to too late; but it was well, even then, to show that the community of right-thinking people were ready to suppress the outrages of the lawless multitude, should there be yet any hidden intentions of future tumult. On our return journey, after this interesting and happy day, my father and Mr. Brown went outside the carriage with their swords drawn; but we reached home safely, and without having to call into play this formidable defence.

Their Majesties now came to Kew, and all arrangements were made for the removal of the Princesses to Windsor for the season, as it was the intention that the Queen should be there confined. A house was taken for Lady Charlotte Finch in Sheet Street ; rooms were appointed for Miss Goldsworthy and Miss Planta in the Lodge, with the three elder Princesses, and Miss Nevin as dresser. The masters were to attend at stated hours, and Mr. Papendick, as page to the Princess Royal, was to wait upon the three, my father, as usual, attending upon the Queen. Miss Hamilton was appointed sub-governess, to remain at Kew with Princesses Mary and Sophia ; Miss Moula, a Swiss, as French teacher, Miss Matthews, as dresser, were also to remain, with Mrs. Cheveley as superintendent, and Mr. Magnolley as page, Mr. Compton having recently obtained that post in the Queen's establishment, upon the death of dear old Mr. White. Mr. Brown, whom I have mentioned as being of our parties, had been a captain of the Lisbon Government packets, and was wrecked a short time before. He found means to ingratiate himself with Lady Charlotte Finch, who immediately told the Queen to place him with the Princes to assist Mr. Powell, which was done. His wife was a good-natured sort of person, and he was also friendly and joined readily into our coterie.

Desolate indeed did Kew appear when their Majesties, the three Princesses, two Princes, and all the attendants left for Windsor. Empty houses, all in retirement at the Palace, that had hitherto been a house of bright but innocent gaiety, and even our dear friend Dr. Majendie removed to Windsor, having, some time back, been made Canon of St. George's Collegiate Chapel there. Mrs. Pohl was a severe sufferer by these changes, for the Queen, of necessity, employed, when there, the tradespeople of Windsor, which also affected the regular orders for the seasons as they came round. Mr. Pohl, too, met with great reverses at this time, from the loss of his employment with Count Bruhl, the Bavarian Minister to this country, upon whom he had every dependence; but upon the Count's marriage with the Countess of Holderness, the scene was changed. Mr. Pohl was an accomplished linguist, and now and then he got a job, but he felt a sad blank in his worldly comforts.

Soon after the release of the prisoners by the mob, a woman and two men broke into Pohl's house in Maddox Street. He, being awakened by something which he could not define, soon found that he must have received a blow on the head. He jumped up and ran out of his room just in time to see these three people get over the wall which separated his premises from a mews. On examination he found that they had set fire to the back parlour, and had taken the few articles of plate in use, with some other trifles; but from under his pillow, where he usually deposited his purse, they had abstracted fourteen guineas. A few months before, a maid-servant of theirs had been committed for a robbery of muslin, lace, and other articles of value, so it was concluded that she had been the ringleader of the thieves. Mrs. Pohl thought it advisable to keep up her cottage at Kew, as it brought her before the notice of the Royal Family, and as some of them still remained there it was better to be on the spot to receive any chance orders. Mrs. Pohl's daughter, too, here had the opportunity of receiving, as day scholar, a very proper education. At home she was taught her mother's business, and by this means and by her own excellent abilities she became at an early age useful to her parents, and able to work her way through life.

We were now alone on our former footing, and I went often as before to the Tunstalls' with the same welcome, and to Mrs. Haverfield, where we had an acquisition to our little meetings in the company of Miss Fühling, whose father had succeeded to the appointment of Clerk of the Works on the death of Mr. Kirby. Mrs. Fühling, from indifferent health, did not go out, but she received friends at home in an agreeable manner.

Finding our life lonely, and knowing that in a short time we should not see my father at all, we prevailed upon him to allow us to go to Windsor, which he did, and took a lodging for us in Church Street. My sister was left with Miss Pullen and the cook to take care of the house, and our other servant went with us.

On September 22, 1780, the Queen was confined with a Prince, who was christened at St. James's by the name of Alfred. Miss Goldsworthy was with her Majesty, who seemed to be away from all her former comforts. Dr. Hunter, who had attended her with all her children, was no more. He had recommended Dr. Ford, who no doubt was eminent, but being a stranger there was a feeling of anxiety. The baby never was healthy. His wet nurse was a Mrs. Williams, a particular friend of Mrs. Cheveley's, and the wife of an East India captain. Mr. Compton was ordered down to take the general wait, as my father was at his post near the rooms of the Queen. Our lodging consisted only of such accommodation as we absolutely required, but nothing more; nor was it very respectable. I fear my poor father considered only the convenience of its being near the Lodge, and never took the precaution to inquire further. Here my mother considered herself free from care, and much as she shunned society at home, she went into it at Windsor.

After remaining at Windsor for six weeks we returned to Kew, where I was left for about a month among my dear friends, while my mother went to St. James's, as was her usual custom, to air and get ready our apartments for the winter, after their having been shut up during the summer. I stayed with Mrs. Haverfield and the Tunstalls, where I was daily in the company of Robert, or as he was familiarly called Bob, Tunstall. I also made the acquaintance of Mr. and Mrs. Miller, who lived at Brick Stables. He was kitchen-gardener to the King by appointment, and was discharged on being told that his prices were exorbitant, but he proved that they were even under par, considering the distances he constantly had to send in vehicles with springs, or by hand, in order to deliver the dainties without blemish. Although his statements were proved to be correct, he was told that such luxuries were in future to be dispensed with, and the appointment was altogether dropped. He had a passionate temper, and being now irritated beyond his power of endurance, he shortly put an end to his existence. Mrs. Miller was a Miss Bain, an intimate friend of Mrs. Montagu's, and while they lived at Brick Stables their house was a little paradise to go to, from his liberality and her extreme sweetness of manner and amiability. His business brought him daily to Kew House, and he always lived in friendship with the attendants.

My sister went with us to London, where my pursuits were much as before.

On New Year's Day the Prince of Wales was introduced at Court as being of age, having passed his eighteenth birthday; and the Duke of York took leave before going to Germany. The parting between the brothers, who had been together from infancy, was very painful. The Duke was to repair to Prussia to witness the King's great reviews, and to study military tactics. He was favourably received, and from his organisation of our army while Commander-in-Chief he evinced proof of the excellence of the instruction he had received. This and other visits to the Prussian Court resulted in a mutual attachment being formed between the Duke of York and the daughter of the succeeding King, which ultimately led to marriage. His Royal Highness was exceedingly handsome, and was called the Apollo of the day.

All was to be gaiety itself in London this year, to attract the attention of the young Prince, but as he was still to remain under the parental roof some little check was sustained over his actions. He was not so handsome as his brother, his likeness being of the Queen, while the Duke of York was like the King; but his countenance was of a sweetness and intelligence quite irresistible. He had an elegant person, engaging and distinguished manners, added to an affectionate disposition and the cheerfulness of youth. In accomplishments the brothers were unequal, as well as in acquired knowledge, the scale turning always in favour of the Prince of Wales. He began his career with varied resources of amusement, rational in themselves, and useful or agreeable to others. He was fond of music, sang well, and accompanied the piano on the violoncello with taste and precision, taught by Crosdill. The Prince joined in the interesting quartett parties, of which Giardini was the conductor and leader, and adapted music for them. These musical evenings, by their regularity and the interest that was thrown into them, for a long while continued to hold the attention of the Prince. Mr. Papendick was seldom absent, and had frequent opportunity to practise with his Royal Highness preparatory to the general meeting. At that period Giardini led at the Opera, and the Prince patronised that as well as the professional concerts led by Cramer, which were started upon the failure of those of which Bach and Abel were the proprietors, and which had been hitherto supported by lovers of music and the old nobility.

It was too evident that the decline of Bach's preeminence preyed upon his health, and his finances were in a worse state than he was at first aware of, which did not tend to ameliorate his distresses. He always maintained his position in the Royal Family and the profession, by whom he was greatly respected; but, alas! scholars fell off, and there was now a new party. Fashion was to erect the standard. Whether reason, consideration, or kind feeling were the supporters, the sequel has pretty clearly shown.

Schroeder was brought forward as the new performer on the pianoforte, and although the small
instrument was still used for the accompaniment of
vocal music in a concert room, as the harpsichord
was at theatres, the grand pianoforte was now introduced for solo playing. The makers were Broad-
wood and Ganas. Bach played occasionally, but
Schroeder was the planet. He was one step higher
in the modern style; a young man, fascinating,
fawning, and suave; a teacher for the belles,
company for the mode, a public performer, or a private player. Bach perceived his excellence in his
profession, and assisted him as a friend, for his heart
was too good to know the littleness of envy. He
gave Schroeder advice from his experience of this
country, and was also of great use to him in the
theory of his profession. He loved him almost as a
son, looking upon his talent with delight, and de-
ploring that his disposition was such as must, in the
end, work to his bane. Schroeder was truly an
enchanting player, and so prepossessing that after
hearing him once one could not but regret any lost
opportunity of hearing him again. He did little or
no good to his fraternity in music. He played when
called upon, but took no interest to forward or assist
any individual, and left no immediate scholar, though
John Cramer studied under him upon the decline of
dear Bach.

The Prince was this season to attend the concert of the new musical band as patron, and where, among other pieces of attraction, Crosdill and Cervetto were to perform a duet concerto. The Cervettos had hitherto led the principal musical performances, but Crosdill, coming down upon them as a home-born subject of equal talent, and instructor to the Heir Apparent, more than divided the spoil.   In the days of which I am writing, little more than the melody of a piece was written down, the performer introducing his own graces, and varying the passages according to his own taste.   Upon one occasion, when Crosdill and the junior Cervetto were to play a duet in public, they had practised together and had arranged the variations of their parts, so that in some movements one was to be first and in some the other. Most unfortunately, in the heat of the moment, Cervetto, who was at a particular spot to follow a passage of Crosdill's, inadvertently put in a grace. Crosdill was on the point of jumping up, but the other quickly apologised, and they played on till the end.   Cervetto promised that he would next day make his mistake public, and again make a sufficient apology, which he did.   He was good-tempered and natural, and many preferred his talent.   It was more from the heart, lively, and touching.   Crosdill's greatness was more from actual labour and study, and produced an effect as his temper dictated, imposing or harmonious. At the same concert, Schroeder played his third concerto of the favourite set. The middle movement he executed with a sweetness and grace that was perfectly enchanting, and the house was in rapture for minutes.

This concert always took place at the King's Theatre, with the orchestra on the stage. We were present with the Zoffanys and Bachs. Bach gave his benefit in the season as usual, and there introduced Miss Cantilo, after two years' instruction. She always sang scientifically, and had a lively and engaging manner, with a natural talent for music; but nature had given a huskiness to her voice which never could be overcome, and which rather increased with age. She was at this time about seventeen, rather pretty than otherwise, with fine expressive eyes, and an interesting little figure.

As Mr. Zoffany's occupation of portrait painting was much diminished by his absence of seven years, he had recourse to the Opera performers for subjects to exhibit. This opened the way to gratis admissions, and often did Mrs. Zoffany fetch me to accompany her. We were constantly in the dressing-rooms of those she was acquainted with, Simonet, Bacelli, Theodore, &c.. and happy am I here to affirm that we never saw anything reprehensible. When the dressing and undressing were over, acquaintances came in to chat as we did, but all was decorum, with the leading characters at all events. Miss Farren was one of our intimate friends. Her mother, with whom she lived in the closest affection, used often to accompany her daughter to the theatre, and her presence would help Miss Farren to decline the overtures of those performers whom, without wishing to offend, she would gladly avoid. We had admission to Drury Lane also, and there I saw the 'School for Scandal' with its original cast of characters; the elegant Mrs. Abington, &c. The nobility, from her great taste and peculiarly distinguished manners, received her at their routs and evening parties ; and consulted her upon their Court and other gala dresses.

To Covent Garden my father could go at all times, through Mr. Harris, and here I heard the famous Tenducci, and Miss Brent in ' Artaxerxes,' for whom the songs were originally written. Also the ' Duenna ' by Sheridan, in which the singular-voiced Leoni was the primo. Mrs. Mattocks, Mrs. Greene, Quick and Wilson were great supporters of comedy.

As I found it very inconvenient to dress my hair, powder being then worn, I cut it off, beautiful as it was, close to my head ; but took care to have a cap most becomingly made, which answered every purpose of dress, half-dress, &c., and 1 had less trouble, and escaped the disgrace I had often before fallen into, of not being tidy with powder, or of being too long at my toilet. My bonnet was of an improved Quaker shape, of the choicest fashionable material, both for winter and summer. We dined occasionally now with a German family in Bury Street, by the name of Bösenberg. He was a renowned cupper and bleeder. His wife and daughters lived after the customs of their own country, and the ease of visiting them suited my mother. Here we met frequently Sir Jacob Wolfe, and his brother the Baron.

This spring, 1781, the whole of the Royal Family returned to Kew, to stay till after the prorogation of Parliament, which brought back for a time our former pleasures with increased gaieties. The nobility, on fine afternoons, came up in boats, other boats being filled with bands of music, to take the Prince to the promenade at Richmond. His Royal Highness was always accompanied by his governor and sub-governor, and returned for the Queen's party in the evening. Mr. Zoffany had a decked sailing vessel, elegantly and conveniently fitted up, on board of which we frequently went, the Bachs being of the party. He used to take his pupil, as he wished to give her every opportunity of being heard. She sang with Madame Bach, whose voice was beautiful on the water.

The fashion in dress this summer was marked. For gowns, alternate stripes of white and buff, or white and lemon colour, in silk or very fine cambric muslin, were the mode; hats, *soie de Paris*, trimmed with Vestris's light blue; or white, trimmed with old Vestris's dark blue, which was a peculiarly bright mazarine. One evening a play was given at Richmond, upon some particular occasion, and all Kew was going. Mrs. Haverfield wanted to take me, but was refused as my father determined upon taking us himself. We were equipped in our best, but, alas! our conductor never arrived. We saw them all go, some in boats, some in carriages, and my mother said, ' I am sorry I agreed to the proposal, as from the first Mr. Albert has been in the habit of disappointing me.'

Mr. Papendiek was often with us. From the time of our first meeting at Streatham he had shown me marked attention, but being only fifteen years of age that summer, I was quite unconscious of its meaning. I thought then of little beyond my occupations, time hanging heavily on my hands when I was taken from them ; but I was not destined to remain long in this state of blissful ignorance. At the time of our being attacked by the highwaymen on Barnes Common, Mr. Papendiek, having a new watch, had put it for security in a corner of the coach, and upon hearing the man say that the ladies were not to be molested, I secreted it. When I restored it to him upon our arrival, he assumed a manner which I could not understand, but which made me feel as embarrassed in his company, as I had done at Streatham the first time I saw him.  As I became more intimate with him, however, this feeling of embarrassment quite passed away, and I was at ease and happy in his company, when, just before his leaving Kew for Windsor, he made a proposal of marriage to me.  I was just sixteen.  I loved everybody that I was happy with; but as to marriage or any sentiment connected with that, I could not feel what it meant.  I was struck with amazement, and with the impropriety of it all, and said that I was surprised that he did not speak to my father, whom I was quite sure would disapprove of it altogether, as it had been his injunction to my mother not to encourage his visits, for he did not wish me to marry anyone in the Royal household.  On this point I was always astonished at my mother's conduct, for on every other question her compliance with my father's will was even greater than is usual.  It arose probably from Mr. Papendick being of her own country, and from his very kind attention to her; and she might not have noticed the frequency of his visits, as she only saw him in company with others.  I was now thrown back into my former state of discomfort, and all enjoyment ceased.  Mr. Papendick told me that he could not speak to my father, to which I answered that I must immediately do so, or I should be acting extremely wrong   I did give my father the whole account, when he said he would not bias my affection to any-one, but that if I could, without sorrow, give up thinking of Mr. Papendick it would oblige him.  We spoke of my return to Streatham, but that did not accord with his ideas, nor was it right that I should now leave my mother.  We both represented the circumstance to her, but she said she decidedly would not forbid Mr. Papendiek's visits, as she thought him a proper person ; but that if my father was of a different opinion, he, being the head of his own family, was the only one to settle the affair. She was perfectly right, but my father did nothing, and though I repeated the conversation to Mr. Papendiek, he continued to call as usual.  My father endeavoured to avoid meeting him, and all was misery.  I at last dreaded the well-known knock, and when the Royal Family left for Windsor, I wit-nessed their departure without repining, as it relieved me from a weighty distress for a time.

# CHAPTER VI.

Bach and Miss Cantilo—Music—Gaiety—Bet between Bach and Fischer—King of Denmark—A lively joke—At Kew with Mr. Albert—Praised at Court—The Queen and Madame Schwellenberg—The Royal Academy—Miss Farren, afterwards Lady Derby—Lady Betty Hamilton—The Duke of Dorset—Bach's declining health—His death—His funeral—Bath—Miss Guest—Public favour capricious—Viol-di-gamba—Abel—Bach and Abel—Illuminations—Fox and North—Pitt—Sukey—Confirmation—General Lake and Colonel Hulse—The Queen's treatment of Mr. Albert—Economy at Court—Mr. Albert an altered man—Changes in the Royal household—Introduction of people of inferior rank—Visits to Hampstead and Tower Hill.

Poor Bach, feeling that his health was fast declining, was anxious to introduce his pupil, Miss Cantilo, as much as possible, and this led to many musical parties, both of evenings and mornings. These brought the King's band into notice, and procured them scholars among the neighbouring families.

Dr. Mingay started the invitations for mornings, and according to the pieces played, such of the band as were required attended. Here we were often indulged with a quartett from the Griesbachs, and with other pieces of music equally interesting, Miss Cantilo being a great attraction.

The singers of the choir were also called upon for glees &c., in which I took a part, as well as in the instrumental performances. Bach heard me rehearse the third set of his concertos, Schroeder's, and other things. The first of my performances was the admired duet for two performers on one pianoforte with himself, which at once introduced me with *éclat*. Among the attendants of these concerts may be mentioned the Egertons, who were very musical; Major Haines, whose daughter, by marriage with one of their family, became Duchess of Bridgewater; and others. Mr. Papendiek was intimate at all these houses, and these musical meetings with the requisite practices brought us often together, but nothing was said, and some partiality, I almost hoped I observed, was shown by Mr. Papendiek for Miss Cantilo, who met his ideas in music, and certainly engaged his attention. Thus was our term finished, and I must say that what with the goings on of the Prince of Wales at the Lodge, the fun with Fischer, the celebrated oboe player, and the various amusements in which I was engaged, the season was one of gaiety, mirth, and enjoyment. The well-known bet of five guineas between Bach and Fischer was made in the presence of his Royal Highness and of us all. The bet was that Fischer could not play his own minuet. He was a very nervous man, and after allowing him to get through a few bars, Bach stood before him with a lemon in his hand, which he squeezed so that the juice dropped slowly. Then he bit another so that the juice ran out on each side of his mouth freely. Fischer tried once or twice to get rid of the water that must, on such a sight, fill the mouth; but not being able to conquer the sensation, he was obliged to own himself beaten. This minuet, which must always remain a favourite, was composed on the occasion of a ball given at Court to the King of Denmark, on his visit to this country some time after his marriage with the Princess Matilda, the King's youngest sister, which ball was opened by the King of Denmark with our Queen, the second minuet being danced by our King with the Duchess of Ancaster.

Another joke was played off upon poor Fischer by the Prince of Wales this merrymaking season, to this effect: after the concert, which Fischer attended twice a week at Richmond or at Kew, wherever the King and Queen were, he used eagerly to seize upon the supper before he went to London. Upon one occasion the Prince came in and said, ' I have ordered something that I know you like;' a dish was brought in, and when the cover was lifted, out jumped a rabbit. Germans have a particular dislike to that animal in every shape and form; therefore it is easy to conjecture poor Fischer's state of mind. This joke cost him only the loss of his supper, but many nights succeeded before he could be prevailed upon to again enter the eating-room.

The middle of November ended our term of ten weeks, and with the exception of my marriage concern, nothing could have passed more happily. I remained a few days at Kew with my sister, until our apartments were aired and ready for us to repair to. Soon after this my father was seized with a bad fit of the gout, which had slightly attacked him for several preceding years, and he did not recover kindly from it. After we had received my brother for his holidays, and Christmas Day was passed, it was proposed that my father should go down to Kew for a few weeks for change of air, and that I should accompany him. Consider me now as the mistress of my father's house, busily employed in every nicety of domesticity, although certainly in miniature. The families who resided there during the winter paid us every kind attention. Hardly a day passed without my seeing the Tunstalls and the Haverfields; and Mr. Meyer, who had always been an intimate friend of my father's, was now often with us, and partook of our homely fare, which I took care should do me credit on this my first essay. He was impressed. He lent me drawings to copy and books to read. The greater part of Johnson's 'Lives of the Poets he read with me, and desired Mrs. Meyer to take me up as a most exemplary girl. This she gladly acceded to, for I had always been kindly received by her, but was despatched when Mr. Meyer was expected home, as he did not allow intruders without his express permission. Other visitors also joined us at meals. At Christmas, Miss Pullen gave up her house and removed to one at Ranelagh, well appointed, and well situated for a school. Miss Pohl joined her on terms of exchange —millinery &c. for education.

Within a few days of January 18 we left our agreeable abode for London, where I was soon busily employed to get my first satin gown made. It was of a puce colour, trimmed with white satin, and a petticoat of the same colour to match the trimming. My hair, which was growing fast, was still confined under a most becoming cap of blonde and white satin. I was welcomed cheerfully at Court on my father's recovery, and complimented on my conduct, with the observation that my dress was no doubt a recompense for my dutiful attention.

At the expiration of the holidays, my brother returned to Hampstead, but was soon recalled on my father receiving a letter from Dr. Majendie informing him that the Queen's nomination for the Charterhouse was now vacant, and that my brother's name stood first on the list. My father lost no time in taking that fine sweet boy to the Queen, rendered still more prepossessing by the animation of his countenance and air of confidence on the present occasion. The Queen received them with less pleasure than my father had anticipated, and said she would speak with Majendie, and let my father know the result. My brother remained at home, and when several weeks had passed after his introduction to the Queen, my father thought it would be advisable to know her Majesty's pleasure, and to ascertain the cause of delay; when, to his utter astonishment, she said that she thought Dr. Majendie had told him that the Schwellenberg had given the nomination to Nicolay's eldest son, as he was educating for the Church, that he was rather older than my brother, and that she concluded that three years hence would be time enough for him. We can easily imagine what my father's feelings were. He told the Queen how serious it was her still allowing the influence of Madame Schwellenberg to direct her actions ; and as for himself, he could only express his regret at her Majesty's decision, which he felt that, as her supposed confidential attendant, he ought at all events to have known before.

At the Royal Academy this year, 1782, it seemed as if all our intimate friends composed the body, as academicians, visitors, &c. This season Zoffany finished his famous picture of the Academy. At their house the society was delightful, with their own set, and others attached to art and science. My brother, being at home now, accompanied me, and many a happy day did we pass in Albemarle Street. This winter Miss Farren, who now appeared in all Mrs. Abington's characters, made a great step forward, for although no one could surpass Mrs. Abington in the talent of enacting, the elegance of Miss Farren made her a general favourite. Her virtuous mind shone through her countenance, and heightened the brilliancy of her fine eyes, her *naïveté* being that of a chaste disposition, and her manner that of a lady. The Earl of Derby had made her an offer of protection, which she immediately convinced him it was not her disposition to accept. He then begged that she would agree to marry him on the death of his wife, who was in ill health. This she in part accepted, but upon condition that he would only see her in company, as she was determined to pay every attention to her profession for the support of herself, her mother, and her sister, and to preserve her character inviolable. Lord Derby agreed, but insisted upon her using his carriage. That she also refused, but at last it was settled that a coach, with every appendage for travelling, and for London work, should be kept for her in my lord's mews; that two footmen should attend, and if at any time pecuniary assistance should be required, that she should apply to him only as a friend. No jewels or presents were to be offered, and every decorum was to be observed, that, should they live to be united, she might be respected. Dear, sweet, amiable creature! indeed she lived up to her determination, and when at last she was married to him, she was received into the best society. Lord Derby, before he came into his title, was married to the eldest daughter of the beautiful Duchess of Hamilton, sister to the no less beautiful Lady Coventry. Lady Betty Hamilton, who was also the admired of the day, certainly did not accept this offer of marriage with affection, but was persuaded into it. Her bridal entertainment, which was given at the Oaks in Surrey, consisted of every amusement that ingenuity could invent. The invitations were general, and the *fête* began at noon and lasted till the usual hour of breaking up. Barthélomon, a violin player, who was always called upon when neither Giardini nor Cramer could be obtained, led the concert in the evening, when his famous rondo, called 'The Maid of the Oaks,' was performed by him with variations, and for years was a favourite. The ballads, dances &c. of the time all bore the title, or sounded the praises, of the maid of the Oaks. Alas! this beautiful maid, after becoming a wife, and the mother of a boy and girl, left her lord and decamped with the Duke of Dorset. They begged a divorce, but my lord of Derby would not agree to it. Soon the Duke deserted her, and she lingered out many years in solitude and ill-health.

Now the Earl, in his turn, tried for a divorce, but as many years had elapsed since the circumstance took place, and the Duke of Dorset was now married, he could not succeed; and his lordship's marriage with Miss Farren must, consequently, await the awful event. Meanwhile, the son and daughter profited by her care and tuition; and so great became the affection of Lord Stanley for her, that he even, if it had been possible, would have gladly been united to her.

We continued to have the enjoyment of Miss Farren's society in private, and still carried on our attendance at Drury Lane. But soon our family, who so short a time before had taken a principal part in all this pleasurable society, were thrown out by illness, and that of an alarming nature. Dear, amiable Bach, after being for several months in a declining state, was now removed to Paddington for change of air. Some kind friends never forsook him, and I believe few days passed without one or other of our family seeing him. The Zoffanys, poor Abel, and others supplied him entirely with provisions sent ready prepared. Mr. Papendiek saw him every day, and assisted him by many kind acts, which are all the more comforting when done by the hand of one we love. Here I urged him to close the eyes of his beloved friend in happiness, by offering marriage to his *protégée*, Miss Cantilo, but on that subject Mr.

Papendiek was deaf to entreaty. The last visit we
paid was together with my father and mother. Bach,
on taking a final leave, joined our hands—I think
now I see his enchanting smile. Not a word was
said; we were motionless. On retiring, we could
not get Mr. Papendiek away, but at last my father
prevailed upon him to hasten to the Queen, with the
news of Bach being so near his end. This roused
him, and after this painful mission, he obtained leave
to return to his friend, who had just passed away
when he reached this room of mourning. The
creditors poured in, but Mr. Papendiek, with the
assistance of Bach's faithful coachman, who had
driven him, I believe, from the first of his coming
to England, kept them from disturbing the corpse.
The Queen, by the hand of my father, sent the widow
a sum for mourning and other necessities, and mourning also for Miss Cantilo, with permission to Mr. Papendiek to remain and report proceedings. Schroeder,
Cramer, and one or two others came to see and to
hear, but no one among his musical associates came
forward with any offer of respect, either public or
private, and this great patron was carried to the
grave and buried with the attendance only of four
friends, my father, Mr. Papendiek, Zoffany, and
Bautebart, but they were indeed sincere mourners.
They deposited their charge, who was a Roman
Catholic, in St. Pancras' churchyard. The Queen,

finding how things were, could not undertake the debts, but the funeral expenses she discharged, and gave the coachman 100*l.* which he had lent to his master.

Mr. Cantilo immediately removed his niece to Signor Rahzini, at Bath, and for five years she was articled to him. The musical department of that city had for many years been in his hands, and he was much respected. He retired from public performance when this engagement was proposed to him, which he conducted with every credit to himself and success to his pupil. Miss Cantilo here formed her friendship with Miss Guest, the renowned pianist, also a pupil, now known as Mrs. Miles, and who, on coming to London to further her professional labours, received the appointment of musical instructress to the late Princess Charlotte of Wales.

Madame Bach, having given up her whole to be divided among those who would not relinquish their claims, now lived among her friends until the time of year arrived that she could return to Italy, her native place. It was the month of February 1782 when Bach died, and it was proposed that before the departure of Madame Bach she should give either a concert or an opera for a benefit, not doubting, from her own and her husband's connections, that it would meet with due response, but among her musical friends no encouragement did she find. A favourite opera and ballet were fixed upon, but the curtain rose before a number not sufficient to pay the ordinary expenses of the night—I mean as regards the artificers employed, for all the performers, including the orchestra, offered their services gratis. This attempt having totally failed, shows how capricious is public favour and private preference. This man of ability in his profession, of liberal kindness in it, of general attention to friends, and of worthy character, was forgotten almost before he was called to the doom of us all, and every recollection of him seems buried in oblivion. The widow, with one friend and the faithful coachman, quitted England in due course for Italy, the Queen allowing her 200*l*. a year for life, and giving her 100*l*. for her journey.

Once more adieu, dear friends, in memory—many a happy hour have we passed together. Madame Bach lived but a short time to enjoy the feeling kindness of the Queen.

Abel pursued his professional studies and performances till within a few weeks of his death, which occurred about two years after that of Bach. His instrument was the ' viol-di-gamba,' smaller in size than the violoncello, but played in the same position. It had six strings, and the tone was peculiarly soft. Abel neither made nor left a scholar. He was too impatient in teaching. Mr. Papendiek studied

composition with him, but not to so good a purpose as
he had zealously hoped, most of what he did learn in
that science having been from Bach, who was just as
gentle as his friend was violent.  Abel was eminent
both as a composer and as a player, but the season
that he lost his friend he lost also much of his power
of exertion from grief, and often had recourse to
stimulants that overdid his intention.  One evening,
at the Queen's concert, he was led to his seat, but he
performed so admirably that the state he was in was
not discovered by royalty.  The same season, on the
occasion of the Musical Fund entertainment, his particular friends dined with him in order to conduct him
to the theatre in safety.  In that they succeeded, but
not in keeping him from indulging in his supposed
necessitous error.  He was led on to the stage between
two persons, and his instrument given to him ready
tuned.  He played almost better than ever, and when
his concerto was finished they dropped the curtain,
for he could not rise from his seat to bow.  Abel was
not received in the higher circles of society as a visitor,
probably from not teaching among them, which introduced Bach.  He was nevertheless a gentleman of refined mind and manner.  From the time that he and
Bach gave up their subscription concerts, he ceased also
to trouble his friends for a benefit night, and supported
his position to the last by the salary he received from
the Queen, assisted by his writings and performances.

He was buried without any honours conferred by the profession, but followed to his grave by a few select friends, of whom Mr. Papendiek was one.

These two professors, Bach and Abel, introduced modern music into this country from Corelli, Geminioni, and Handel, followed by Schroeder, Clementi, Haydn, and Mozart. The principal composers and performers who followed these great masters were Pleyel, Dussek, Steibelt, Beethoven, Fischer, Cramer, Salomon, Crosdill, the Cervettos, Hummel, &c., all moving on by degrees to the present system, which, although great in itself as surprising, is a suppression of nature; sentiment being overlooked, sweetness annihilated, art and the marvellous alone supported.

During this season, 1782, we had splendid illuminations for Rodney's great victory over the French fleet in the West Indies, where he took the Count de Grasse prisoner, and brought him home on board his ship, the ' Ville de Paris.' The public rejoicings were also for the taking of Pondicherry in the East, also from the French. These victories in some measure drew off the malignity of the public against Ministers, but only for a time; for in March so determined was the House no longer to support the Government, that when a division was called, the numbers were found to be equal. The Speaker's vote turned the scale once more in their favour.

However, this soon led to their resignation, and ultimately to the coalition between Fox and North that surprised the whole world.

On this eventful day, my mother and I were taking a quiet dinner at Zoffany's, when Mr. Papendiek came to conduct us home immediately. It was then about four o'clock. Every shop was shut, and only a few stragglers were to be seen in the streets, hurrying home like ourselves, while at the House multitudes had collected. All was dismay, discontent, and want of confidence, and so it continued for some time—until the change, in fact, was settled, when Pitt's long administration began.

Nothing of private interest marked our *séjour* at St. James's, and we moved to Kew as usual; but before our return thither, Mr. Zoffany began my sister's portrait, which when finished was an excellent likeness, and was a great solace to my mother when some years later she died.

I continued to visit the Tunstalls, and Mrs. Haverfield, as before; and the latter took me to Mrs. Trimmer's parties, where Mr. Papendiek, introduced by Mr. Ernst, assisted in their musical evenings. I was also constantly at Meyer's, at Montagu's, and at my aunt's, where the inimitable Sukey taught me to make pastry and confectionery as I have ever since made them; also pickling and preserving by the same method as that I now pursue. I went on with my writing, as Mr. Roberts was anxious to perfect the beautiful hand that he was forming; but this could only be occasionally, as the Royal Family had this season removed to Windsor immediately after the birthday, and Mr. Roberts was but seldom at Kew. His health was in a very declining state, supposed to have been brought on by his not obtaining the consent of the friends of the lady he wished to marry, one of the nieces of the great Garrick.

Though, as I have said, I was a good deal amongst my friends, it only amounted to a small number of hours altogether, and I was much at home, and dull.

In July there was a Confirmation at Kingston, for which dear Dr. Majendie examined and prepared me, as did also Mr. Bellamy, our vicar. He laid down maxims for my future conduct, gave me excellent practical advice, and appeared satisfied with the manner in which I had been taught my religious duties, and pleased with the feeling I expressed. The little party consisted of my mother, as protectress, Miss Howlett, Miss Pigot, my cousin Charlotte, and myself. About this time we had to go into mourning for Prince Charles of Mecklenburgh, and my black silk gown I was to wear new on this day of Confirmation, and a very pretty white cap, with my hair laid a little in curl, as it was beginning to grow. In my own conceit, I looked animated and well. Miss Pigot had a cap like mine, made by Mrs. Pohl, who interested herself in our appearance, and set us off cheerfully. She had all ready for us on our return, and sat in my father's place at dinner. In addition to our happy family party, we had the company of our kind friend Dr. Majendie, who, having witnessed the day's proceedings, gave us his encouragement to go on well.

By some means Mr. Papendiek had heard of this day's business, and rode over to Kingston from Windsor to meet us at the church door. On coming out after the ceremony, he was again there, and congratulated me. This, of course, struck all my friends, and from this time our marriage began to be talked of as a certain thing.

A circumstance which occurred at Windsor about this time aided the rumour, while it marked a new era in the Royal household, which not only destroyed the respect due to those about the persons of Royalty, but subverted order, checked the harmony of the community, and annulled all confidence between them. The degradation, too, of the affair, we suffer under to this day. In this year, 1782, the Prince of Wales was twenty, and though no longer under tutors and governors, he had not yet a wholly separate establishment, but had a suite of apartments in the Castle at Windsor, a house at Kew opposite to their Majesties, and a range of rooms at the 'Queen's House' in town, so that he was still to some extent under the parental eye. The attendants were not on board, but took their meals in the King's establishment. General Lake and Colonel Hulse had been attendants alternately on the two elder Princes, from their infancy, during their hours of recreation, and were now by his Royal Highness appointed equerries. These gentlemen privately overlooked the domestic vices and irregularities of their charge when young, and managed the intrigue of the elder with Mrs. Robinson, the renowned 'Perdita,' while only a lad, by conducting her from the ait at Kew through the garden gate at the back of the house, to the Prince of Wales's apartments. His Royal Highness was not fond of her, and the affair soon ended ; but as the cost was very great, his Majesty was called upon to pay it, and apparently no inquiry was made. On coming to Windsor for the season, the wife of one of General Lake's grooms either accidentally caught the eye of the Prince or was purposely placed in his way, and his Royal Highness ordered her down to his apartments, desiring that some appointment might be made to keep her there. She was a tall slim person, with rather a pretty face and dark eyes, but a great slattern, and more low and vulgar than that class of people usually are. Her husband was a dressed-up horror, impertinent and disgusting ; but General Lake, nevertheless, took him from the stables, and placed

him about the person of the Prince. At the dinner hour this fellow was shown into the dining-room of the attendants, being announced as Mr. Mills, when Mr. Kamus, who at once discerned that all could not be right, asked by what authority they were to have the honour of his company. He answered that he had been appointed valet and hairdresser to the Prince of Wales, and had been ordered by General Lake to join the pages at dinner. This was an insult that could not be suffered, and the gentlemen desired that their dinners should be served to them on separate tables. Lake and Hulse dined with the King's equerries. Mr. Kamus saw Lake afterwards, who told him the whole affair, but he could not succeed in obtaining an interview with the Prince till the following morning, when he met with no satisfaction. He then saw the King, but no better success attended that interview. He therefore solicited an appointment in the East Indies, to enable him to join his brother and sister, Sir John and Lady Day, or anything equally respectable with the post he now held; but could obtain nothing. 'Ernst begged to have his situation changed to one in Hanover, for, having been for some years at the University of Göttingen, he preferred Germany; but he met with no better success than his companion.

My father now addressed the Queen, and entreated that, if no alteration were made, he might be permitted to return with his family to Strelitz, either on pension, or with some appointment in the establishment of the Prince Charles, now the reigning Duke; but the Queen objected upon the same plea as when it was before proposed. My father now gave vent to his feelings; spoke of her Majesty's wish that he should accompany her to England, of her suggesting that he should marry, and, combating all his objections, eventually gaining his consent, saying that she would be his friend always. He reminded her, too, of the disappointment she had caused him about my brother, adding that he hoped her Majesty would give him credit for having faithfully fulfilled his part of the compact by never quitting her or failing in any one point of duty. The Queen acknowledged all this, lamented the circumstance of Mills, but said she could not interfere, as the King had not expressed his disapprobation to her. She went on to say that since it had been found necessary to exert great economy in the civil list, perquisites would be less, and they would in future take into their service such persons as they could more generally employ; that they were compelled to suffer certain privations themselves, and they would be obliged to make some changes, which those who had hitherto been in every way considered, and had lived like gentlemen, would, she feared, feel also. My father then spoke of me, telling the Queen that he had

arrangements in the Windsor Lodge were never altogether favourable to company, for the family began
to reside in it before it was completed, and it always
had the appearance of a scramble. Mrs. Montagu
now lived at Windsor, which took her husband from
the Lodge ; Mr. Compton was callous upon the subject, for he had lost his wife in the preceding spring,
just as he had taken a house in Charlotte Street,
Pimlico, and was looking forward to comfort. She
fell, poor thing, in alighting from a carriage, which
brought on premature labour and death in about six
weeks. When not in attendance, he lived secluded
in this neat little house with his only child, a daughter, whom he educated. We knew nothing of these
proceedings till my father came down to Kew, and
when he told us the news we were, as may be supposed, greatly distressed.

During his stay the Dresslers and Hoffhams passed
a day with us. I was to conduct the whole entertainment, as a first essay. My cookery was first
stewed carp, secondly à-la-mode beef. They succeeded well, and I obtained much praise for these
excellent dishes, as well as for my additions, according to the fashion of the day.

This led to an invitation from both these families.
So on the following Monday I left Kew in the Rich-
mond coach alone, which set me down at the ' White
Horse Cellar,' Piccadilly. I walked from thence to

Tottenham Court Road, and there got into a Hampstead stage, which set me down at the Dresslers' door. With these amiable people, together with my brother and George Papendick, I spent some happy days. From thence I went with Miss Dressler to her sister's, Mrs. Hoffham, who lived at Dock Head, on the Surrey side of the river, opposite the 'Iron Gates' on Tower Hill. The house was good, and stood pleasantly in a garden, with a full view of the river. Here we stayed for about a week, and returned to Kew by walking from the 'Iron Gates,' to which we were ferried over, to Piccadilly, and then taking a chance seat in one of the stages. Our Sunday was passed in the usual mode of the citizens of that period. We breakfasted early, walked, after ferrying over, to the Savoy Church in the Strand, then to Piccadilly, and went in a stage to Kensington. There we took a bit of lunch and ordered our dinner, and then walked a considerable time in the Gardens. After dinner, back to Buckingham Gate, and into the Park, which was filled with company for the evening promenade. There we saw the Count de Grasse, Rodney's prisoner, on parole. He was a fine man of unusual height, aged, with white hair, and a commanding presence. From the Park we returned as we came.

After these two pleasant visits I returned to my parents at Kew.

# CHAPTER VII.

Bitter disappointment of Mr. Albert—Mr. Papendiek again on the scene—Mrs. Albert encourages him—Marriage arranged—Description of trousseau—Visit to Streatham—Advice from Mrs. Kay and Miss Fry—Return home—First sitting to Zoffany—The wedding fixed suddenly—Arrangements—Married at St. George's, Hanover Square—Mr. Albert did not attend—Mr. and Mrs. Papendiek go home—First dinner, not a success—Visit to the Queen at St. James's —In the evening to the younger Princes and Princesses—Present from the Prince of Wales—Mr. Papendiek to Windsor—Arranging the house in Charlotte Street—Presents from the Queen—First party goes off well—Zoffany sails for India—Grand concert— Salomon.

My father was bitterly disappointed at my not obtaining an appointment of any kind about the Princesses, and was sorely perplexed and troubled about my future. He could not bring himself to like the idea of a marriage with Mr. Papendiek, yet he felt hardly justified in forbidding it, as he was a good man, and at any rate in a respectable position. The match was proposed under embarrassing circumstances, but, as I was at first only fifteen years old, and even now only seventeen, surely one word to the purpose, spoken with the smallest degree of firmness, would have put a stop to the whole thing; but this word he never spoke. How and why my mother, in this case, acted in direct opposition to his injunctions and wishes I never could define, unless it was imperceptibly brought about by the ease she experienced in Mr. Papendick's company, who was a German, and of the manner she was yet in her own mind accustomed to, and one who paid her every attention for the privilege of being now and then permitted to pass an hour or two in friendly intercourse with us. Mr. Papendiek understood from the first that I would give him no encouragement unless my father's consent and approbation could be gained; but this he always hoped he might in time get over. My father said to us both that he never would destroy my happiness, but in the present instance he did not think it would be promoted, as Mr. Papendiek did not settle comfortably or contentedly in this country, and he, moreover, considered that his income was too small, especially as there was no prospect of improvement in it. Besides, he had contracted an engagement in Germany, which was only just broken off by the father of the young woman, who did not wish her to leave her own country. Under these considerations, my father trusted that we should see the undesirability of a marriage, and that we should at once give it up. It was after this conversation with my father that I returned to Streatham for six months, as I have already related. On my return home I found to my surprise that Mr. Papendiek

had been visiting at our house as usual, and I
saw him constantly in that way. Then music was
introduced, all to my regret and discomfort. I
dreaded his knock. I pined; I felt dismayed. Miss
Cantilo seemed to attract his attention, but she being
suddenly removed to Bath on poor Bach's death, the
field was again left open, and no fence put up, as
there should have been, by my mother. Of this he
took advantage, as well as of the unhappy occurrences among the dependents of the Royal Family.
He took strong measures to advance his suit, and
upon the slight expression of mine that I had no
objection, provided my father would say the same,
he appeared determined to carry it through. One
more obstacle arose in his brother, George Papendiek,
being suddenly thrown on his hands; but it was to
be, and I need hardly add that he at last prevailed.
Our marriage was to take place as soon as he could
get leave from Court, and my mother determined to
have all preparations put *en train*, so that there
might be no hurry at the last.

Mrs. Pohl promised her assistance to mamma, and
with her kind advice and help my trousseau was
soon put into good hands, so that when required all
would be found ready.

I wished to pay one more visit to my beloved
friends at Streatham before my wedding, and wrote
to ask Mrs. Kay to fetch me any day after Sunday,

November 10, on which day Mrs. Pohl was to take me with her to the Sacrament at St. George's, Hanover Square, as at that time she still lived in Maddox Street, where I was born. On that Sunday mamma and I proceeded thither in a hackney coach. My mother, as a German, did not go up to the table, but remained in the pew to give me her blessing. This act of devotion gave me a feeling of peace and serenity of mind that I must fail in describing. I was quieted ; perturbation ceased. My book was a comfort, as I now knew how to use it. Mrs. Pohl gave me a Prayer-book, handsomely bound, just as we entered her pew. Dear soul! she was a true friend to me, and our affection ceased but with her death.

A short description of the dresses prepared for my wedding may be amusing, and will make my daughters smile, as the mode of to-day is rather different.

Purchased the preceding spring, as the high fashion for walking in St. James's Park, in the morning, or rather at noon, and to vie with Madame Hüniber's two daughters (one of whom eloped with Captain Fitzgerald of the Guards, and is at this moment living at Hampton Court, as sempstress to Queen Adelaide), I had two white dimity jackets and petticoats, handsomely trimmed with muslin frills. These, and a fawn-coloured silk of two summers' wear, were now newly vamped up ; my puce satin new trimmed with white, and two or three ordinary gowns and morning wraps were purchased and made up. Also a Manchester cotton, as they were then called, a stripe of cotton and wool mixed, and a narrower one of satin. Mine was of two shades of red, and was trimmed with a pretty fashionable trimming. Besides these dresses, I had a new white lustring, to be made up at pleasure, and a print ; with aprons, a hoop, a horsehair petticoat, a new white hat, a black bonnet, and a cap or two appropriate for dress and for daily wear. The white fox-skin trimming of my cloak was put upon a new white satin, and my muff was cleaned. Then I had a pair of black satin shoes, with diamond-cut steel buckles, a present from Mr. Papendiek. For walking commonly, a pelisse or great-coat of Bath coating, a black silk muff, and my dear black silk Quaker-shaped bonnet. Everybody had also in those days a black silk cloak trimmed with lace.

The black silk and a dead-leaf silk I had, newly done up, and a morning gown made a neat equipment for Streatham. whither Mrs. Kay fetched me on the 12th. Mr. Kay met us on the top of Brixton Hill with the blunderbuss as usual, and we arrived in safety, finding Mr. Fry, I verily believe, in the same chair in which I had left him a year and a half ago.

Nancy waited at tea. She was now parlourmaid, housekeeper, and needlewoman, with a helper, in the place of Mrs. James. There was no change of masters, so I rubbed up all my elegancies and my usefuls, and renewed my acquaintanceship with friends. Elizabeth Barton was still there, so we formed our parlour party with Mr. Fry for French and English readings as before. We walked in the sweet grounds, and ran riot with Mrs. Kay *comme à l'ordinaire.* Peggy Pitcher was on the eve of marriage with the blind Lord Deerhurst, so there was no visiting beyond morning calls to talk of nothings, and to kiss affectionately, for she really was glad to see me. All gone by at the Thrales' also. Their two youngest girls and the two youngest Pitchers were now pupils at Mrs. Kay's. We passed a day at Mrs. Grove's, and had two gala evenings at Russell House, to take leave on the approaching weddings. The topic of mine was introduced, as one truly interesting, but much to my distress.

In our mornings of retirement I received salutary lessons of conduct from dear Mrs. Kay and Miss Fry. They lamented the affair as being irrevelant to the intention of my father; but now that it was to be, my conduct, they said, must be that of duty to my husband, with care and watchfulness. I must rise at a given hour—never waver for ailments, of which numberless would doubtless now occur; I must fix an hour for devotion, and never deviate from it, for even in illness that could still be kept up; I must set an example of punctuality, and the old rule must strictly be followed, ' never to leave for the morrow the work of the day.' These, and many other precepts, and much good advice I received from these inestimable women, and I earnestly desired to be given grace to follow them. But oh, how hard it was! I had to fight alone, when too young to inspire confidence. I soon had young children, a weak frame, a small income; and many difficulties in my position arose. I cannot exculpate myself from error, but I have prayed to be forgiven, and yet do, fervently.

So happily passed the time while I was yet in that blessed abode. A day or two before Christmas I returned home, dining on the way with my dear friends, at Mrs. Langford's, on Ludgate Hill, where they now resided. In the evening they set me down at St. James's, where I once more bade adieu to those who had always befriended me. I was placed under their care when I was six years old, remained with them until I was fourteen, and afterwards returned to them for six months. I had now again been five weeks under their hospitable roof, and now it was really adieu, for little did I ever see them after—Mr. Kay never, though he visited my eldest daughter; and Miss Kay died shortly after my last visit. Those years were years of happiness indeed. They did not return ; they could not.

On Christmas Day, when Mrs. Pohl and her two children dined with us, and my brother and sister were also with us, we enjoyed our beef, mince pies, and plum pudding, as usual. A good tea, muffins heaped up, and German cake, with the delicious punch, finished our day, and the Pohls went home in a coach.

The next business was to send for our hairdresser, Kead, the cavalier of the day, to contrive a head-dress for me. My hair was growing fast, but was not yet of a length to be like others. This he managed beautifully, and I now sat for the first time to Zoffany for my portrait. I passed the day with them, the Farrens met us at dinner, and in the evening we all repaired to Drury Lane to see Miss Farren act. I am ashamed to say I have forgotten in what.

After this day we devoted ourselves to arranging all my things ready to be transported to the lodgings that Mr. Papendiek had taken in Charlotte Street. At the beginning of January my father came home from Windsor, dull, absorbed, and no cheerfulness about him. He looked at my things, and said he thought they would do, particularly admiring the Manchester cotton. We walked together, but not to Charlotte Street. He would not go there.

On Monday, January 13, as we were sitting down

to tea, a sharp ring at the house bell surprised us, and in walked Mr. Papendiek. The Queen had that morning said to him, ' I dare say you wish to be in London. I spare you until Saturday next, the birthday, when you will attend as usual.' Our wedding was then fixed for the following Thursday; and the next day, Tuesday, the 14th, mamma and I and our gentlemen proceeded to Doctors' Commons for the licence. Then to Birch's for our luncheon, and to Willerton's in Bond Street for the ring and the little hoop safeguard. We dined and spent the rest of the day together. Wednesday Mr. Papendiek fetched his brother from Hampstead, and there paid all expenses. Meanwhile, I went to our lodgings with mamma, deposited and arranged my possessions there, received our servant, settled all requisites with her, and returned to my old quarters to pass my last day under the parental roof. A trying time for every female; for whether or not we have been happy, natural instinct binds us to those from whom we have received all wants from infancy, who under all circumstances afforded us shelter, and comfort under every pain and sorrow, who took us to the font for baptism, who saw that we were confirmed in our faith, who led us to the Table to make there our public confession of it, and who, by precept and example, encouraged us to every good work. Blessed parents, I thank you for my education, liberally given, for my maintenance, for every indulgence and advantage of society, for every intention of good towards me, and for all affection shown to me with the desire to lead and guide me in the path of righteousness. Once more I acknowledge every benefit received, and thank you in grateful and loving memory.

I dreaded the parting hour, and went off early to my room. I was a favourite child of my father's, and a companion to him, and I feel it now, as I did then, a point of distress that he should not have been happy in my marriage.

My sister was asleep. Georgy boy was sitting up waiting for me. He had moved his little bedding on to chairs in my room, as he would not leave me while I was still at home.

The next morning, no sunshine. It was damp, dull, and cheerless when I rose to quit my home, January 16, 1783.

Mr. Kead dressed me well and becomingly. A white jacket and petticoat, my satin cloak, and a white hat, formed my bridal attire. At ten, the party arrived. Finding my father did not come forward, I went to him, when he handed me to my uncle, saying, 'Louis, this is your affair; you will give my daughter to this man.' I was sensibly hurt, but nothing could be said then. My father had ordered no carriages, nor had he interested himself

in any arrangements for us. We therefore went to
hackney to St. George's, Hanover Square, where
the ceremony took place. A bad omen occurred, for
Mr. Papendiek having omitted to take the ring from
the paper, it fell on being disencumbered. The clergyman urged my mother's being lent, as the proper
hour was already past, but I determinately refused,
and fully meant to return home, when fortunately
the young ones picked up the missing ring, just in
time. The ceremony being ended, my uncle said,
'I will have the first kiss,' when the clergyman said,
'I almost wished it. The bride is very young, and
I feel greatly impressed in her favour. Madam, I
sincerely wish you well; and you, sir, in your care of
her.' We then drove off to a house at Ranelagh,
where they provide those sort of things, and had a
wedding breakfast. From thence we proceeded to
St. James's, where we dined at three o'clock. No
change of dress. My aunt met us, and my father
received us. When dinner was served, he placed
Mr. Papendiek next my mother, myself being, of
course, next my husband. The party consisted of
my uncle and aunt, cousin Charlotte, who was
bridesmaid, Mrs. Pohl, Ungerland, and the Clays,
George Papendiek, my brother and my sister. The
dinner was first mock turtle soup and cod's head
and shoulders; removes, à-la-mode beef and roast
turkey; sides, sauerkraut with sausages, and a chine

of pork; in the centre a pigeon pie. Then a company pudding, and mince pies. In the evening my boy cousins arrived and Mrs. Pohl's two children. Wedding cake was not then the custom in our rank, but favours, so mamma took care to please the young ones with these, and a few niceties also. She took us home at ten, George Papendick accompanying us as an escort back for her. We then found ourselves alone for the first time, and our conversation naturally turned upon the events of the day. The marriage service is very impressive, and in thinking of it one could not help feeling affected. In our case we had the distress of knowing that, though the marriage was permitted, consent was not given, and we resolved that our conduct should be such that we might hope to be forgiven in time, and that we might secure God's blessing.

The next morning I rose with a composed mind, which for some time before had not been the case. At our breakfast we were annoyed by different people calling for *douceurs*. Then followed Mr. Clay's elegant present of tea-board, waiter, bread-basket, snuffer-tray, and four little stands, all alike; a black ground with a silver pattern. The tea-board is only just now, fifty years after, worn out. Our dinner, my first attempt, was a knuckle of veal in soup, with parsley and butter, and a rice pudding. Too great a falling off from the Windsor table, and a sort of reprimand followed. To our great delight, at six o'clock, in walked papa and mamma to tea. We then had servants who took pleasure in serving their masters, and mine ran out for muffins, and brought them up hot and hot. Good London porter, and oysters cold and broiled, made our supper; with a little warm mixture of wine or spirits, with cake, before parting. We played a cheerful pool at quadrille, and all passed off well, this visit from my beloved father making me very happy.

The next morning, the 18th, Kead came to dress me, and put on my very pretty and becoming cap, for, in those days, no head of my age was uncovered; and dressing myself in my satin and all my best, we proceeded to St. James's in sedan chairs. While dressing, the Queen desired to see me, and on entering her Majesty said, 'I am glad to see you; how neat you look! Well, my dear, your father has been anxious to educate you well; you will now have an opportunity to reward him. You are very young, but I am sure you know your duty; practise it strictly, and all will go right. Your mother was always an industrious person, and I hope she has taught you to be so too. I make no doubt that on my inquiries we shall hear good reports of your conduct.' I began to feel in what light I stood before her; and the lady in attendance, perceiving my distress, took my hand and led me to look at the jewels, or I think I should have fallen. Upon which the Queen said, ' I will not keep you,' her kind formula for closing an interview, and I backed out. I had not courage to look at the company, and retired upstairs. There my visitors came to pay their compliments. Mr. Devaynes, the household apothecary, brought me a silver cream jug ; Mr. Kamus a pair of diamond-cut steel shoe buckles. Mrs. Pohl dined and passed the day with us, and, as she was in attendance, brought us many little accounts of the dresses &c., which to this day amuse me. We all have our little weaknesses. In the evening at eight o'clock, when the younger Princes and Princesses went home, the Prince of Wales only attending the ball at St. James's, I went down to see them. They were all so merry and so friendly, and Lady Charlotte Finch bowed most condescendingly. And so ended this gala day.

The next day, Sunday, Mr. Papendiek had to attend the Prince of Wales, so my brother came to take me to church. We went to the pages' pew in Charlotte Street Chapel, and met my uncle and aunt there. The latter was shocked at my appearance, with my Quaker bonnet, Bath coating pelisse, and black silk muff; but I always preferred dressing quietly for church. When Mr. Papendiek returned to dinner, he brought me, as a present from the Prince of Wales, an enamelled watch and key, the same that my daughter, Mrs. Planta, now has, damaged by Elizabeth having, when a child, thrown it down in a pet. At afternoon church, Mr. Butler preached, strongly advocating attendance at the evening services; to enforce which, he introduced a striking anecdote, which I will repeat. A merchant, whose affairs were embarrassed, had not the courage to meet his creditors, and determined to leave the country at night, unknown to anyone, when, according to his usual habit, he went to evening church. It was the 7th of the month, and the 37th Psalm, one of those appointed for that evening, described so pointedly his own case, that he resolved on attending to the voice of the Psalmist—to remain in this country, to set his house in order, and to follow the blessed precepts of the Almighty with more assiduity than before. What wholesome, fine advice for a young person! I hope I have profited by it. At least it has been imprinted on my memory.

The morning following, Mr. Papendick went to Windsor. Linen day, and I found plenty to repair, which would keep my servant and myself employed for some time. I now began to be alone, and, of course, at liberty to make such arrangements as would be for the comfort of us all. George Papendick was to live with us, so I made him put all his own things in his bedroom, which adjoined the parlour. That room which was to the front I kept for meals

and for evening use only, so that it should always be
tidy to show anyone into who might happen to call.
The dressing-room upstairs I arranged for Mr. Papendiek's own use, and moved all his music into it, so
that here he could practise undisturbed, which he
did for at least four hours every day, and receive his
friends, and feel quite independent. I established
myself, with my little all, in our bedroom, placing
the bureau drawers between the windows, which, by
letting down the flap, served for writing and dressing
table. Our rooms were not over furnished, but with
a few good books, and some pretty ornamental things
neatly arranged, I began to feel quite at home; and
although Gussy [Mrs. Papendiek's youngest daughter
and my mother.—ED.] will scarcely give me credit
for it, I hoped something like gentility appeared.
Two of our rooms were furnished by her Majesty,
and a case of plate was also sent by her, which contained cruets, salt-cellars, candlesticks, and spoons of
different sizes, silver forks not being then used. From
the Queen came also six large and six small knives
and forks, to which mamma added six more of each,
and a carving knife and fork. Our tea and coffee
set were of common Indian china, our dinner service
of earthenware, to which, for our rank, there was
nothing superior, Chelsea porcelain and fine India
china being only for the wealthy. Pewter and Delft
ware could also be had, but were inferior.

A few days after this, I went to Zoffany's for the second sitting of my picture. A dreary morning in winter, and the fidget of not being at home to receive Mr. Papendiek, added to the cramped attitude for many hours, no doubt caused that expression of countenance so distasteful to my family. I reached home in time for dinner, which seemed to please, and the smiles returned. The arrangements in the house I had made were highly approved of, particularly that of Mr. Papendiek's own room, where he could, and did, have his friends to practise their duets &c. with him.

His hours of waiting were now changed. He was to be in attendance at breakfast at nine, at dinner at three, and to remain until the Princess went into the Queen's Room, which was about six o'clock, as their Majesties dined at four. Our hours were now, therefore, eight o'clock breakfast, half-past one dinner.

We received our first invitation for Wednesday, the 29th, an evening party at Mrs. Clay's, where we met Mr. and Mrs. King, whose town house was in King Street, Covent Garden, the business being carried on in Pall Mall, as I believe it still is, by his sons. Mr. King was all kindness. I had often passed a day with them, under Mrs. Montagu's care, at Sutton Court, near Kew Bridge, and now he proposed a repetition of these visits, which would no doubt have come to pass, but to Kew we returned no more till their home was broken up.

Then we began to sum up our accounts, which we found had dipped low. The quarter's salary was about 46*l.*, and Mr. Papendiek had incautiously paid the whole of Dressler's account for the wedding breakfast, hackney coaches, licence, *douceurs*, &c., which he certainly was not prepared for. We reminded my father of his promise to furnish the 130*l.* for the debt, but in a moment I saw that it was not forthcoming. As I knew that Duberly, the army clothier, had already asked Mr. Papendiek to get orders for him from regiments, I proposed borrowing that sum from him. He lent it willingly, but at a high rate of interest. We paid away 100*l.*, and reserved the 30*l.* in case we should find ourselves without money. I never had an allowance, so was somewhat helpless; but experience soon taught me the value of money and the necessity of carefulness, and the sequel must speak for me.

On February 3 our first party was to take place. Mr. Papendiek had willingly agreed to it, provided there was no bustle. I borrowed candlesticks for the supper table from mamma, but where to get a coffee pot I did not know. I went to our old fish shop in Vigo Lane, and brought home two lobsters for three shillings. When I got home there was a basket directed to me from papa and mamma. With what delight I opened it! First came out the sweetest little round fat turkey, next the yellow Dresden china, still in being, and thirdly a silver coffee pot. Mrs. Pohl came early, and we arranged the room prettily before our guests arrived. We then had a small pianoforte, and first we played a trio. Then cards, and supper in another parlour, as it was stipulated in our agreement that, whenever we had friends, we were to have the use of this second room. After supper we sang trios and quartetts, which I accompanied on the guitar, which instrument Mr. Papendiek had given me some time before.

After this party, my third and last sitting to Zoffany took place, and then he sailed for India. He was permitted to assume the title of Sir John Zoffany by the King, as he thought it more appropriate than that of Baron, which had been conferred upon him by the Emperor Joseph II. at Vienna. Poor Mrs. Zoffany, with her little girls, Theresa and Cecilia, went down to Strand-of-the-Green after depositing her jewels, plate, and other valuables, with her banker; disposing of the superfluous furniture, and letting the house in Albemarle Street. We just saw her, but she was too wretched to be amongst her friends. Her loss was indeed great to me. Zoffany stayed in India fourteen years, and then returned to England, where he remained till his death in 1810. He was buried at Kew.

We went to a party at the Lockleys', and often went to the Palmans'. She was a German, and made her little evenings interesting. She only received four or six friends at a time, and the repast was only a secondary consideration.

On Friday, February 14, was the concert for the new Musical Fund, which always took place as early as possible, in order to introduce to the public the foreigners engaged for the season. Salomon was this year the great star. He called upon us, and when Mr. Papendick returned his visit, he was fortunate enough to find him at home, and cordial friendship seemed at once to rivet them. Crawford had the Opera House then, and their Majesties patronised it. Tickets, gratis, were always ready for the attendants on the Royal Family, and Crawford gave us a box on the tier immediately above the pit, and so near the stage that everything was brought to view. For this first grand occasion, Kead dressed mamma and myself at St. James's in the afternoon, and there Mr. Papendick and his brother called for us. When we were seated, my husband presented me with a beautiful opera glass. Augusta now has it, ever in the same case.

Mr. Papendiek first went to see that Miss Planta, and her party, a few boxes off, were all right, and then joined his friend behind the scenes. The orchestra was, as now, upon the stage, and in due course the concert began. Salomon was to play first, and the desk was brought on, as it still continues to be. Then he appeared, introduced by Abel, Fischer and Mr. Papendiek following. He was not handsome nor of an imposing figure, but the animation of his countenance, and the great elegance of his manner, soon caught the public eye. Having bowed, he so placed the desk that not the smallest particle of his violin was hidden, and the 'Tutti' of his favourite concerto, by Kreutzer, commenced rather mezzo-piano, and increased to a crescendo that drew down volumes of applause. Now came the solo; a repetition of the melody an octave higher, which he played with an effect perfectly sublime. It was in the minor key, and the cadence he introduced was a long shake, with the melody played under—something new, which put Fischer almost into fits. The adagio movement he performed in such a manner that Fischer was heard to say, 'I will play it no more; he has outdone me.' Then the rondo followed in the same key as the first movement, and Salomon introduced one short variation that struck upon the ear in such a manner that it was difficult to keep quiet. Having finished, he returned his instrument to the attendant, but retained the bow, which assisted his graceful bow. Abel, who had been permitted to sit, now rose, and they went off arm in arm. Such a *début* has scarcely ever been experienced. We were jumping from our seats.   Schroeder played in the first act, and made a most successful *début* also.   His graceful and sweet manner of touching the pianoforte found its way to the approbation of the public.   Such, pupil of Fischer, was also introduced, and his performance was masterly in the extreme.   A quartett finished the first act, performed by Salomon, first violin; Borghi, of the Opera, second; Watts, tenor; and the inimitable Duport, violoncello.   Beauty after beauty seemed to be the order of the evening.   Now Mr. Papendiek entered our box with Salomon.   We soon found the way to converse interestingly, and ever after he was at home in our humble dwelling.   The Haverfields and Tunstalls, with Mr. Fühling, were in the pit just under us, and Mr. Fühling and Bob Tunstall came up to us and said many kind things.

So ended this delightful treat.

# CHAPTER VIII.

The Miss Linleys—Oratorios—Playhouses—Tragedy and comedy—
Captain Broughton—Slough—Salomon—Emperor's eye—Mrs. Mag-
nolley's school—A dinner—Question of the Prince of Wales's es-
tablishment—George Papendiek—Day in town—Birth of Princess
Amelia—Caudle and cake—Birth of Mrs. Papendiek's first child—
Received her friends—Caudle and chocolate—New Year's Drawing-
room—Christening of the little girl—Present from Mr. Papendiek—
Visit to the Queen—The Queen's interest in nursery arrangements—
Stag hunt—The Prince of Wales—Party feeling—Mrs. Siddons—
Drury Lane—Covent Garden—The King, Mrs. Siddons, and Miss
Burney—New house near Grosvenor Place—Household arrangements
—Duchess of Devonshire—Canvassing for Fox—Great excitement ·
Fox chaired—Mr. Clay—George, the button-maker.

It was now Lent, and the Royal Family went to
Windsor on Mondays, returning to town on Wednesdays. Oratorios were given at the Covent Garden
playhouse on Wednesdays, where the Linleys, father
and son, conducted, and led the orchestra on the
stage, and the three Miss Linleys sang. It was the
most perfect performance, particularly for Handel's
music and that of other ancient masters, that could
be imagined. Description falls far short of the reality.
The eldest Miss Linley married Sheridan, and never
lost her power to sing, but then only friends could be
gratified. The second married Tickell, some public

character, while the youngest remained single, and continued to sing in the oratorios at Covent Garden till they were given up for the Abbey performances. There were oratorios also at Drury Lane, where Miss Harrop was the principal singer, and very good, and Tenducci also. The playhouses then consisted of one tier of boxes entirely round the house, so as to be quite clear of the pit; then two tiers above, on each side only, as the first gallery joined the second tier of boxes, termed 'green,' and the shilling gallery joined the third tier. On oratorio nights the seats in the pit had backs, and were covered, the price being 10s. 6d., the same as the boxes. The first gallery was 5s., and the second 3s. 6d. Their Majesties attended the two houses alternately on the Wednesdays and Fridays. There were tickets always for us, and when we could walk there and back we never failed. Now my black bonnet and cloak came into use for the upper accommodation. For the pit one dressed the same as for the boxes. When mamma joined us we had a coach, which was far more comfortable. To the Opera we also sometimes went. Late in the season Vigononi and Allegranti were attractive in the comic line, with Morigi the bass. The dancers were perfection, Vestris, father and son, Simonet, and Bacelli. Gardelle was ballet master, and Giardini leader. At Drury Lane the tragic performers were Henderson and Mrs. Yates; comic, Mrs. Abington and Mrs. Palmer, with Miss Farren second to both, and great in her own especial character, Maria, in 'The Citizen.'  At Covent Garden Miss Young was the first, both in tragedy and comedy, Wroughton principally for the former, and Lee Lewis decidedly for the latter.  In 'The Duenna,' written by Sheridan, and brought out with great splendour, the principal actors were Mrs. Mattocks, her husband, Messrs. Wilson, Quick, and Bannister, Mrs. Greene, Miss Harper, &c.  The prices then were: for the boxes, 5s.; pit, 2s. 6d.; galleries, 2s. and 1s.

All was going on most happily, when I was suddenly seized with the effects of matrimony, and I do believe no creature ever suffered more than I did. I was more dead than alive, and, till towards evening, I could seldom do anything.  Mr. Papendiek nearly lost patience, but at last was convinced that I did use every exertion to overcome the lassitude, and he was more satisfied.

The parties were now over, except my aunt's, which was impeded by the loss of her brother, Captain Broughton, in the West Indies.  He had been promoted to the rank of commander, and to get his new ship ready for the voyage to England it is supposed that he over-exerted himself, which brought on fever, and he died after a few days' illness.  He left all he had to my aunt; 2,000l. in the Funds, and 500l., with plate and other effects, delivered up to her

from the West Indies by dear Captain Broughton's
faithful servant.  The Captain possessed every quality
that could make a man amiable in private life, and in
his public character he was meritorious, as his conduct
during Keppel's engagement with the Channel Fleet
proved.

As soon as Mr. Papendiek saw what a great sufferer I was, he proposed taking me in the chaise with
my father and himself, on Easter Sunday, on their
way to Windsor Lodge, and depositing me with Mrs.
Blackman at Eton.  The weather was peculiarly fine,
and I was indeed comfortable.  The parlour opened
upon steps leading to the garden, and the fresh air
revived me.  Here again I picked up much domestic
knowledge, which I have found very useful to me.
In my walks with my father we got as far as Slough,
and there found that the house Herschel now has
was to let.  We were delighted with it, with its convenient arrangements, and very pretty garden of one
acre, at the end of which was a gravel walk, with a
row of high elms on each side.  On the side next to
Windsor, from whence there was an imposing view
of the north side of the Castle, was a raised terrace,
with a few trees, just enough to break the scorching
rays of the sun without impeding the view.  All our
family were so greatly pleased with the place, that,
although it was too far from Windsor for convenience,
my father decided upon taking it for three years.

After a fortnight's *séjour* at Eton, we returned as we came, and I was certainly recruited, if not brought back to my usual health. My brother had returned to school, disappointed at my absence.

When this house was put into tenantable repair and beautified, my father had all his things removed from Kew to this sweet place. The furniture was placed and appropriated in the best manner possible, the crib, nursing chair, and a few other things needful being sent to me in town at once.

During the remainder of the summer we passed many agreeable days with Mrs. Pohl, at her own little dwelling and at St. James's. My mother went often with us to public amusements, and was, I should say, more happy than during any former seasons of her life, for she doted upon Mr. Papendick. Schroeder often breakfasted with us, and if I were pretty well we had a little music in the way of a lesson. Dear Salomon often and often called to plan some entertainment or to practise. See me he always would, which, as Mr. Papendick was often from home, the world censorious, and all of us warm-hearted, might perhaps as well have been avoided. Yet I am sure that in Salomon's mind only rectitude the most honourable, and sincerity the most pure, had place. Dear friend, we appreciated, we respected, we loved you! Farewell to thy memory.

We now looked over what mamma had left of

baby linen, and purchased the requisite additions, with patterns to make from during the summer. We then made arrangements with Ungerland, our landlord, to have our rooms cleaned during our absence in the country, for it was settled that we were to spend some weeks or months at my father's new house. George Papendiek was to remain in town, visiting us only occasionally, with this understanding, that he was to go off upon the first contentious word, so that we might keep friends. His temper was so trying that it was necessary to make certain stipulations.

Mr. Papendiek wished to make me a present on my birthday, and being very much struck with the colour, then perfectly new, called 'Emperor's eye,' a most brilliant tint of, I should say, what is now termed 'knife steel,' he bought a gown of it and had it made up for the King's birthday, June 4. On that day I went with Mrs. Palman, Miss Wadsworth, and Miss Eves, to see the company, and spent a happy day at St. James's, but I did not see the Queen, as she was not well. My brother always came home to make his bow to the King, who was his godfather, which added to my pleasure. To our surprise, Mrs. Magnolley came to the Palace. She was the wife of the page to Prince William, and kept an elegant ladies' school at Grove House, Knightsbridge. Under her care my sister was to be placed after the midsummer holidays. Judge of my feelings not to have Streatham preferred! My father's reason for this extraordinary step was that, as the house stood on the high road from Windsor, he could always see my sister, while to Streatham he might not be able to go once through the summer. There was some weight in the observation, and to this effect I wrote to my dear friends, whose answer could, of course, only be politely to express regret. Mrs. Magnolley's establishment was conducted upon more of a school plan, and consequently there was less of the feeling of a family, but in no other way was there any inferiority. The best masters attended, and in the house everything was well regulated. Mrs. Magnolley was herself fascinating and clever, and possessed every requisite qualification for the mistress of such a house. My sister remained with her for about seven years. We were asked to dine at this sweet place, just after the King's birthday, by way of seeing it, and making my sister acquainted with her future surroundings, and I will give one more account of a dinner of those days. We sat down ten in number. After soup and fish, there was a round of beef at the top, a roast goose at the bottom, at the two sides a leg of lamb, boiled, and a loin, fried, and four appropriate vegetables, all put on the table at once. Peas were eaten with a broad-bladed knife, best forks only having three prongs. These viands being removed,

in their place came two gooseberry pies, at the top
and bottom, baked and boiled custard at each side,
Swiss and other cheese, radishes and butter.

For our summer dress, my father presented my
mother and myself with the most beautiful lemon-
coloured fine cambric muslins, with a white lace
pattern running over them, and a little glazed. He
met with them accidentally, and being of his favourite
colour we profited by his taste. They were pretty
in the extreme.

We now set off for Slough. A glass coach and
four horses for us, and the servants by the stage.
They would not drive a coach so far in those days
with a pair of horses, even if one changed half-way.
My father and Mr. Papendick came down about a
week later, when the Royal Family moved. In this
pretty house I had two rooms, and a closet adjoining,
and all was beauty and delight, the only drawback
being the distance.

At the close of this session of Parliament the
King proposed the separate establishment of the
Prince of Wales, as he came of age in August. It
was decided that his Royal Highness should the following winter live in Carlton House, and that he
should retain the apartments in Windsor Castle, as
well as the house at Kew where he and the Duke of
York had been brought up. These were to be put in
order for him. Among other numerous appointments,

Mr. Powell, who had been dismissed from his post with the younger Princes, was now made librarian, and George Papendick sub-librarian, at a salary of 100*l.* a year.

Our first step in this business was to increase his stock of attire, and a day in town was proposed for that purpose. I took it for granted that I was to be of the party, but found that was not Mr. Papendick's intention. Young person like, I was affronted, and urged the holiday, and we set off. We met with an accident to our horse on the way, but reached London at last and made our purchases, a piece of cloth for shirts, with cambric frills and ruffles, cravats, &c., and ordered a suit of clothes for State days. The Prince's people were to have a uniform. Although extremely costly and elegant, yet a uniform it was ; another innovation upon the attendants as gentlemen. We left George Papendick in town, and returned safely to Slough. I found by this day's occurrence that Mr. Papendick did not expect me to have any opinion opposite to his, and considered his having agreed to my going to town an excessive indulgence. It had been a great expense, and was not to be repeated. I felt hurt. This George Papendick was to run away with everything ; confidence, money, and favour. However, no other opportunity for pleasure occurred at present, and the affair passing over, we were all reconciled and happy again.

My brother was placed at Eton upon our arrival in the remove under Dr. Langford. His tutor was the Rev. S. Goodall, his dame Mrs. Hexter. On his return after the vacation, he, at the age of eleven, was moved to the upper school.

At the beginning of August, as the Queen hourly expected to be confined, the pages were ordered never to leave the house, so my father and Mr. Papendick took leave of us for the present. On the 7th the event took place, with a Princess, who about the middle of September was christened Amelia. On the day caudle and cake were given to the public at Windsor only, another evident mark of economy. I would not miss it, it was too good, so we ordered a chaise and made a day of it, bringing plenty home, as members of the family, which we distributed among our friends.

At the end of October I was to leave Slough, and it became necessary that I should once more ask my father when he intended to fulfil his promise to pay the 130*l.* He gave me a part of it, and said that in consideration of his having kept us on and off for five months, he thought he had amply done all we could expect. Certainly the saving in housekeeping was a great help, yet we were somewhat embarrassed. Nevertheless we reduced the debt to Duberly as much as we could. Soon after our return home our landlord gave us notice to quit, which

I thought very unfeeling of him in my present situation; but of course we agreed to it so soon as I should be able to be moved.

On November 30, 1783, at a quarter to ten o'clock, just when the drums beat the night call, my baby was born; a little girl, now Mrs. Planta. The next day by coach we informed the papa of the joyful event, and between his 'wait' of breakfast and dinner he rode up on horseback to see us. He asked if the little girl could see, when she, as if by instinct, opened her eyes, which were, even at that early age, declared to be fine. My father was always particularly fond of children, so at every possible moment that he had to spare he devoted himself to nursing the sweet doll.

On December 12, I sent out my cards of thanks, as it was then the custom to receive your friends in your room, baby being visible whether awake or asleep. Caudle and chocolate with cake was always ready, and those poor souls who took the trouble to call laid their 2s. 6d. in the saucer, a *douceur* expected by the nurse. Papa was at home, and gave me for my present six Nankeen double-handled cups and saucers.

The Royal Family arrived in town on the 22nd, and Mr. Papendiek asked the Queen if she had any commands with respect to the christening of his little girl, to which she answered, 'Have her named Charlotte Augusta: Princess Royal and Princess Augusta shall be her godmothers, and Compton shall stand for your old master, Prince Ernest.'

On New Year's Day there was always a Drawing-room. The Poet Laureate wrote the poem, Wiede-mann, then at the head of the King's band, composed the music, which was performed by the band, the vocal parts being sung by the choristers of the Chapel Royal, the bishops giving the blessing. This year it was more than usually splendid. It was the first at which the Prince of Wales appeared since he came of age, and also the first which the Princess Royal attended, as being introduced.

In the evening was our christening. We assembled at six. The Queen sent word that she could spare no one to act as proxies for the Princesses, that my mother and my aunt must represent them. Somewhat of a disappointment, for all our best was prettily set out. I had had my white lustring made up, new cap, Kead to dress me, and sweet baby so prettily dressed. However, Schräder in his canonicals arrived, and the ceremony proceeded. I was also churched. Our first refreshment, tea, coffee, muffins, &c. The canonicals off, cards and music. Then our second repast, christening cake, caudle cups, egg wine, mountain and tent wine in decanters, German relishes of 'Metwurst,' anchovies, &c., and their appendages, mulled beer, and a bowl of punch.

The party consisted of Schröder, the German chaplain at St. James's, uncle, aunt, and two cousins, grandpapa and mamma, my brother and sister, Mrs. Pohl, Ungerland, and Mr. Hünnemann.

The last named was the son of the physician to the Court of Hanover, and had lately come over, strongly recommended to the King as so fine and accurate a copyist of paintings that the most critical judges were often puzzled to distinguish the original from the copy. He was also a good miniature painter. Having letters of introduction to us, Mr. Papendick employed him to paint his portrait in miniature, and had it set as a bracelet clasp, having a corresponding one made with his hair and cypher, and he presented the pair to me on this christening day. We thought it only kind to invite this stranger, who had taken so admirable a likeness of my husband, and had the whole finished off with so much taste.

Mr. Papendick was frequently absent of an evening at this time, for the Prince of Wales was still at the Queen's House, Carlton House not being yet ready for him, and often called upon him to give him an hour or two practice, as his Royal Highness preferred him to Giardini. After the Queen's parties were over, the Prince's began, and two or three times a week he would have a quartett party, and sometimes quite a grand concert.

The Queen's birthday on January 18 next en-

gaged us. I dressed myself, putting on the pretty
christening cap, the dark satin, as on the preceding
year, and in our sedan baby and I went to St.
James's. There the Queen called for me, greatly approved my account of nursery improvement, my close
attention to the duties of a mother, thought the little
girl had already grown much, and all seemed right.
The Princesses were delighted with her, and the
whole was agreeable. I then returned to my father's
apartment, where friends came up at all hours from
three to ten o'clock. On the Queen's birthday a
turkey with many other good things was always put
upon the table at three o'clock to remain till five.
On the King's birthday a goose and peas, with various
etceteras, also at three o'clock. Then tea and coffee,
cakes, wines, and niceties, according to the season.
Among others Mrs. Magnolley visited us, after seeing
the company. She lamented that my sister would
probably be the only one from the Royal household
that would be placed under her tuition, and from her
she expected not much credit. Poor little Sophia,
then only eight years old, already showed that peculiar morose manner ever and anon attached to her.
She had pretty things, learned to dance, to do easy
needlework, had encouraging books, but all seemed
disregarded. She never expressed any regret at
leaving home, but appeared apathetic in everything.

Until Easter this year, 1784, their Majesties were

less at Windsor than usual. One day in each week, either Tuesday or Saturday, was devoted to the stag hunt, at which the Prince of Wales was expected to attend. That sport had been revived a year or two before, as one of those hoped to give amusement to his Royal Highness. Parties of the most elegant description were given at Buckingham House with the same hope, and as a sort of form to introduce him to the nobility generally. But every parent must here lament that nothing under the parental eye or roof could afford either pleasure or one spark of filial gratitude. No expression was manifested to cheer the endeavour their Majesties were making to show the Prince favour, and by every possible means to draw him to that affection which should bind every family in unity. Party feeling ran very high at this time, and every rank of the nobility beset and assailed the Prince. The standard of pleasure, too, was raised very high, and the Royal victim drank the noxious draught to the very dregs.

The new Musical Fund concert was in February, and at the Opera House as before. I did not go. Abel introduced the great star on the violoncello, Crosdill. He made a successful *début*, and was a favourite of the public during his life. He was an Irishman, and his playing studied, practised, and finished, both in *adagio* and *bravura*, but in his style there was no pathos. The Cervettos were all enthusiasm,

Duport sublime. The first act finished with a quintett, which Salomon led, and then Duport made his bow on quitting England. Crosdill was to teach the Prince of Wales, and would have most of the private concerts. Cervetto had the Opera and leading public music meetings. Therefore for Duport nothing remained. great performer as he was. This concert also introduced Clementi, and most successfully did he ingratiate himself with the public. He was a man who never visited among his own rank or those of a higher position, but went only where he was sure of being well paid. He succeeded in getting extensive teaching at a guinea a lesson ; all others, Schroeder included. receiving only half that sum ; and Clementi taught sixteen hours every day. Fischer brought forward another scholar of the King's band. Kellner, who played with his master and Such a trio oboe concerto, very fine and spirited. and much admired for its novelty.

At Drury Lane the most brilliant star that perhaps ever appeared, shone forth this season in Mrs. Siddons.[1] Tragedy she played to the public, it was

[1] Walpole in one of his letters thus refers to Mrs. Siddons : ' I have been two days in town and seen Mrs. Siddons. She pleased me beyond my expectation, but not up to the admiration of the *ton*, two or three of whom were in the same box with me. . . . Mr. Crawford asked me if I did not think her the best actress I ever saw ? I said, " By no means ; we old folks were apt to be prejudiced in favour of our first impressions." She is a good figure. handsome enough, though neither nose nor chin according to the Greek standard, beyond which both advance a good

her line; but to their Majesties she played sentimental comedy, and read plays to them at Buckingham House. She first appeared in Isabella, which character, with that of Lady Macbeth, she herself considered her two leading ones. I have seen her in every tragic part she acted, and to me she seemed equally great in all. The parts of Ariadne and Desdemona her years would not permit her many seasons to personate, but they were perfect while she attempted them. This February I saw her in 'The Fair Penitent,' with Palmer as Lothario. It was perfection indeed. Mrs. Yates and Henderson went to Covent Garden, as did Mrs. Abington after her inimitable acting in 'The School for Scandal' at Drury Lane, where she had been engaged for many years. She certainly was the first in her line of genteel comedy; and although she may since have been equalled, she has never been excelled. She was received at the houses of the nobility, and was looked to by ladies for the fashions of the season. Drury Lane, being brought into repute by Garrick and the

deal. Her hair is either red, or she has no objection to its being thought so, and had used red powder. Her voice is clear and good, but I thought she did not vary its modulations enough, nor ever approach enough to the familiar, but this may come when more habituated to the awe of the audience of the capital. Her action is proper, but with little variety; when without motion her arms are not genteel. Thus you see all my objections are very trifling; but what I really wanted, and did not find, was originality, which announces genius, and without both which I am never intrinsically pleased.'

elder Sheridan, was always considered the leading theatre, and had the most renowned company. This comedy of 'The School for Scandal' was written by Brinsley Sheridan, in order, if possible, to support the establishment upon the same high standing as before the retirement of Garrick from the stage. It succeeded, and the first night of its representation the society of *litterati* engaged nearly the whole of the lower circle of boxes as a compliment to the author. When the curtain drew up, the *litterati* stood up, which was the signal for the house to do the same, and Sheridan led on those who were to appear first with a speech of introduction, then made his bow and retired amidst deafening plaudits. We went to Covent Garden to see Mrs. Yates as Lady Macbeth, and Henderson as Shylock the Jew. That and Macbeth were his two finest characters, and in neither of them has he ever had a rival, nor has Miss Young as Portia. Mamma, Mrs. Pohl, and George Papendiek accompanied us, and we were all much gratified with our three nights' amusement, and baby at home was as happy asleep as we were awake.

The King was a very great admirer of Henderson, and also of Mrs. Siddons, who was about this time appointed to teach the two youngest Princesses to read and enunciate. Mrs. Siddons was always anxious to act with Henderson, as she considered him one of the greatest, if not *the* greatest actor of his day, and it was unfortunate that they were engaged by the two rival houses.

[Miss Burney relates a conversation she had with the King, upon one occasion when she met his Majesty at Mrs. Delany's, upon the subject of plays and players, which seems *à propos*, and I hope I may be pardoned for quoting it. He, the King, was sorry, he said, for Henderson, and the more as Mrs. Siddons had wished to have him play at the same house with herself. Then Mrs. Siddons took her turn, and with the warmest praise. ' I am an enthusiast for her,' cried the King, ' quite an enthusiast; I think there was never any player in my time so excellent—not Garrick himself; I own it !' Then coming close to me, who was silent, he said, ' What? what?' meaning, what say you? But I still said nothing; I could not concur where I thought so differently, and to enter into an argument was quite impossible; for every little thing I said the King listened to with an eagerness that made me always ashamed of its insignificancy. And, indeed, but for that I should have talked to him with much greater fluency, as well as ease. From players he went to plays, and complained of the great want of good modern comedies, and of the extreme immorality of most of the old ones. ' And they pretend,' cried he, ' to mend them; but it is not possible. Do you think it is ? — what ? what ?'—ED.] [1]

The oratorios were drooping a little. Mrs. Sheridan was missed, although Miss Linley outdid herself. Salomon often took his two o'clock meal with us, after a practice at home, and sometimes with the Prince; for he was generally engaged for the private concerts, Giardini having the Opera, and Cramer the established concerts. At the Queen's House, the fondness for the ancient masters kept him aloof, much to the annoyance of Abel and Fischer.

My father and mother doted on baby, so every fine afternoon we went to St. James's, either carrying

[1] In another part of Miss Burney's *Diary* she says: 'Mrs. Schwellenberg told me Mrs. Siddons had been ordered to the Lodge to read a play, and desired I would receive her in my room. . . . I received her by the Queen's commands, and was perfectly well inclined to reap some pleasure from the meeting.

'But now that we came so near, I was much disappointed in my expectations. . . . I found her the heroine of a tragedy—sublime, elevated, and solemn. In face and person, truly noble and commanding; in manners, quiet and stiff; in voice, deep and dragging; and in conversation, formal, sententious, calm, and dry. I expected her to have been all that is interesting; the delicacy and sweetness with which she seizes every opportunity to strike and to captivate on the stage had persuaded me that her mind was formed with that peculiar susceptibility which, in different modes, must give equal powers to attract and to delight in common life. But I was very much mistaken. As a stranger, I must have admired her noble appearance and beautiful countenance, and now regretted that nothing in her conversation kept pace with their promise; and as a celebrated actress, I had still only to do the same.

'Whether fame and success have spoiled her, or whether she only possesses the skill of representing and embellishing materials with which she is furnished by others, I know not; but still I remain disappointed.'

baby under my cloak or outside, as weather permitted, the maid following at her leisure. Baby was undressed at her usual hour, laid in grandmamma's bed to sleep, and a little before ten she was wrapped in her blanket and carried home as we came. I had the maid with me, however, on returning, and we walked through the Park with the Relieve Guard as a protection. We never were, I think, in the least the worse for it, and we all enjoyed the meeting.

After fruitless attempts to obtain a lodging to suit us, we took a house opposite the turnpike, where it then was, just at the turn into Grosvenor Place from the Pimlico Road, and where the pastrycook's shop still is that was once so famed for Chelsea buns. Being much out of ornamental repair, we were able to engage this house for one year at 40*l.*, and thither we moved in April. The back parlour was pretty, as it opened down a few steps into a small garden. This was our common room, the front parlour being entirely for Mr. Papendiek, to be used only on great emergencies as a dining room. I met with a proper aged person as cook, who proved of infinite use in our little *ménage*. She was spirited in managing, cleaning, washing, and preparing our meals, with my assistance, but nursing tired me, and I spared the maid with reluctance.

We were asked and persuaded to pass a day with the Meyers, who had come up from Kew to remain at their house in Covent Garden during the contested election between Charles Fox, Lord Hood, and Sir Cecil Wrey. Several of the nobility almost ruined their property in canvassing for the Fox and Holland party, and it will be remembered that the celebrated Duchess of Devonshire, during the six weeks, was indefatigable in her exertions on their behalf. Many anecdotes are related of her, both for and against her female delicacy. It was principally to her great charms of person that she owed her success in canvassing. She was very beautiful, and her manner was so engaging, so sprightly, and withal so gentle and polite, that all who came in contact with her at once became subservient to her influence.

[Miss Burney says of the Duchess: 'I did not find so much beauty in her as I expected, notwithstanding the variations of accounts; but I found far more of manner, politeness, and gentle quiet. She seems by nature to possess the highest animal spirits, but she appeared to me not happy. I thought she looked oppressed within, though there is a native cheerfulness about her which I fancy scarce ever deserts her.' Later on, she says: 'I now saw how her fame for personal charms had been obtained; the expression of her smiles is so very sweet, and has an ingenuousness and openness so singular, that, taken in those moments. not the most rigid critic could deny the justice of her personal celebrity. She was quite gay.

easy, and charming; indeed, that last epithet might have been coined for her.'—ED.]

So great was the public ferment, that private individuals and moneyed men of every rank supported Charles James Fox, many to the half of their fortunes, and to the detriment of their families and interests.

At eleven o'clock, we were to be at the Meyers' to see the procession come in, which lasted till quite one, when the polling began. Entertained indeed we were, if it may be so called. Fighting, drumming, screaming, singing, marrowboning, hooting, hurrahing, &c. were going on the whole time. Elegant carriages passed, Fox coming in that of the Prince of Wales, with dress liveries, fox-tails, ribbons, flowers, &c.

The High Bailiff made no return on account of the illegal votes predominant on Fox's score, and I know not how that was settled; but when the House met, a petition was presented by Hood and Wrey. However, Fox was to be chaired, which took place early in May. The procession was conducted in the following manner: bands of music, cat-call noises of all kinds, emblems of every insignia of a fox, twelve carriages of commoners and gentry, with their best liveries and every possible decoration, twenty-four horsemen, dressed in blue coats and double brass buttons, waistcoats and shorts of buff kerseymere with the same buttons, silk stockings, dress shoes, yellow or gold shoe and knee buckles, buff Woodstock gloves, and cocked hats ; the horses handsomely caparisoned, and ornamented with fox-tails and heads, flowers, &c., and buff and blue ribbons. These made a dashing appearance. Then came Fox in a decorated chair, with a good brass band preceding him, and immediately following the chair were twenty-four gentlemen of the Prince of Wales's household, of whom George Papendick was one and my cousin Hugh, page of presence, was another, in the same dress, Quentin bringing up the rear on a beautiful horse, strikingly ornamented with appropriate designs. Then six of the carriages of the nobility in State costume. The Devonshires last, with four footmen behind, two at each door, and a groom at the head of each of the six horses, the five other carriages having each their complement of attendants. Last of all came the State carriage of the Prince, with the full equipment of horses, men, dress, &c. The procession of course began from the hustings, St. Paul's, Covent Garden, from whence it went three times round the square or market, down King Street and Bedford Street, just round Mrs. Clay's corner into the Strand. At the corner of Cockspur Street and Pall Mall, all the barrels for refreshment were put ready by the brothers Harry and Sam House, the great spirit merchants of the day, the former of whom had expended on the election 25,000*l.* and the latter 15,000*l.* Then on went the procession to the courtyard of Carlton House, which it went round three times, the Prince and his friends being at the windows to cheer Fox; then down Pall Mall, up St. James's Street, to Devonshire House, where a platform had been erected against the wall in Piccadilly, within the courtyard, for the Prince and others to receive Fox, and whither they had arrived in private carriages through back streets. The Duke would not permit anyone to enter his gates save the member himself, although he had allowed his Duchess to waste his property and degrade herself. After shouts of welcome the day's sports ended there. At the public-houses it finished with the needful.

This election brought Mr. Clay to town again, and with him a button, which he had for some time been perfecting, and now introduced. It was for gentlemen's mourning attire, and, improving by wear, was in use for years. He also had greatly improved snuff-boxes, which were now made to open with hinges, miniatures being introduced or settings of hair; so by his button and his box a second fortune was rapidly accumulated. My father's friendly acquaintance with this worthy and ingenious man commenced in agency on the Queen's business, who had added largely to her stock of usefuls and ornamentals from Mr. Clay's manufactory. She now again gave encouragement certainly to the snuff-box —taking snuff being one of her weaknesses; as did the King to the button, for in his youth one of his favourite occupations had been turning and button-making. Of a German in Long Acre he had learned how to make the loop and attach it to the button; so upon this occasion he said to Mr. Clay, 'Send me several sets of buttons, for as I am called George the button-maker, I must give a lift to our trade.'

During the election, and on the day of the chairing, we were invited to Mr. Clay's corner house, but I had had enough of that sport at dear Mrs. Meyer's, and we declined, particularly as our gentlemen were at Windsor. Here ended our pleasant friendship. A farewell leave-taking was all we ever again saw of dear Mr. Clay, for on quitting London after this last visit to the metropolis he remained in Birmingham, and his son dying at an early age, he lived in retire-ment.

At Ladyday 1784, George Papendiek received his first payment, 25*l.* I proposed that now that he was well stocked with clothes he should keep this salary for running expenses, and save as much as he could, so as not to be any expense to us when we went away for the summer—he living with us when in town as before. Our income was now 196*l.* a year, and this assistance from George Papendiek would be a great boon to us.

# CHAPTER IX.



DURING the Easter recess, Salomon was making every
effort to introduce with *éclat* one of the greatest
singers ever heard in this or any other country—
Mara. In the opinion of some, Mrs. Sheridan surpassed her in feminine sweetness in a few of Handel's
sublime airs, while Catalani may have, in one or two
instances, equalled her in *bravura*, but I can
scarcely admit that it was so. Mara was perfect in
every style, and had an astonishing compass of voice,

clear from the upper treble D to the third leger
line A, and that without effort, and pure. Higher
and lower notes she could produce by trick or
management. She knew the properties of every
instrument, so that when singing a duet with an
instrument she was always perfectly in tune, being
careful never to touch the imperfect tones of it. She
played an accompaniment upon the pianoforte, organ, harp, or guitar in excellent style. Salomon
engaged the Pantheon for four private concerts, and
succeeded in getting the Prince of Wales, the Duke
and Duchess of Devonshire, the Bessboroughs, &c. to
patronise them, and had the Prince's side very
elegantly fitted up; the King's being, as it was,
opposite, and the parterre for the general company.
When Salomon brought this wonderful woman forward, there was perfect silence. She was not handsome; had projecting teeth, a German face with a
determined expression, though not ill-natured or
repulsive. On the contrary, her countenance was
animated. Her eyes were black and excessively
beautiful. She was rather above the common height,
and upon this occasion was dressed in black velvet,
with a magnificent diamond tiara, and looked more
like a queen than a singer. She tried her voice in a
sort of prelude, a new idea among us. Then the
*tutti* or symphony of the air commenced, and led up
in *crescendo* to a high note, upon which Mara began.

She held it for a few bars, then brought it to a long shake, and from it ran down an octave or more in notes as clear as bells. When she had finished her song the excitement was intense. The people almost screamed. The Prince came down and spoke to her as she descended the steps of the orchestra, and said how greatly he admired her. She answered, ' Then I hope for protection, as I offended my sovereign, the King of Prussia, by marrying. Yet on quitting his dominions he forgave me, as these brilliants will show. The necklace I do not wear, as it impedes my singing.' The Prince engaged her constantly, and went to hear her everywhere that she sang. She went always under the protection of her husband, who was engaged also where she sang as orchestral violoncello, and had he been in the least a gentleman, they would have been received generally, as she was ladylike and very obliging. Though she was naturally aware of her very superior talent, she was encouraging and friendly to others, and always willing to give advice or assistance.

A female singer was required for the King's concerts of ancient music, and when Mara was proposed, there was fear lest her pronunciation of English should not be sufficiently good for Handel's music. There was a meeting of the directors, therefore, to decide this point, and she sang before them portions of the ' Messiah,' accompanying herself in an ancient style on the pianoforte in such a manner that they were enraptured; and her rendering of the sublime words was so pathetic and the foreign accent so slight that they were unanimous in her praise, and at once requested the King to engage her for the next concert. This was done. She pleased, surprised, and gratified, and when, at the conclusion, she sang 'The Prince, unable to conceal his pain,' out of 'Alexander's Feast,' the King rose, and expressed his great delight, saying that he perceived she was capable of undertaking anything that might be required of her. After this, her success was assured.

On their Majesties' return to town after Easter, an account of the private rehearsals at the Abbey was presented to them, the long-expected music meeting being now determined upon. It was to be for the benefit of the Royal Society of Musicians, and as a commemoration of the death of Handel, twenty-five years before, and was in every respect to be done on a magnificent scale. The performances were to last for three days, and the music was to be of an ancient stamp, either oratorios or selections from them, and other sacred pieces. The tickets for the public rehearsal were fixed at half-a-guinea each, and it was to take place in the daytime; morning dress, hats and bonnets. For the evening perform-ances, the tickets were to be a guinea; no reserved seats, no preference. On each ticket, the name of the sub-director, who was to show you to your seat, was mentioned, and the door at which you were to enter. Evening dress, with the exception of feathers, which were forbidden. The Queen wore the same character of dress as that in which she appeared at the ancient concerts—a *sacque*, which had a bodice to fit, which met to the lower point, where it branched off, and was trimmed down each side, the petticoat underneath being trimmed to correspond, and the stomacher being covered with jewels. The part of the gown that denoted the *sacque* was the fulness required for the back breadth which was laid in deep double plaits between the shoulders, and only once confined about an inch below the original tack, and hung loose from there. The Queen's train was about three yards in length, and was held up by a page of honour; those of the Court attendants were two yards long and could be looped up elegantly. The sleeve was close to the arm, with rows of lace from the top, terminating in three deep ruffles at the elbow. The material was gold or silver gauze or silk tissue for the dress in summer, and for the winter the tissue in satin. The headdress was a cap with Court lappets, and jewels, but not in profusion. The three elder Princesses were in tissue silk frocks, with a lace cuff turned over the bottom of the sleeve, and simple caps with no jewels; and as they, with the exception of the Princess Royal, had not yet been introduced at Court, they wore no lappets. Their trains were about one yard on the ground, which was then considered a walking length.

They, with Lady Charlotte Finch, sat on one side of their Majesties' box, the Princes on the other, each with a multitude of attendants. The King, his sons, and gentlemen attendants were in the Windsor uniform; dark blue, with red cuffs and collars, and gold-laced button-holes. The noble directors, the bishops, and the prebends were placed immediately under the Royal Family, so that the King could converse with them when he wished. The ladies all wore hoops, but that of the Queen was much smaller than the Court hoop, and those of the Princesses only of a size to lift the dress from clinging. The principal lady singers were in silk dresses, the men in bags and swords; the ladies of the company in silk or India gold muslins, the men in evening dress without bags and swords.

The King, with his usual kindness, asked Mr. Papendiek what part was assigned to him. When he only bowed in answer, ' Oh,' said his Majesty, ' we must have Papendiek's flute, so I shall desire that he takes the high leading parts in the " Te Deum " and in the Dead March in " Saul." '

Miss Burney's account of the whole performance is so excellent, that I will not repeat it, but refer my daughters or any other readers to it.[1] My own little private remarks, however, *re* the dress &c. on this grand occasion, I thought would be interesting to any females who may peruse these pages.

George Papendiek was among the violins, but Salomon had no part in this memorable meeting, nor had he in one extra concert given at the Pantheon, when Mara sang by command some especial piece, to the astonishment of professors and amateurs alike.

Alas, poor me! all this time I was in my bed, to the great disappointment of Mr. Papendiek, with a feverish cold, and was covered with blotches like great bites, so I missed this magnificent entertainment at Westminster Abbey. I think I had lately over-exerted myself, for as we had but one servant besides the nurse, my 'place' was no sinecure. As Mr. Papendiek liked to be able to ask any friend, who might happen to call, to sit down to dinner with us, we always had one good thing at the top, with makes-up at the bottom, and all pastry, confectionery, and general arrangements of neatness and order fell to my lot, with all superior cooking. Dr. Khrone had poor baby weaned, but she did not mind it, and at this time we put her into short coats. We made her four white frocks and two coloured ones, with

---

[1] It is not known to which of Miss Burney's works this remark refers, as the *Diary and Letters* of Madame D'Arblay were published many years after Mrs. Papendiek's death.

the skirts full and three tucks and a hem; the bodies plain, cut cross-ways, and the sleeves plain, with a cuff turned up. These, with converting of underclothing, nurse, I, and a workwoman finished off in a week. The rest of her attire was, long cotton or thread mitts, without fingers, tied round the arm high above the elbow, a double muslin handkerchief crossed and tied behind in a bow, or if cold a silk pelerine, with the same coloured bonnet, close front, high caul, with a bow in front. Baby's was blue, and very pretty did she look.

On the King's birthday we went to St. James's, and grandpapa took her in to see the Queen, who desired that I should be called. She said, 'You look ill, but your baby does you credit.' Then she desired Princess Amelia to be brought in, who was three months and three weeks older, but the Queen was struck that my babe appeared more lively, and more intelligent than the Princess. Her Majesty also admired her cap and frocks, and wished me to make one of each for Princess Amelia, the cap only being finally determined upon, which I did not much lament. Her Royal Highness's nurses, Mesdames Cheveley and Williams, were very angry with the Queen's remarks, when the same lady who had seen me the first after my marriage, perceiving it, said in the kindest way, 'Her Majesty is gracious in encouraging a young woman in exemplary duties; and considering that this child has just been weaned, it is striking that she should be looking so well.' Then my nursing was approved, and the Queen was determined to be kind. The babies hankered to play, and the King, coming in just then, set them going for a moment, and then our visit was ended. The day was passed as usual, but I kept quiet, being still very weak.

Now, for good luck to me and to many, it was proposed, as Parliament was to sit longer than usual, that there should be two more Abbey concerts. Tickets went off faster than they could be printed, both for the rehearsals, two, and the performance, which promised to be as grand as those of the former occasion.

With Mr. Papendiek, I went to the first of these rehearsals, and with my ' Emperor's eye,' and petticoat trimmed to match, a new summer white silk cloak, a pretty cap with ties under the chin, and Kead's inimitable dressing, I really looked interesting. I was alone in the middle aisle with my book and my opera-glass, but knowing all the royalties, and their attendants, the directors, &c., I soon made friends.

To describe the sight is quite impossible. The Princes and Princesses were more than beautiful. They were animated, elegant, affable, and good-natured. The Queen was that day in light green and silver, with ornaments of emeralds and rubies; the Princesses in lilac and silver, with pearls.

The overture in 'Esther' was the first piece, in which Crosdill and Cervetto were first violoncellos in unison, Mara (the husband) and another as seconds to them, and in the obbligato part my old dancing master, Villeneuve, one of the principal double basses. The second piece was the 'Dettingen Te Deum,' the whole assembly rising with the first words, 'We praise Thee, O God.' These are too well known for me to attempt to describe them. Suffice it to say that they were performed to perfection. In the second act came the Dead March in 'Saul.' To endeavour to represent the funeral as coming from a distance, it began *pianissimo*, gradually increasing in loudness as the procession was supposed to come nearer. It was at first proposed to have minute guns really fired, but this was given up, as it was feared that they could not possibly be a success, and Kellner undertook to play the double drums. This he did so exquisitely as to cause a vibration in the pianoforte, and the sound was like an echo more than the firing of a gun. When the funeral was supposed to be in sight, it being that of a king, the whole company rose, and the orchestra worked up to a *fortissimo*, and so grand was the illusion that handkerchiefs were in requisition. Then, as it appeared to pass on, we were all seated again, and the orchestra had so practised that the sound of the instruments seemed to die away in the air. The performers were quite exhausted, and afterwards said that to excel in the effect they desired to produce was as fine and difficult a performance as they could be called upon to execute. We must give one tribute of praise to the poor flutists (of whom my husband was one), for on their instruments depended a great part of the effect. Most of the company walked home through the Park, which being observed by their Majesties, the carriages were ordered to be driven slowly, so we were again one party. The last performance of this season I also had the pleasure and gratification of attending, as the Queen gave me a ticket. Mr. Papendick walked to the Abbey with me, and falling in with Mara and her husband, he said to her, 'You look very smart in that white silk, but how loosely it is put on!' To which she answered, 'You forget what my voice must do this day—it must have room to do itself justice.' Indeed her voice was taxed, for in that fine anthem, which was performed, 'O sing unto the Lord,' she had first four bars solo, then had to take the C seventh line, and hold it for four bars, while the chorus falls in, above which her voice sounded distinctly. Fischer in the greatest excitement said, 'Her voice was louder than my oboe, I heard it.' It was repeated, and was, if possible, even better executed. We heard Mr. Kennedy, a remarkably fine counter-tenor, in 'Worship the Lord in the beauty of holiness;' and also in the Coronation Anthem, which began when the King stepped from his carriage, and was so arranged that as he entered his box the words 'God save the King' were sung. We had a splendid selection of music, and thus ended my supreme delight for this season.

Now we quickly prepared for going to Slough. Baby's crib was taken this time in addition to the pianoforte, and a little more luggage. One coach took mamma, baby, nurse, myself, and one servant, and we called for my sister at Mrs. Magnolley's on the way. In her pretty pink bonnet, covered with a small-leafed India muslin, and pelerine the same, I thought she looked something brighter. My brother was ready to receive us, glad enough to board again at home. The garden and fresh air made my baby thrive vastly, and adding to her little wardrobe one coloured and two white frocks, we considered ourselves arranged for the summer. My gowns rubbed on well. Straw bonnets being introduced for the first time this year under the name of 'Dunstables,' I got one—price eight shillings. It was trimmed with a wide sash ribbon tied round the crown with an even bow in front. The hair was dressed full in front, with the curls still pinned, so the strings of the hat were contrived between the two curls, and tied loosely under the chin.

This year we visited the neighbouring families, and with my increased intimacy with the Pitt family, who greeted us in a most friendly manner, I found my *séjour* very agreeable. Mr. Papendick, soon after our arrival, had a horse offered to him for seven guineas. He consulted my father about it, who, thinking it would be a great convenience, persuaded him to buy it. Mr. Papendick had the stable got ready, received the mare, broke her in, and found that she was without fault; so my father, my husband, and my brother rode her backwards and forwards to Windsor and Eton as required, and it was a great convenience, and the plan answered well. So quiet, tractable and easy was this mare that Mr. Papendick put me on her back, and after three lessons I took a ride of eleven miles. Often after this I used to have a ride before breakfast with Mr. Papendick; and a most pleasant amusement I found it.

We invited my uncle and aunt to stay with us, but the latter, hearing of an alarm of thieves that we had, would not accept a bed for fear of my uncle getting into danger. Our dog was always at night stationed in the hall, near the garden and house doors. One night poor Rover barked sadly, and we were all up, but could see no one from the upper windows, so my father and Mr. Papendiek fired into the air. The following morning we found footmarks along the garden path, and that the stable door had been tried, but fortunately without success. We, however, added further safeguards, and had no more alarms.

We always went to the Ascot, Egham, and Maidenhead Races. This year the Pitts and Davenports, of the Crown Inn, proposed to join us to the latter, and that we should afterwards dine at Marlow. October was rather late for such an excursion, but as we found it would please, we consented. Our party consisted of nine, so two carriages were in requisition. The day was fine, the scene almost gayer than usual, and the dinner excellent and not profuse. Altogether a charming party, although, unfortunately, poor Mr. Papendiek could not be with us. My father and Mr. Pitt called for the bill. None was brought; and then we found that we had dined at Mr. Davenport's expense—as a small return, he said, for the preference we had always shown his house. We appreciated his kind civility; we were happy and grateful.

[At this point there is another break in the memoirs, but I cannot find that any event of interest occurred in the private life of Mrs. Papendiek during the interval that elapsed before we can again take up the narrative a few months later. In the way of public affairs, too, nothing took place that in any way concerned her or her family. The country was at peace, and ' the lifelong and hereditary struggle between Fox and Pitt' now began. Their fathers, Lord Holland, and Lord Chatham, had been rivals, and the sons carried on the strife with a nearer approach to equality, but their measures are matters of history, and have no place in these pages, except in acting as landmarks to connect the thread of events.

Mr. Papendiek was made ' page of presence' early in the year 1785, and where we resume Mrs. Papendiek's discourse we find her describing the perquisites attached to the appointment, which seem to have been considerable. Linen of different kinds for the house, coals, any leavings of meals served to the Princess in her own rooms, with the candles allowed for them, besides two tallow candles a night, and wood. Two bottles of wine were also allowed on every royal birthday, and on the anniversary of the Accession, the Coronation, and on New Year's Day. The salary also was slightly raised. To resume in Mrs. Papendiek's own words.—ED.]

These additions to our income of 220*l.* were most acceptable, and we felt happy and thankful for them.

On the King's birthday, 1785, my father led his little grandchild in to the Queen, who was delighted with her. Her Majesty recommended leading strings —a band round the waist, with a loop on each side, of a length to hold, so as to support the child in case she should stumble, and I immediately attended to this advice.

This day we saw the company, and at night the ball, when the Princess Royal danced for the first time. She was always shy, and under restraint with the Queen, and after making her courtesy, while retreating the four steps, off came her Royal Highness's shoe. Shoes were then worn with diamond buckles, and no sandals. The master of the ceremonies instantly replaced it, her partner, the Prince of Wales, holding her hand by way of support, and in the most graceful manner, giving the effect of retaining it, in order to lead her back to her place; so the accident caused as little bustle as possible, and by many was unperceived. The Princess was never elegant in exhibition, although her figure was good and imposing. Timidity, with a want of affectionate confidence in the Queen's commands and wishes, always brought her Royal Highness forward as ill at ease, while out of the Queen's presence she was a different being. The Prince, on the contrary, showed an elegance indescribable in everything that he did before the public, whether in dancing, music, or what not. It was a brilliant Court. The dresses were very showy, as steel embroidery was introduced this season, and very generally worn. My puce satin, for this fourth year, I had trimmed with a row of flat steel down each front, the white being taken off, cap and petticoat being trimmed to match, and steel buckles on black satin shoes.

The Prince of Wales this season had public days, when George Papendiek, with the rest of the household, attended in their uniforms. The two librarians were stationed in the library to receive the cards, and insert in a book the name of each individual who was presented, with his rank. This was the first introduction of that form, for hitherto at the Drawing-rooms, and at the King's Levées, the simple introductions had been considered sufficient. In those days the Court was confined to the nobility, and a few of the gentry who were well known.

At this time Mr. Hünnemann made an offer of marriage to Miss Wadsworth, which, after much consideration, and several disagreeable circumstances, was accepted. Mr. Papendiek obtained the King's permission for the marriage to take place, but, when it did, the allowance from the King was to cease. He, however, promised a continuance of his patronage, and as all poor Hünnemann's friends were strenuous in recommending his miniature painting, he never failed in business, and from his careful habits he realised more than could have been expected under the painful occurrences that ensued. Miss Wadsworth's friends were against the match, but were eventually prevailed upon to allow it to proceed.

The new Musical Fund concert next engaged us. An oboe player, of the name of Kamm, arrived, who was equal to Fischer in concerto and orchestral playing, but not so great in the different styles of ancient music. This Kamm had travelled with Mr. Papendick and Wendling, so it will be easily imagined how constantly he was at our house, enjoying a practice, and talking of old times. Schwestre, a fine bassoon player, also came to this country, and both were to appear at the Fund concert. Kamm played a duet concerto with Fischer, who introduced the octave shake in his cadence. The effect drew down applause scarcely ever equalled, and Fischer was extremely gay to have succeeded in this new trickery: Schwestre also astonished the public, for no performer had before been able to do so much with the bassoon as he did. Abel, as he sat, expressed in dumb show every sign of approbation. A quartett, led by Salomon, supported by Kamm, Kellner, and Schwestre, pleased beyond description. In the second act, Cervetto and Crosdill played a duet, and the former inadvertently put in a few notes that had not been decided upon, as I have already described his doing once before; but this time, though he made every apology, Crosdill would not be pacified, and they never played together again.

This season I saw Mrs. Siddons in 'Venice Preserved' and the 'Grecian Daughter,' and also Mrs. Jordan, who made her *début* in the 'Romp.' I met the latter often afterwards at Höppner's, to whom she sat for Thalia, as being esteemed the greatest comic actress of the day.

Höppner had been in the Chapel School at St. James's, and represented that he had neither power of voice nor sufficiently good health to follow the profession of music; that drawing and portrait-painting were the bent of his mind, and in that line he hoped for patronage and encouragement. Mr. West, the friend of no one who might possibly interfere with his success, pronounced poor Höppner as the possessor of a talent too inferior for royal notice, and he left Windsor with blighted hopes. He had previously taken the likenesses of the five Princesses in crayons, upon a petition he presented to the King, and during that time we had become intimate with him and his wife. She was a spirited, handsome woman, and being acquainted with Mr. Giffard, the tutor of Lord Belgrave, they were introduced through him to Lord Grosvenor, who took him by the hand. The Prince of Wales, the Duke of York, all the Whig nobility, and most of the leading people of the day sat to him, and in two years he had overcome all difficulty.

Mrs. Billington appeared this season under the protection of his Royal Highness the Duke of Cumberland, brother of the King, which fact, added to her being an Englishwoman, handsome, and a fine singer, shook Mara's position a little, who, however, never wavered in her own mind. She felt her superiority to be such that no real disadvantage could ensue, and, much to the credit of both of them, no enmity ever subsisted between these two talented creatures. They were often engaged at the same concerts, when they previously arranged together what they should sing, so that neither should depreciate the other, or render any special point inferior by comparison. Mrs. Billington was the daughter of Mrs. Weichsel, a German, and a good singer, who was engaged at Ranelagh and Vauxhall, which places of amusement were in those days the mode, and considered quite in good style. Bach was intimate in the family, and improved the mother's knowledge of music, and taught the little girl the pianoforte. She, at the early age of six years, played a duet with Bach in public. She had a genius for music, but never cultivated it enough to feel the beauties of it. Mara had studied the science with industry and perseverance, so that besides the great volume and sweetness of her voice she possessed the knowledge and taste requisite to render her performance of every style of composition perfect. She was engaged at almost all concerts, and often at the Queen's House; Billington also.

At Carlton House, there were not the same grand concerts or gala nights as heretofore. The Prince only gave small parties this season, at which he himself played the violoncello in a quartett or trio. When Salomon led, all was right, and gentlemanly deportment observed; but when Giardini or Crosdill was at the head, or when there were a set of singers with whom the Prince took a part in glees &c., then much disorder took place. Quentin was one of the leading associates, and this improper company generally dined or came in to wine. Mr. Papendiek, seeing how things were, told his Royal Highness that he held himself responsible to the Queen for his character, more especially as he was engaged as attendant upon her Majesty's daughters; that he would, with the same pleasure as he had always felt, obey the Prince's commands whenever the evening was to be spent in music, but that when he was asked to join a set to which he could never bring himself to belong, he must forbear to obey. The Prince with feeling at once said, 'I am glad that the Queen has an honest man in her service.' Then turning back to his now habitual manner of levity he added, ' When I am King, you shall be my sergeant trumpeter, a good sinecure.' After this, there were several pleasant evenings at Carlton House, with Salomon and others to assist in the music.

This was quite a musical season, and our friends were often with us at dinner, or in the evening Schwestre was full of spirits, and would come into our kitchen to assist in making his favourite liver dumplings, sauerkraut, dumplings of bread, stock-fish pie, and other dishes. Vegetables, dressed in various ways, and different sorts of grains were also in great repute.

We had taken a house at Windsor, so as to be more convenient for Mr. Papendiek's attendance at Court, and now gave notice to our landlord to quit our house at Pimlico on the day which completed our year's tenancy. The answer was, that as no agreement had been made, at the time we took the house, about giving notice to leave, we were bound by law to keep it till Michaelmas. We felt our want of experience, and no redress could we obtain. So we determined to stay on in town till we could let the house, and put a man and his wife into the other one, to take care of it and clean it. A married pair were recommended to us by Mrs. Delavaux. The woman being a black, few would employ them, so we got them cheap, and most excellent and trust-worthy did we find them.

Great excitement was caused just at this moment by the announcement that a man, named Lunardi, would ascend in a balloon from the artillery ground on Easter Monday, which this year fell on April 23. Hünnemann had procured a window for us and the Wadsworths, when suddenly the weather assumed to itself a winter aspect of the most severe character. There was a heavy fall of snow for some days, and a frost hard enough to produce skating, so the balloon speculation failed for the present. In the summer, however, this feat, which was novel to the English, was successfully accomplished. and our friends were not deprived of their gratification, but we had then left London.

A series of concerts was established at the Hanover Square Rooms, from Easter to the end of the season, something after the plan of those once held by Bach and Abel for the nobility, but in addition now the Prince of Wales was to be at the head. They soon found that the subscribers, even by introducing friends for the night, could not support the intention, so they were obliged to admit the gentry. Cramer led, and his party assisted, with Crosdill, of course, and the foreigners. I went to the first two concerts. One night I wore white silk, the other the Emperor's eye, with a beautiful French gauze cloak, and a hat of the same, with a wide brim, called a balloon hat, worn low down on one side, and high up on the other. Kead dressed me, and the effect was very becoming.

We decided, after all, to move to Windsor at once, and to leave our house in town in charge of the cook, with George Papendick. Therefore, about the second week in May, a post-chaise took me, with the nurse and baby, and several small things, down. We found Mr. Papendick, and Blacky and her husband, there to receive us; our luggage soon after arrived, and in a day or two we were settled. It was a pretty little house, with a passage running right through, there being a parlour on each side. In our living room we placed our pianoforte, and our furniture all fitted in as if made for the room. In those days the chairs were always arranged in a row along the walls, and carpets were not fitted to the rooms, but made up in a square, with a border round, and placed in the centre. Mr. Papendick picked up a few articles cheap at a sale, and we were soon very comfortable. The drawing-room was to be upstairs, but this we could not afford to furnish at present. Mr. Papendick's dressing-room was one floor higher, near our bedroom, and here I arranged all his books, music, and everything for study and practice. It had a good window, a fireplace, a pretty bit of carpet, and all comfortable about him. We also had a good garden and outhouses.

The Delavauxs called, and other Slough friends,

and I soon found how best to arrange our hours and regulations for our convenience and accommodation. We breakfasted at eight, or rather before, as Mr. Papendiek had to be at the Lodge by nine. By twelve o'clock everything was ready for visitors, from that hour till two being the visiting time. At two o'clock everyone dined, unless company was expected, and then it was generally made three o'clock. Needlework and tea went on between the hours for walking—that requisite for health being regulated by the seasons and the weather; baby ran about in her go-cart. Once she fell with it, but no harm can happen to a child if on even ground. The go-cart was originally of Italian invention.

On Sunday, May 22, 1785, after eating a slice or two of melon at dessert, I did not feel very well. Nevertheless, we walked in the Home Park after tea, and did not return till eight o'clock, and at half-past nine or thereabouts my baby was born. Dr. Wilmott was with me, but no nurse, and Mr. Papendiek at once gave him three guineas for his very attentive kindness. He then rushed off to the Lodge, but it was past ten before he reached his post, and the family were already seated at supper. A look from the Queen made him ask the lady in waiting to explain to her Majesty, when opportunity permitted, the cause of his inexactitude, which she did at once. The King, hearing something of what was said, cried out, 'What? what? What's that?' Upon being told, he said, 'Poor little Papendiek! I saw her at eight o'clock. She has been quick. I will name the little stranger Elizabeth Mary, if the Queen has no objection, and her Majesty will appoint a godfather,' which was Prince Ernest again. On the morrow the Royal Family and attendants moved to London.

It was now the time for the three Abbey performances, with the three rehearsals. No alterations were made in the arrangements, which were precisely the same as those of the year before. Marchesi, a most exquisite tenor singer, supplanted Perchierotti this season, who returned to the Continent. He was placed between Mara and Billington, the latter being this year also engaged at the Ancient Concerts. All this enchanting excellence I lost. Mr. Papendiek tried to console me by telling me that the extreme brilliancy of the first year surpassed these performances; but for sublimity, science, and excellence, every one of them was perfect.

After the King's birthday, my father and family came down to Slough, where the poor horse and lad were ready to receive them. Mr. Papendiek thought that Mr. Pitt, in whose care she had been left, might have done more for the animal, but his health had been very indifferent, and, no doubt, he had left it to his people. My father settled with Mr. Papendiek that he should pay all expenses, and share the use of him with papa and my brother, as before.

I was feverish and not well, and baby, too, was delicate. Poor little thing, she never throve well, and was taken from us at the early age of fifteen, after a very suffering sojourn here, though we did everything in our power, as time went on, to strengthen her. My first visitor was Madame Mara, who stayed to dine with us, taking only a little white soup and cold chicken, as she was going to sing at the King's concert in the evening. Little Charlotte, then eighteen months old, was brought down for her to see, but not looking pleased, having just awakened from her morning sleep, Madame took up my guitar, and played to her. With this she was delighted, and when Mara added singing to it the little thing was ready to spring from her nurse's arms. She showed love for music from the very first, and talent for it very soon. Her nurse had a good ear for music, with a fine voice, and had been urged to sing at Sadler's Wells, but had prudently declined. Mara, after this, made that unfortunate visit to Oxford when she was hissed, hooted at, and offered every indignity, because she would not sing in the choruses or stand while they were being sung. To the first she answered that she never did sing in chorus, it was useless, and deprived others of the merit. To the second charge she answered, that in a sacred edifice she always did stand while they were sung, but that in a theatre or playhouse, she could not feel that any command to that effect ought to be given. The outrage was dreadful. She stood up with her music in her hand, and the orchestra performed their part amidst the most unbecoming yells. She stood during the sacred choruses, but the scene was shameful, and her voice could not be heard. She stopped at Windsor on her way back, but the King would not allow her to sing. She therefore, immediately upon her arrival in town, called a meeting of the directors of the Ancient Concerts, but they, not wishing to lose her, would not consider the circumstance as being in any way connected with their regulations—a very proper decision, which was submitted to the King. He, however, rather cooled towards Mara, and it must ever be lamented that any disaffection should have fallen upon such matchless excellence.

Our half-crown visitors, for caudle and cake, were few this time. I was churched on the Sunday four weeks after baby's birth, and on Wednesday, June 22, she was christened. Miss Planta and Miss Nevin stood for the Princesses, and my father for the Prince. The former brought me fifteen guineas as a present from the Queen, and my father gave me a new kind of instrument, a kind of organ and piano-forte combined, which I found as a surprise on coming downstairs. The next day we went to the Lodge to return Miss Planta's and Miss Nevin's visit, and saw the Queen and Princesses.

# CHAPTER X.

An unpleasant surprise—Dr. and Miss Herschel—Stag and hare-hunting—The King's hunters—The Pohls—Lace—Price of provisions· - The Queen's birthday—Weather-bound in London—Drury Lane— Dr. Herschel and his telescope—History of Dr. Herschel—The Astronomer Royal—Discovery of the planet Georgium Sidus or Uranus —Death of Mr. Pitt—Horn, organist of St. George's Chapel—David, the tenor—Debts of the Prince of Wales—He declares himself a bankrupt—Presents on coming of age—Attempt on the King's life— Thoughtful kindness of the Spanish Ambassador—Sunday schools— Baron Hordenberg—He leaves England—Illness of Princess Elizabeth—Birth of Mrs. Papendiek's third child, Frederick—Seriously ill—Presents—Loss of 15l.—Inoculation—Re-arrangement of the royal household—The Duke of York in Germany—Mr. Magnolley associated with Mr. Papendiek—Mr. Brown—Lady Charlotte Finch— Death of Prince Octavius—Mrs. Harris—Princess Elizabeth ordered to ride—Review on Ashford Common—The ' Messiah '—The Marquis of Carmarthen—Alterations in fashion—The Eton Montem—Dr· Herschel and Mrs. Pitt.

A HOLIDAY we now had to Slough, and little Charlotte's delight was unbounded. Could we have remained there for a few days what a mutual comfort it would have been! but servants then, as now, would not assist beyond their engagements.

Our house in town had been let this last quarter, so that, at last, was off our hands, and George Papendiek became our inmate again at Windsor.

Then I had a surprise—an unpleasant one, I must

admit, as I did not feel equal to it—by a visit from Mr. Papendiek's father, who came over with the quarterly messenger from Hanover. He was very jaded when he arrived, poor man, and sadly oppressed by the rapidity of his journey, but we all did what we could for him. The children interested him, and he was very happy with us, and at Slough; and also with old Delavaux, who took him often to his garden, where they played skittles and smoked together, and drank a tankard quite after a foreign fashion. But at last his real desire came out, which was that we would take care of his youngest son, Carl. It was rather hard to expect his eldest son, scarcely established himself, and married, with two children, to provide for his two younger brothers; and my father made up his mind to speak to old Mr. Papendiek upon the subject. This he did, and it put a stop for the present on Master Carl's coming. My husband contrived to pay the expenses of his father's travel, and sent presents to his mother and sister, who shortly afterwards married a Mr. Schmidt. Mr. Papendiek got leave of absence for a few days, and took his father to London, showed him the sights, and took him to the theatre to see Miss Farren in 'The Chapter of Accidents,' which was a perfect performance, and then saw him safe on board the packet. Then these poor things parted. They did meet once again when Mr. Papendiek went over to Hanover with the Princess Royal in 1796 or 1797. The old gentleman wrote to us afterwards, expressing himself as having been much pleased with his visit, and sending little presents to the children. These farewells are very painful, and I was glad afterwards that poor old Mr. Papendiek had had the gratification of seeing his son once more.

Time was now verging on towards autumn, and nothing particular occurred. As it was my father's last summer at Slough we exchanged visits as often as we could. The poor horse was sold for 3*l*. 10*s*., and my dear, neat and pretty bridle and stirrup for 1*l*. 10*s*. We had all made the acquaintance this summer of Dr. and Miss Herschel, who were then living on Datchet Common, and it was finally settled that he should take the house at Slough when my father's three years' lease was up, so at next Ladyday he established himself in this pretty place, much to my satisfaction.

My father and mother now returned to St. James's, leaving my brother to board with us at 25*l*. a year, which, as we were so mutually fond, was an arrangement that gave us the greatest delight.

Hunting was now carried on with great spirit, the Prince of Wales coming down, even when settled in London for the winter, on Tuesdays and Saturdays for the stag, and Mondays and Thursdays for hare-hunting. Mr. Papendiek was foremost in the throng, and was often desired by the King to ride his hunters to try them for his own use. Those in at the death of the poor animal were always marked on the cheek with its blood by the yeomen prickers, and seldom did Mr. Papendick miss this distinction. Many a time the stag was taken after a run of thirty miles or even forty, with the same number of miles to return. This the King often did on horseback, but he sometimes returned in his carriage.

My children often went to the Lodge, which made them feel at home there. I still continued to make the caps for Princess Amelia, and had the pleasure to retain the Queen's good opinion.

My dear friends, the Pohls, were just now in extreme trouble, as, owing to great difficulties in business, they were not able to meet their liabilities, and their goods and property in trade were seized. Mr. Pohl had returned from the continent, having arranged to enter into a partnership in the lace trade, but as yet there had not been time for any lucrative returns, though it would doubtless be a successful venture in the end, as the price of lace was very high in those days. Imitation laces had not been invented, and those for ordinary dress and common usages cost many shillings a yard, while a drawing-room suit could not be bought for less than 70*l*. Mrs. Pohl entreated that all might be kept quiet till after the birthday, but Cobb, the principal creditor, would not; so she, with her son and daughter, took refuge under the hospitable roof of Mrs. Müller, whose husband was page to Prince Edward. Mrs. Pohl had also free access to my father's apartments, and mamma did all she could for her and her children.

In mentioning these prices, I should add that although most articles of dress were considerably more expensive in the days I am writing of than they are now, a good thing once purchased became an article of property, and such things as lace were handed down from one generation to another as heirlooms. Fashion, too, was not then *exigeant* in the matter of continual change. A silk gown would go on for years, a little furbished up with new trimmings—and a young woman was rather complimented than otherwise when she exhibited care of her possessions, and might, with no discredit to herself, appear time after time in the same attire. There was, perhaps, quite as much time and thought expended upon dress then as there is now, but as long as it did not interfere with more serious duties this was considered a proper and useful employment for women, and the neatest and smartest appearance produced on the smallest amount of expenditure was a matter of comment and praise. While I am speaking of expenditure it may be interesting if I mention the prices of provisions and other necessities of life in those times. Meat, taking one kind with another, was fivepence a pound; a fowl, ninepence to a shilling; a quartern loaf, fourpence; sugar, four-pence a pound; other groceries about the same as now, except tea, which was very much more expensive—six shillings a pound, and upwards. For ordinary earthenware, a large plate cost twopence; a small one, one penny; and other things in proportion. I should say that as a rule ordinary every-day things were cheaper, and luxuries decidedly dearer; but people were content without them, and were not despised for living economically.

I and my babies were to appear on the birthday in the Queen's dressing-room, so dress had now to be attended to. Hoops were no longer worn, but a horsehair petticoat, quilted in fine glazed stuff, which had almost the same appearance, and was much more convenient, having no whalebone, and a pad was added at the bottom of the waist behind, resembling our present *tournures*. In front of the dress from the top of the bodice to the collar bones, was a network of silver, called a 'titonier,' which supported a double handkerchief of muslin, crape, or gauze, of a yard or more—square, worn over the gown, trimmed or plain. My puce satin was once more done up, and, with a white gauze handkerchief trimmed with narrow blonde, with the same on the sleeves and cap, looked very neat and smart. My babes were in clean white frocks, and blue satin sashes; Charlotte and Princess Amelia being both in caps of my make. These two kept pretty fair pace with each other in improvement, and were fond of each other in their play.

We had come up to town to stay with my parents a few days before the birthday this year, 1786, and now, as a very severe frost had set in, we, as well as the Royal Family, were weather-bound in London. This annoyed my mother, as we overcrowded her rooms, and I was sorry to so inconvenience her by our protracted visit; but it could not very well be helped, as I feared my young baby might take cold on the journey, being, as she always was, so fragile. My brother had been obliged to return to Eton, and remained for the time with his dame, and my sister also returned to school at Mrs. Magnolley's, which, being so near at hand, she was able to do, in spite of the weather. Beyond the regret at inconveniencing my mother, I naturally had none at this extension of my pleasant holiday.

While we were still in town, we saw Mrs. Siddons twice, and Miss Farren's *début* as the leader in genteel comedy at Drury Lane. She appeared first as Lady Teazle. An address, penned by herself, was read to the audience by the deputy manager, to express that she had undertaken to follow Mrs. Abington by the encouragement of the manager, and not trusting in her own abilities; that she had taken every pains to qualify herself for this arduous task, and that she therefore hoped for their indulgence, &c. It is hardly necessary to add that her success was complete. She had been a most efficient second both in tragedy and comedy, and had made a great impression, during the summer, by her acting in 'The Chapter of Accidents.' She was taller than Mrs. Abington, and had a remarkably good figure, fine eyes, and a most expressive countenance, which was illumined by virtue, and peculiar amiability. She, Mrs. Siddons, and Mrs. Jordan filled the house every night to an overflow, while at Covent Garden, Mrs. Abington and Miss Young, with Lewis, Quick, and Munden equally divided the public opinion. I must not omit to name the two Palmers, Smith, and King, at Drury Lane. Indeed, the stage was in its zenith, although Garrick had retired from it. Their Majesties gave every encouragement to it, by appearing every week at one or the other house.

About the middle of February the frost gave way, and as Mrs. Deluc was going to Windsor in the post coach, she very goodnaturedly took charge of Eliza and her nurse, and I returned about a week later with Charlotte. The latter began now to spell out words of one syllable from her nursery pictures, and the amusement of letters, pictures, pencils, and paper were more entertaining to her than toys, and she picked up much information by that means.

Dr. Herschel took possession of the house at Slough at Lady Day, 1786. His first step, to the grief of every one who knew the sweet spot, was to cut down every tree, so that there should be no impediment to his observations of the heavenly bodies. Then he erected in the centre of his garden his wonderful twenty-feet telescope. Every movement of this ponderous machine was easily accomplished by two persons, even when the mirror was in the tube, the interior of which measured five feet in circumference. The gallery for spectators held six people, and Dr. Herschel had a seat which was moved up and down at pleasure by himself. At the bottom of the erection were two small rooms, one for Miss Herschel to write down the observations as they were made by her brother, the other for the man who assisted in the movements when required. Company and friends were never denied admittance to view this extraordinary piece of mechanism, nor in the evening to look at the moon and planets, either through the large telescope, or another of ten feet, also fixed in the garden.

The stabling had been converted into a small dwelling-house, where Miss Herschel had her apartments and study contiguous to the smaller telescope. The stable yard was now a pretty garden, on one side of which were buildings for chemistry, on the other, rooms for polishing the mirrors, which was done by rubbing the iron with a preparation at a temperature of ninety to one hundred degrees, which process, when once begun, could not be left till finished. Two persons, therefore, relieved each other at short intervals, the one beginning while the hands of the other were still actually at work. These mirrors, both of ten feet, and of five feet, were sent all over the continent, many of them to Catharine, the renowned Empress of Russia, and by this traffic, Dr. Herschel established his fame as one of the greatest mechanists of his day, and also set himself at ease in pecuniary matters.

His story is an interesting and most curious one. He had come to this country a few years before as a deserter from a military band in Hanover, his native place, having, by a circuitous route, reached Calais, and from thence crossed, and landed at Dover, with only a French crown piece in his pocket. He was fascinating in his manner, and possessed a natural politeness, and the abilities of a superior nature. He worked his way up to London by music, either as a writer, or a performer on a pocket instrument of the guitar or lyre construction, as an accompaniment to his singing. In London, he fortunately met with Ranzini, who, just then going to Bath to settle, took Herschel with him, and made him conductor of the concerts at the Subscription Rooms, the Pump-room, the public gardens, and leader of the orchestra at the playhouse. He was also engaged as organist at one of the principal churches, and divided the teaching with Miss Guest. A vacancy for a violoncello player occurring in the band, he sent for his brother Alexander from Hanover, who at once came over, and with him his sister, who afterwards lived with the Doctor. Miss Caroline Herschel was by no means prepossessing, but a most excellent, kind-hearted creature, and though not a young woman of brilliant talents, yet one of unremitting perseverance, and of natural cleverness.

The Doctor, who was always at work, now exercised his ingenuity upon making opera-glasses, which were eagerly sought after from their excellence, and which, therefore, greatly aided his coffers. This led on to his trying the telescope, and when he had completed one of five feet, he ran about the streets at night making his observations, and at a proper moment took it to Dr. Maskelyne, the Astronomer Royal at Greenwich, who so greatly approved of it that, with every encouragement from this great man, Dr. Herschel returned to Bath, and there worked at a ten-feet telescope. He was then introduced to Sir Joseph Banks, who took him, with his telescopes, to the Royal Society, of which he soon became a member.

After this he returned to Bath, and, finding his place in the musical department filled up, he arranged his affairs, and took a final leave of the place, and of all those who had been kind to him, and to whom he was attached with ties of sincere affection and regard. With Ranzini the parting was painful, for ingratitude and want of feeling had no part in Dr. Herschel's nature.

He now settled himself on Datchet Common, and Sir Joseph Banks suggested to the King to appoint him as Astronomer at Windsor, with a trifling salary to enable him to prosecute his researches, for his Majesty's own occasional amusement. The King, however, being just at this time much harassed by public business, and also deeply wounded by the conduct of the Prince of Wales, paid no attention to the President's proposal, and Dr. Herschel remained for the present unnoticed by Royalty. Not so by the Royal Society, and through their assistance and patronage the Doctor soon became known and introduced to men of learning. From Datchet he came to Slough.

It was in the year 1781, on May 21, that he made his great discovery of the planet 'Georgium Sidus,' so called after his Majesty King George III. It is sometimes also called 'the Herschel,' and by foreign astronomers 'Uranus.' Rather later, the Doctor discovered a volcanic mountain in the moon, and, continuing his researches with unremitting zeal, he added much valuable information to the existing knowledge of the planetary system, and of the heavenly bodies generally.

Dr. Herschel showed every kind of attention to Mr. and Mrs. Pitt. The former being in a declining state of health, the Doctor passed many hours with him in his well-chosen library, and avowed that he derived much instruction from his remarks, and great pleasure from his society and conversation. At the end of the summer, this excellent man died, leaving the property to his widow until her death, when it was to revert to their son, Paul Adee Pitt, my brother's Eton friend and companion.

I was only in town for a very short time this year, and missed the Musical Fund concert, but no new leading stars appeared upon that occasion. Mr. Horn, a pianoforte player, was brought into notice by publishing a set of sonatas, of which the second particularly attracted the notice of Abel. It was chromatic, the melody of the *adagio* pretty, and the whole sonata of a superior cast. The Marquis of Stafford, while travelling in Germany, met with this Horn, and, engaging him as his valet, brought him to England. He then married the housemaid, whose situation soon caused my Lord to dismiss the pair. Horn immediately made music his study, and by teaching earned a tolerable livelihood. Abbé Fogler was his friend, and, it was supposed, greatly assisted him in these sonatas. Be this as it may, they introduced him to notice, and he ultimately taught the Queen and Princesses, and died organist of St. George's Chapel, Windsor. His wife remained just what she was, but Horn was of a good disposition, and by no means a low or vulgar man, and brought up his children well. His second son was the renowned 'Casper,' in Weber's 'Freischütz,' at Drury Lane, and was for many seasons the favourite singer on the London boards.

I made another short visit to town, in order to attend the Abbey concert. David, the tenor, was the novelty this year, and fine indeed he was. The solo, 'Thy rebuke hath broken his heart,' was repeated. Tears flowed. It was glorious. Mrs. Kennedy was also very great, and Mara, dear Mara, and Mrs. Billington maintained their power and might in all their excellence.

After the King's birthday, which I attended as usual, I returned home.

At the end of this session, the Prince of Wales solicited that the sum stipulated for the repairs of Carlton House should be paid to him, and the answer was that it was ready, and would be given to the commissioners, on proving their accounts. This his Royal Highness would not listen to ; it was represented that the screen alone had cost more than the Crown had allowed for the whole, and he wished to have the disposal of any money he could lay his hands on. The King was aware of his son's debts, of the house fitted up for Mrs. Fitzherbert, of the hunting seat purchased in Hampshire, where, in the family of Gascoigne, the Prince had a seraglio, the brother of the females being raised from groom to the head of the stud stables, and at his death buried with the honours of the Royal liveries, and his sisters being afterwards taken into the Queen's household as assistant dressers. Of these, and many other extravagances, was the King aware, and as the Crown would not pay his debts, the Prince threw up his establishment, declared himself a bankrupt, and all the appointments null and void.

Mr. Powell, my cousin Hugh, and George Papendick were now thrown out of employment, and on our hands again. When the accounts were looked over, the old pages, Lockley and Sontague, brought theirs correct to a mite. They now begged to retire on pensions; the former returned to his native country, Germany, and, dying soon after, the Prince educated and provided for his son, who is now practising as a surgeon in London. Du Paché, Choie, and Mills were now the attendants, and Weltze, the maître d'hôtel, who fitted up the Pavilion for his master, and a house in the adjoining buildings for Mrs. Fitzherbert, at a cost of seventy thousand pounds.

Lake was made a Lord, and Hulse a Baronet. These men were still at the call of the Prince, and when at Windsor Lady Lake had evening parties at her house for card playing of every description.

[The following passages from Dr. Doran's 'Lives of the Queens of England' show very clearly the state of the Prince of Wales's affairs, both as regards his pecuniary embarrassments and his relations with the King and Queen, at about the time of which Mrs. Papendiek is here writing :—'The eldest son of Queen Charlotte began life very amply provided for. Parliament gave him 100,000*l.* as an outfit, and 50,000*l.* annually by way of income. Three months after the birth of his youngest sister, Amelia, in November 1783, he took his seat in the House of Peers, joined the opposition, gave himself up to the leading of the opposition chiefs, whether in politics or vices, was praised by the people for his spirit, and estranged from the King, who did not like the principles of those who called themselves his son's friends, and who held in horror the vices and follies for which they were distinguished. . . . The Prince of Wales was already overwhelmed with debt. The domestic comfort of the Queen was even more disturbed than that of her consort, by the solicitations made by the so-called friends of the Prince of Wales,

to induce the King to pay the debts of his eldest son.
Her Majesty's confidence is said to have been fully
placed at this time upon Mr. Pitt.  A conversation
is spoken of as having passed between the Queen and
the minister, in which he is reported as having said :
" I much fear, your Majesty, that the Prince, in his
wild moments, may allow expressions to escape him
that may be injurious to the Crown."  " There is little
fear of that," was the alleged reply of the Queen.
" He is too well aware of the consequences of such a
course of conduct to himself.  As regards that point,
therefore, I can rely upon him."  Mr. Pitt inquired if
her Majesty was aware of the intimacy which then
existed between Mrs. Fitzherbert and the heir-
apparent, and that reports of an intended marriage
were current ?  " He is now so much embarrassed,"
added the minister, " that at the suggestion of his
friend Sheridan he borrows large amounts from a
Jew who resides in town, and gives his bonds for
much larger amounts than he receives."  In the
family dissensions caused by this unhappy subject
neither sire nor son behaved with fairness and can-
dour.  In 1784 the Prince had been required to send
in an exact account of his debts, with a view to their
liquidation.  The King had, at least, intimated that
he would discharge the Prince's liabilities if this
account was rendered.  The account *was* rendered ;
but after having been kept for months it was re-

turned as not being exact. . . . By the following year his debts amounted to 160,000*l*., and he could see no chance of relief but by going abroad. His first idea was of a residence in Holland, and he was ready to proceed thither as a private individual, should the King refuse to consent to his leaving England. All that he wished for, according to his own declarations, was to economise, to live in retirement and remain unknown, until he could appear in a style suitable to his rank.'—ED.]

On my birthday this year, 1786, I was of age, and my father presented me with a round silver waiter, bearing my initials, and I was lucky enough to receive several other kind presents and remembrances from friends and relations.

We attended the Egham and Maidenhead races as usual this year, and mixed with our friends in the neighbourhood pleasantly. My mother stayed with us during the first month of my father's 'wait' at Windsor, and occupied the two sweet little rooms at the end of our drawing-room.

On August 2 we all had a terrible fright in the attempt made upon the King's life by a mad woman, named Margaret Nicholson. His Majesty had gone up to town to hold a levée, and just as he was stepping from his carriage at the garden gate of St. James's Palace, this woman bent before him presenting a petition, when suddenly, without any warning, she drew a knife from her bosom with her left hand, and made a plunge forward, aiming at the King's heart. He, however, was fortunately not in the least hurt, and the woman was seized by the attendants. His Majesty at once returned to Windsor without holding the levée, so that he might be with the Queen before any rumour of the attack could reach her. The Marquis del Campo, the Spanish ambassador, was quicker still, having started off post haste to Windsor the moment after the occurrence, with the kind and thoughtful intention of engaging the Queen in conversation until the King himself should appear, and thus keeping any possible report of the affair from her Majesty's ears. In this laudable desire he succeeded, and only retired when the King himself came in briskly and cheerfully with the words, ' Here I am, safe and well, and no harm done ; but I have had a narrow escape ! ' and then he related the whole story to her. The Queen and Princesses were all greatly agitated, to say nothing of the attendants of both sexes ; for his Majesty was so greatly and deservedly beloved that any evil coming near to him was felt by all as members of one happy family. But the King's extreme gaiety and cheerfulness was infectious, and soon all around him recovered their wonted spirits. On the following Sunday, the Terrace, which was always gay and bright, was more than crowded—all the King's subjects being eager to show their devotion and thankfulness for his merciful deliverance. After this occurrence all petitions, which his Majesty had hitherto received in person, were given to the lord in waiting on public days, and handed by him privately to the page, who passed them on to the King.

Mrs. Trimmer's great movement in establishing Sunday schools in many parts of England came to pass during this year, and her Majesty hearing of it, and being much struck with the excellence and advisability of such a plan, desired that the same might be instituted at Windsor. The Queen interested herself greatly in the scheme, and being so thoroughly imbued as she was with the sense of religion in all its bearings, was most anxious that the benefit of a religious education should be extended to all with whom she came in contact. Her Majesty had several interviews with Mrs. Trimmer, and being much impressed with that lady's clear understanding and sound judgment, requested her to write a work on education, which she did, and it has ever since been considered an authority upon that question.

Nothing else of particular moment occurred either to us or in the world around us. We were constantly with Mrs. Pitt, at Upton, enjoying the homely fare of cake or bread, with wine, in the dear, brick-floored parlour. She, poor woman, complained much of the dulness of her life, and we did our best to cheer her, as did also Dr. Herschel, who often walked over to her house with his sister of an evening, and as often induced her to join his snug dinner at Slough.

Just before the hunting season began, Baron Hordenberg engaged the house at Old Windsor that Huddlestone afterwards lived in, in order to enjoy the sports of the field, and also to be near the King. He was Hanoverian Minister, and much in request at the Lodge. His wife was a fine woman—rather of suspicious material from her inelegant manner, her repugnance to restraint and her want of real respect to Royalty. With her husband she attended the Queen's evening parties, and after the Prince of Wales had seen her, he attended the hunt more regularly, and was often at the Lodge. On one of the days, the stag making a home chase, the Prince concluded he would not be missed, and popped in to see the Baroness. Her husband soon discovered the delinquent, and before night the Hordenbergs, with their suite, were on the road to Harwich, leaving the Prince to tell his own tale. The Baron resigned his appointment, and upon arriving at home he lived in retirement, never again mixing with a Court. The Prince did not show himself at the Lodge for some time, at least not till New Year's Day.

The winter set in unfriendly, the weather being damp and chilly, so we could not get out much, particularly as I was not well, and all felt depressed. George Papendiek began to be troublesome. He was bored with the dulness, and with the babies, poor little things, and did not make the best of matters. On Christmas Day I took the sacrament in the parish church, and whether from the fatigue or what I know not, but in the evening I had a fainting fit, and ventured out no more.

The Pohls visited us for a few days when she came down to Windsor with a small *demi-saison* order of dress for the Queen and Princesses. They had been in great distress for some time, but Mr. Pohl was now beginning to weather the storm, and took the short lease of a spacious house in St. James's Place. Vigilant as ever, he soon, with a little sashing-paint, and other domestic assiduities, made it a very desirable abode, and here Mrs. Pohl began to get her connection together again.

Before Christmas the Royal Family removed to town agreeably to their usual custom, but after the New Year's Day drawing-room they returned to Windsor, which they continued to do weekly through the season as before, on account of the pleasure of the hunt to the King. The two elder Princesses, being now both introduced, always accompanied their Majesties. Princess Elizabeth's health now assumed such symptoms of alarm as to prevent her attendance at Court, as had been intended, and through the whole of the season her Royal Highness was confined to her own apartments. She had a scrofulous abscess on the left side, which was many weeks coming to a state to admit of its being lanced, and at her present age, nearly seventeen, this naturally weakened her considerably. She was born fat, and through every illness, of which she had many, she never lost flesh. Her good humour never forsook her, but her spirits now were low, and whenever she saw those whom she knew felt for her and loved her, she invariably shed torrents of tears. This proved her weak condition.

On the Monday previous to the Queen's birthday (January 18) the Royal family went to town, but fortunately for me, the Princess Royal, having a slight feverish cold, was left at Windsor with her lady-in-waiting, and poor, disappointed Miss Planta. Poor, but not disappointed Mr. Papendiek, being at home, was able in the middle of the cold frosty night of the 19th to fetch Dr. Wilmott to me from Eton. At half-past nine on the morning of January 20, 1787, dear angelic Frederick was born. When Mr. Papendiek went at ten o'clock to the Lodge, the Princess Royal sent a carriage for my other two children, who remained with her Royal Highness the greater part of the day. I was in great danger all that day and through the night, but towards morning sleep assisted the doctor's skill, and I rallied.

On February 18, the churching and baptism took place. This time the Royal Family had not offered to be sponsors, so we kept it among ourselves, the two grandpapas and grandmamma standing for my sweet babe, who was christened by the names of Frederick Henry. My father gave me five guineas, and my presents from Mr. Papendiek were a solid silver mustard pot and spoon, with purple glass inside; four plated salt cellars, gilt inside; and four silver spoons. My mother's present was rosettes for the boy, as long as he should wear them.

Mr. Papendiek now took lodgings at the house of Clarke, the Queen's footman, in Eaton Street, Pimlico. They were rather more expensive, but convenient to the Queen's House, which was all he had to think of, as his attendance would no longer be required at Carlton House. We thought it better that George Papendiek should now settle in town, so as to be more among his friends. Poor fellow, he took an affectionate leave of me, and we never met again. Mrs. Zoffany then came to stay with us for a week. She told us that a friend had lent her a house in Hart Street, Bloomsbury, for one year, while her house at Strand-of-the-Green was being repaired. She wished us to go to her whenever we liked so to do, but it was too far from our beat to afford any convenience.

Just before she arrived, Mr. Papendiek came to

the bureau in my room for the 15*l.* reserved for the rent of the Christmas half-year. Alas, it was gone! and no trace of it could ever be found. No stranger had been in the room. Nurse was the only one who knew of the money being there, and she appeared in every respect to answer to the excellent character we received with her. We never recovered it, and it was indeed a sad loss.

About a month after, Mr. Papendick took Charlotte up to stay with her grandmother, but finding that there was small-pox in the next apartment, he brought her back again, and a few days after the three little dears were inoculated by Dr. Mingay. They were all very sick and ill, but recovered nicely.

In April, Princess Amelia, the King's aunt, died, leaving her estate of Gunnersbury and all her other property to her brother-in-law, the Prince of Hesse-Cassel. After his agent had settled all the affairs and had paid legacies &c. the estate was sold, and subsequently bought by Mr. Copland, the great master builder of the day, who paid 10,000*l.* for it. This he divided into three parts, reserving for himself land that he still called the Park, with the fine cedar trees and the sheet of water. The house he fitted up with great taste, and ornamented it with elegant articles of *vertu*, collected by him in Italy in his summer excursions. Mr. Copland died in 1834, and his widow sold it to the great Rothschild, who, however, never lived in it, as he died in 1836.

The early part of this year, 1787, saw many changes in the arrangements of the Royal household. The six Princesses were now divided into three parties, which necessitated some additional attendants to wait upon them, and changes in those already holding appointments about them. The apartments, also, were all rearranged. Lady Charlotte Finch had a house found for her in Sheet Street, Windsor, and also had extensive apartments at St. James's. Miss Planta had good rooms there too, and most of the other ladies were lodged in Buckingham House. On account of the conduct of the Prince of Wales, the King kept the Duke of York abroad, but unfortunately with no good result, for upon the death of the Great Frederick of Prussia, his Royal Highness left Berlin and was established at Hanover, where he played the same game as his Royal brother did in England. Prince William Henry, our present King (I write this in 1836), was established at St. James's, at the house where he at present lives, which has been, of course, greatly enlarged and repaired both substantially and ornamentally. This Prince was sent to cruise about our settlements in the Western Hemisphere; the Prince Edward was sent to the University at Geneva; and the three younger Princes to that at Göttingen. None of them had any English person in attendance upon them, with the exception of Prince William, who having entered the navy at the usual early age, had the youngest son of Dr. Majendie to be with him as tutor.

The Queen availed herself of this opportunity to insure the services of Mr. Magnolley (page to Prince William) to assist in the wait upon the three elder Princesses, to relieve Mr. Papendick. He desired that he might share the perquisites, and this was arranged to his satisfaction, rooms also being provided for him at St. James's, at Kew, and at Windsor. He was to board with the other pages. The perquisites of the Board of Green Cloth we kept wholly— tablecloths, napkins, store candles, and pitcher wine. The perquisites to be shared were those used in the Princesses' own room,—wax candles, the night wax mortars, and the remains of any meal served to them separately, with wine, or whatever it might be. Mr. Papendick observed the same rule with my father; whatever remained untouched he took, but anything that had been tasted he allowed the page's man to take. Not so with Magnolley. He grasped all he could.

Mr. Brown, who had remained sole page, after Powell's dismissal, to the three younger Princes, was now established in the nursery under Lady Charlotte Finch, and in this situation he became all in all to her. He retained his rooms in the Prince's house at Kew, also at Buckingham House, and one was found for him at the Lower Lodge, Windsor. The assumed powers of Lady Charlotte Finch increased as the Queen's opportunities of attending to the education of her daughters decreased, and through her influence Mr. Brown's little girl was introduced to, and was constantly with, the Princesses. Her ladyship tried hard to obtain permission to educate her grand-daughters, the three Miss Fieldings, with the younger Princesses, partially, if not wholly; but there the Queen was inexorable. The King had elevated their father in the navy as high as he could, the Queen had made Mrs. Fielding bedchamber-woman, and more could not be considered. Miss Finch came only by invitation. She was perfectly a lady, much liked, and very deservedly so.

These arrangements having been formed, all was working satisfactorily, when a catastrophe occurred which threw a gloom over the Royal Family not soon to be overcome; the death of Prince Octavius from inoculation. He, with Princess Sophia, was taken to Kew for the benefit of the air, and to be constantly under the eye of the surgeon, Pennel Hawkins, who lived in our house. Princess Sophia did well, but this dear child and most interesting boy was supposed to have caught cold just when the eruption should have come out, the King having taken him into the gardens late in the evening, towards sunset. Only twenty-four hours did this angel suffer, and died apparently from suffocation which nothing could relieve.

For children under seven years of age, no mourning is worn at Court.

The dear child's coffin was taken in a coach to Westminster Abbey, where he was interred. At the door stood Mrs. Harris, his Royal Highness's wet nurse, who entreated to be allowed to enter, which was granted. The King was touched by the circumstance, and desired that she might be written to, and told how much his Majesty approved her dutiful attention.

The Royal Family went down to Windsor, and public business was suspended, the Easter recess being prolonged. The Easter Monday hunt, the last meet of the season, did not take place, for upon this occasion there was always a large assembly of company to meet the Queen and others, and at the spot where the stag was turned out, this sweet little Prince used to appear dressed in the appropriate uniform, with all the correct paraphernalia of long whip &c., the King calling out, ' Turn out the little huntsman also.' Oh! it was a severe visitation. The King was devoted to all his children, and this one seemed in some respects to be the flower of the flock. He was a lovely child, of a sweet disposition, and showed every promise of future goodness. A portrait was painted of him by Gainsborough, who was the Queen's favourite portrait painter, and who afterwards took the King's likeness by her desire, as also one of the Queen herself.

Princess Elizabeth now recovering, was removed to Windsor; and horse exercise being recommended, the King desired Montague to begin to teach her Royal Highness to ride, and to have proper horses broken in for her. The Duke of Montague was Master of the Horse to the King, the Earl Harcourt the same to the Queen, the former being also Governor of the Round Tower. Both these noblemen came down to attend, and Mr. Papendiek was not only to try the horses, but was to ride with the Princess. This was flattering, and was kept up through a great part of the summer. It afforded amusement to the King, and was productive of much benefit to the Princess Elizabeth's health.

Public days were resumed at Court, the three elder Princesses moving always with the King and Queen. The King, for whom every one thought much, appeared to be resigned, and patiently to fall into his usual habits, but the theatre the Royal Family did not again attend this season. The first gala was a review on Ashford Common of General Goldsworthy's regiment of cavalry. To make the spectacle gay, he had tents erected in the form of a crescent for the lady spectators, the Queen and Princesses occupying the central position. The Delavauxs took a coach and insisted upon my accompanying them, which with Mr. Papendick's consent I did; and much gratified indeed I was. It was the first review I had seen, and by this indulgent arrangement of the general's, we did see the whole without the slightest impediment or inconvenience.

The Abbey concerts now again drew general attention, and as I had not been in town during the winter, Mr. Papendick wished me to go, which I did, with great satisfaction to myself. Charlotte went to St. James's, but the two babies I took with me to Eaton Street. I wished to hear the 'Messiah,' which was to be opened by Mara, and I need hardly say that the performance was exquisite. The 'Comfort ye my people' was as perfect a performance as could possibly be heard, and when the quick part came, 'Every valley shall be exalted,' every person stood, following the example of those in the Royal box, and Mara's manner of singing it, with the ancient trill, was equally fine, or even more so, than the *Adagio*. The Princes being all far away, the Queen took her five daughters, the three elder being accompanied by the Ladies Elizabeth and Caroline Waldegrave, and the two younger by Lady Charlotte Finch and Miss Goldsworthy. The maids of honour, and other ladies in attendance, arranged at the back of the two Royal boxes, made a brilliant appearance. The Prince of Wales was present in his own State box, with Lake and Hulse; and the directors all went up to him in turn, and paid all proper attention. The most conspicuous of these was the elegant and handsome Marquis of Carmarthen, who was just on the point of being divorced from his wife, she having gone off with Mr. Byron. So great was the Marquis's love for her, that he hastened the divorce, so he said, to see her happy with the one she appeared to prefer to himself. She was the only surviving child of the Earl of Holdernesse, a handsome woman, elegant and accomplished, and of a good figure. She did not live long after this unhappy affair. leaving one daughter only, Lady Mary Osborne, who was brought up by her grandmother, Lady Holdernesse, and turned out a fine, amiable young woman.

A little change in dress occurred about now. The great cushion was abolished, and the hair was frizzed tight, so as to support a round cap with a ribbon round. One curl just behind the ear, and a second one down upon the neck even with the chignon. The sleeve was now over the point of the elbow, with a double frill of white lace.

After the concerts were over, I returned to Windsor in a postchaise, leaving Charlotte in town, in time to be present at the Eton Montem. It was indeed a gay scene, and to see our dear boys walking high, as they were in the fifth form, was most gratifying. Their Majesties not attending this year, Mr. Papendiek was obliged to remain in town, and I therefore went alone with my nurse and babies. The crowd alarmed me, but our postboy soon brought us to a snug spot, from whence we saw the whole comfortably, and being the first Montem I had seen, I was very much pleased.

Dr. Herschel was begged to go over to Windsor whenever any appearance in the heavens was likely to interest the King. This he willingly undertook to do, and a ten feet telescope was placed so as to be always ready, but whenever anything very particularly beautiful or unusual was to be seen, he would send down a twenty feet telescope without making the slightest trouble. The King was gratified, and the whole family pleased with the astronomer royal. Sir Joseph Banks was flattered at the appointment, and the Royal Society also.

Among friends it was soon discovered that an earthly star attracted the attention of Dr. Herschel. An offer was made to Widow Pitt, and accepted. They were to live at Upton, and Miss Herschel at Slough, which was to remain the house of business. All at once it struck Mrs. Pitt that the Doctor would be principally at the latter place, and that Miss Herschel would be mistress of the concern, and considering the matter in all its bearings, she determined upon giving it up. Dr. Herschel expressed his disappointment, but said that his pursuit he would not relinquish ; that he must have a constant assistant, and that he had trained his sister to be a most efficient one. She was indefatigable, and from her affection for him she would make any sacrifice to promote his happiness. This brought us together again, and many happy days and hours did we pass in that sweet garden at Upton, the young ones passing their spare time in rambles and joyous merriment.

## CHAPTER XI.

St. George's Chapel at Windsor—Painted windows—New College, Oxford
—West—Fashion set by the Prince of Wales—Grand pianoforte—
Art and science—Rodgers—Lady Mexborough—Miss Haines—Housebreaking and robbery—Hart Street—Mrs. Pitt and Dr. Herschel
again engaged—Epidemic fever at Eton—Precautions against infection—Death of a canary bird—Mr. Papendiek takes to a wig—Mr.
Lang, assistant surgeon of St. Bartholomew's Hospital—Mrs. Albert's
great strictness—Mrs. Papendiek gives a dance—The supper—Visit
from Salomon—A private concert—Charlotte writes a letter—Mr.
and Mrs. Duberly—Approaching death of Mrs. Pohl—'Back Stairs'—
Fashions for evening dress—Fashionable work—Mrs. Hünnemann—
Mrs. Duberly—Höppner and Mrs. Höppner—Charlotte's portrait—
Signs of the King's serious illness—Mrs. Magnolley—Dr. Heberden—
The Princess Royal's rooms refurnished—Dr. Herschel marries Mrs.
Pitt—Troubles at St. James's—Ramberg—Drawing of the Papendiek
children—House at Kensington—The Zoffanys—Charlotte goes to
school—The King tries wine—Death of Miss Laverocke—Miss Pascal,
now Mrs. Theilcke—The party for Cheltenham.

ANOTHER branch of art and science had, a short time
before this, been brought to the King's notice.

St. George's Chapel at Windsor was being, by his
Majesty's command, repaired and beautified, and it
was suggested that the windows should be painted.
Mr. Jarvis was introduced, and shortly after he
began his work. He took the large house at the
bottom of Peascod Street, with a fine garden and

outhouses, which he appropriated to his furnaces for burning the glass, and having only a wife and no family, the lower rooms of the dwelling-house were used for the painting.

He had just completed the window of New College, Oxford, of which the subject was the 'Nativity,' designed by Sir Joshua Reynolds.

The 'Resurrection,' from a design of West's, was fixed upon for Windsor, and it was a great success. West was painting the altarpiece, subject the 'Last Supper,' and he had also settled himself at Windsor, in Park Street.

Mr. Forrest, who assisted Jarvis, was a pleasant man, and his wife a friendly woman who received most agreeably in their small abode. He was very musical, and, with Mr. Papendiek's assistance, brought his flute-playing to such perfection that he often performed a duet concerto with him at the King's concerts.

The Wests were Americans, originally Quakers. The eldest son, Ralph, was delightful. He had a fine, tall figure, with an expressive countenance, and invariably sat to his father for the portrait of St. John. His dress was simply elegant, which was striking amid the large cravats, curled hair, and other extravagant fashions set by the Prince of Wales, I verily believe to laugh at people, for his Royal Highness became every dress, however overdone. Ralph and I were sworn friends. He came in and out of our house at pleasure, and his society was always agreeable to us all.

No presents marked my birthday this year, but towards autumn a surprise awaited me. A foreman of Bautebart's, the original pianoforte maker, invented a new instrument, which he termed a grand pianoforte. It was the shape of a harpsichord, but with brass tubes. A superb instrument, but a little hard in the touch. Frisker was the man's name, and he sent it down to the Lodge on speculation, but there, ancient music bearing the palm, the organ and harpsichord were not to be superseded.

This new grand pianoforte, therefore, reached our dwelling, and Frisker took ours of Goner in exchange, with 25*l.* addition. Schroeder was delighted with it, and was of use to the maker. He at once taught me three of his concertos, to set both off; then his sonatas, and three difficult ones of Haydn's just published, with violin and violoncello accompaniments.

Art and science thus hovering round us, combined with the new instrument, attracted others, and we became the centre of a charming *coterie*. Rodgers asked Mr. Papendiek to take up his son, a boy of twelve, with a most beautiful voice, and a wonderful intonation and genius for music. He attracted notice as one of the leading choir boys at the

Chapel, and was engaged at all public concerts round the neighbourhood. Through us he was invited to private parties, and I hope gathered friends. We gave him the opportunity of being present at all our little meetings, and in return he kept all our instruments in tune, which he did admirably.

He was to teach little Charlotte her notes and gamuts, but this did not very well succeed, for although he was clever, his temper was peevish and stubborn, and he could not conciliate or encourage the poor child in her task. In other things she did well. She could stitch a pocket, she read prettily, and now began to write.

My mother passed now and then some time with us, and we had our parties to the races—Egham, Ascot, and Maidenhead, as usual, with a pic-nic dinner afterwards.

One of these days, when we were amusing ourselves by singing glees, Lady Mexborough, who was fishing with a party near, heard us, and brought us fruit. Then, finding we were old friends, expressed her pleasure at meeting us again. She was a Miss Stevens, a member of one of the old established families of Windsor, and her father compelled her to marry the Earl of Mexborough by holding a loaded pistol to her, to shoot her or himself, should she persist in her refusal. This severe remonstrance settled the point, but I do not think she eventually regretted it. Another of our musical friends, Miss Haines, married Colonel Egerton, who became Earl of Bridgewater.

The Royal Family going for a week or two to town, on account of some foreigners, we took the opportunity of paying a long-promised visit to Mrs. Zoffany. Her house in Hart Street was at the corner of Church Passage, and one watchman's box was close to her front door, a second being stationed up the passage. It was a comfort to feel so well protected, for just after the war housebreaking and robbery of every description were very prevalent.

Just after I left, having stayed a week in every comfort of friendship, Mrs. Watkins arrived from India, and by Mr. Zoffany's desire, made his wife's abode her home *pro tempore*. She was protected on the voyage by Maddison, the great stockbroker, who managed all Zoffany's affairs, and of whom Zoffany painted such an admirable portrait that it was engraved.

In those days, when London was very different to what it now is, Hart Street was very desirable, both as to light and air, but the approaches were bad, through Monmouth Street and St. Giles's. I always avoided dark streets in going or returning from St. James's, when possible, and never met with the least unpleasantness.

A few days after our return home, Mrs. Pitt called to tell us that the offer from Dr. Herschel had been renewed, and again accepted, under the following arrangement. There were to be two establishments, one at Upton and one at Slough ; two maidservants in each, and one footman to go backwards and forwards, with accommodation at both places, and Miss Herschel to have apartments over the workshops. A tube was arranged for the Doctor to communicate with her, direct from his post of observation, so she was able to write minutes of his proceedings without being exposed to the open air.

Sir Joseph Banks and ourselves were the only friends entrusted with the secret of their engagement. All preparations were begun, and spring, when the mourning was to end, and the marriage to take place, was anxiously anticipated.

At Christmas my brother and Paul Adee Pitt were to leave Eton, but in November an epidemic fever broke out, first in the College and then spread through Eton and a part of Windsor, which caused the dispersion of as many of the scholars as were able to leave. My brother was one who had it severely, and my nursery-maid also, who, as she would not be attended by Dr. Mingay, was removed to her friends and died after four weeks' illness. We nursed my brother at home, and through Dr.

Mingay's excellent precautions, the infection did not spread, and all the rest of us escaped. The doors of all the rooms were kept wide open to create a thorough draught, and small fires kept burning in each sleeping room. Twice a day a large pan of vinegar, boiled with certain spices, was placed on each of the three landings of the staircase.

My father and mother principally nursed my brother, assisted by us and an excellent maid, sent by Dr. Heath, who remained with me afterwards. He was bled twice, and fed with port wine, spiced, with a rusk softened in it, sometimes a little diluted with water, and, as he began to recover, meat and chicken panadas. At the end of six weeks he rose up better than he had been for some time before falling ill.

The doctor pronounced it nervous fever, bordering on typhus, but fortunately it did not amount to that dreadful illness, though it was bad enough, and many died in both towns. The school having broken up at the commencement of the epidemic, did not re-assemble till after the Christmas vacation.

Two more events in this year distressed me; the one was the death of my canary bird, which we had cherished among us from the time of my marriage. On returning to the parlour after a few days of indisposition (Milly, the servant, having always taken charge of it during my absence), I called to my little favourite, who not jumping upon the perch as usual at the sound of my voice, I stood up to look into the cage, and, to my sorrow, saw the poor little thing lying on its back dead at the bottom of the cage. It had plenty of seed and water, and we think it must have dislocated its neck in getting at the food, the glass not being quite opposite the aperture in the wires. Poor little fluttering innocent! I trust the pain of death was momentary. Tears fell over it, but they could not bring it back to imprisonment. It was released.

The other event, though of a very different kind, was a source of great trouble to me. Mr. Papendiek had long threatened to wear a wig, as his head was bald at the top, and he complained of the cold, and now, in spite of all my remonstrances, he was determined, and did carry his threat into execution. Wigs were not then what they are now, a covering made to imitate the hair, but real frightful wigs. Mr. Papendick looked older, his fine forehead was hidden, and his beauty greatly diminished by this horrid wig. I said it even lessened my love for him, but he was inexorable, and time reconciled us, though I continued long to grieve at it. For two or three mornings, not feeling the cold as before, he forgot his hat at starting, and had to step back for it to the amusement of us all.

My brother and Pitt were now both to enter on

their respective callings. With the former, who was then sixteen, I lost my companion, and the 25*l.* allowed me for his board ; in Paul Adee, an open-hearted friendly acquaintance, who had endeared himself to us in every social tie.

My brother having determined upon the medical profession, my father asked the advice of his friends upon the subject of his training, not wishing again to apply to the Queen, when Mr. Meyer, who was my brother's godfather, recommended his being articled to an assistant surgeon of a hospital, surgery being the branch of the profession that he preferred. The surgeons about the Court were eminent men, but aged, and not in general practice, so it was judged best to bring my brother into active business. Mr. Lang, assistant surgeon of St. Bartholomew's Hospital, and surgeon of Christ's Hospital, was the one preferred, and my brother was introduced to him, approved, and all finally settled. He was a clever man, a member of the Literati Society, and eminent in his profession, though not a great operator. He was an intimate friend of Mr. Meyer's, and of that party—Hayley, Cowper, &c. He was a rich man and a gentleman, so all appeared favourable.

The premium was high, but it included the payment to Mr. Lang, and to the hospital for the use of instruments, admission to the library, the attendance at lectures, at the visits of medical men, at operations, and in fact, all matters relating to the business of that most excellent establishment. The hours of attendance were from ten to four or five, Mr. Lang giving a list of the proper books to study when at home. Pott, the great surgeon, was at the head, Earle, Blick, &c. being under him, and all progressed most favourably. My brother became every day more attached to the profession, and being of a studious disposition, and showing great ability, he was much liked in every department, and his progress was rapid. The expense of placing him had been great, but no doubt was felt of an advantageous result.

His friend Pitt was near him in the hours of study, as he had been apprenticed to his uncle, Mr. Baldwin, a wholesale chemist, but their happy meetings were no more during their leisure time. Mr. Baldwin was rigid, and my mother allowed few indulgent privileges to her children. That of cultivating friendships and forming acquaintances she almost prohibited. Perhaps it was for a wise purpose, for it made us dependent upon our own resources for filling up our time, and may have given my brother that habit of study which now so greatly accelerated his improvement, and in the variety of situations he has been thrown into through life, this may have constituted a happiness where otherwise there must have been a blank. When we were in town, he was fond of having my children to amuse him at his meals, and during the early part of the evening he would join us in our games of cribbage, picquet, whist, quadrille, or backgammon, retiring early to study for the next day's attendance.

Before the departure of my brother and young Pitt, it was proposed to give an evening party as a sort of farewell. A dance was the wished-for merriment, but where was the room?

Our large kitchen was put into requisition, and with argand lamps, laurel boughs, and other pretty decorations, a most complete chamber for dancing it made. The approach to it was through our common parlour, where tea and refreshments were served, the front parlour and side room being appropriated to the supper, which was all prepared at home, according to the custom of that time, and the drawing-room being reserved for cards. New Year's Day, 1788, was fixed upon for the entertainment, as the Royal Family intending to go up to London only just for the drawing-room, Mr. Papendick was able to obtain leave of absence.

The Misses White and Stone were invited the previous week to assist me in the preparations. The rooms were lighted with wax candles, and the passages &c. with lamps. The supper consisted of an épergne on each table with pickles and preserves, wet and dry: Then, placed neatly and prettily on the table, were cold roasted poultry and game; the same boned in aspic jelly, decorated with lobsters and prawns ; potted meats ; eggs, hard-boiled in forcemeats ; blanc-mange, as eggs supported on cake softened by brandy, with whipped cream round ; tarts in very small glass pie-dishes ; mince pies, equally small, pigeon pies, savoury patties, cheese, butter, anchovies, watercress, and such delicacies, all decorated and prepared so as to require no cutting ; fruits, fresh and dried, blanc-mange, yellow, green, and red, jellies all colours ; these ingenuities being much attended to, a round of beef, fillet of veal, ham, and salads on the side tables. Mulled beer, negus, and punch were the warm beverages, and for cold, wines of different sorts, including home-made wines, and currant and raspberry water &c. We engaged a part of the Freemasons' band from that tavern.

Mr. Papendick and Salomon dined at Dr. Herschel's and joined us at the hour appointed. I led off the dance, opening the ball with young Pitt out of compliment to him, and we kept it up till about four o'clock in the morning. Our guests numbered about one hundred and fifty.

Salomon remained on with us, and during his visit we had quartetts of a morning, selecting those of the King's band to assist us that we required, the Griesbachs being generally of our little parties. Our friends were amused and gratified. One of the minor canons, Mr. Gibbons, who had married a lady of fortune, came now to settle at Windsor, and took a house in Park Street. They made their *début* in the society of Windsor at a private concert given at this time. The glee party, four in number, were there with Rodgers to accompany. We took Salomon with us, which was a great favour, and I with him and Mr. Gore, who played the bass, performed two sonatas of Haydn and one of Schroeder. I also took a second to Rodgers in singing, in which I could always succeed with musicians.

This concert brought me many visitors and invitations, but I at once declined the card parties on the plea of my little family and the uncertainty of Mr. Papendiek's presence. These two evenings were a subject of sarcasm with the Delavauxs for many a day—the 'Kitchen dance,' and the 'Minor Canon concert.'

The Royal Family, with their attendants, left Windsor a few days before the birthday, for the season, and little Charlotte went with her papa, on a visit to her grandparents at St. James's. In the hurry of departure she took up her little box of toys, but left the key. I sent it by the first conveyance, but in the meantime she wrote me a letter for it. It was of her own inditing and was simple and natural, the description correct, and the words very fairly spelt, the letters being formed some like printing, others to imitate writing. This was in January 1788, and she was only four years old the end of the previous November.

Mr. Papendiek had given up Clarke's lodgings, and had this season engaged those of Gates, a hairdresser and perfumer, in Queen's Row, Pimlico. They were cheerful, clean, and much less in price than Clarke's, and the people civil and attentive.

Mr. Papendiek told me of Duberly's intended marriage with the daughter of a late general in the army, then living with her widowed mother. None of his family approved of the match, but he nevertheless proceeded with it and married, taking a private dwelling-house in Soho Square, and extensive premises in Dean Street for his business of army clothing. We had paid our debt to him, and Mr. Papendiek had procured for him another regiment, and now he was anxious to introduce his wife to us, and to renew our friendship upon the old easy footing.

They also engaged the large room in Brewer Street, Golden Square, to let out for dances, concerts, or routs, and began by instituting a subscription series of twelve alternate nights for music, which was to consist of a professional quartett, with permission to amateurs to perform if they desired it. Some of the twelve nights were to be devoted to dancing, and for these occasions a band was engaged consisting of two violins, violoncello, tabor and pipe, the then fashion.   The room was small, but they mustered two cotillons and about twenty couple for the country dance.

As Mr. Papendick wished to keep up the connection, we took tickets, intending to go when we could.

The spare room at St. James's was fitted up for my brother.   His bed was put into a recess with curtains neatly hung over it, so that it had all the appearance of a study, where he could receive his friends, and occupy himself without causing any inconvenience to mamma.

I went up to town for a week, taking up my quarters at Gates's, and was present at the first of Duberly's subscription nights.   I ran in to Mrs. Pohl to speak about a bonnet, and to see how she was.   I had heard that she was indifferent, but little did I expect to find my dear friend on her deathbed.   She was supported on her bed taking stock of what remained of her once flourishing and elegant business when I went in.   She hoped to recover, and was cheerful.   I stayed with her some time, but we never met again.   She wished her daughter to continue the business, and was glad that I required a few things.

My white bonnet of the previous summer was to be trimmed with the now fashionable colour of orange, in compliment to the marriage of the

Hereditary Prince of Holland to the Duke of York's sister—now King and Queen of Holland.

I paid my visit to Mrs. Duberly, who was not at home, but when she returned my call at St. James's we were in. She was horrified at being shown up the 'back stairs,' but I took care to show this proud woman that they were the private entrance to the King's and Queen's apartments as well as to ours. Nobody, however, appeared that afforded her any interest.

The first of Duberly's evenings was a dance, beginning at eight and ending at twelve o'clock, and it went off very well. I danced with Duberly and Salomon. My dress was the puce satin, with the trimmed sleeves and gauze handkerchief as before, the ends of it being fastened in front by three white satin broad straps, buckled with steel buckles. The last addition was a gauze apron as long as the gown, which met behind at the waist and was finished off with two equal bows and ends lying upon the bustle, and a large nosegay of artificial flowers, given to me by Princess Elizabeth, and tied up by her for the occasion. Headdress the same, but Kead's attendance being suspended in favour of Mr. Theilcke, I thought I was not so becomingly finished.

Evening dress for gentlemen at that time was a cloth coat, lined with silk or satin according to the season, waistcoat like the lining, slightly embroidered, black satin shorts, white silk stockings, and shoes with buckles, lace ruffles and shirt frill, a smaller bag, and the sword without a knot. Mr. Papendiek's colours were a very dark dead brown, with light blue lining, the waistcoat being worked by me with a rose pattern.

My dress was particularly admired, as being of the last fashion, and Miss Strong immediately borrowed the nosegay, which I lent with pleasure.

At that time everybody made flowers, as the fashionable work for the season. Prince Ernest had written to Mr. Papendiek to procure for him the proper instruments for the work, which for a complete full blown rose with buds, leaves, wire, and silk, cost about twelve guineas. These commissions from the Prince were always to be paid for by the Queen. This one she rather cavilled at, and as Mr. Papendick had some difficulty with it, and also in procuring the instruments for Princess Elizabeth, my nosegay was given as an acknowledgment of all his trouble.

I finished my week in town by calling upon my friends. I saw Mrs. Hünnemann, who had just given birth to her eldest son, Bladen, and was looking ill and quiet. Mrs. Wadsworth told me that the husband allowed all requisites cheerfully, but the conversation always turning upon the saving of expenses was a little depressing. As I had at that time never seen death, I would not call again upon poor Mrs. Pohl. I paid my bill, and she was pleased with my order, and with my long visit; but though that was but a few days before, she could not have borne it now, so fast did she decline.

As I sat in the Windsor coach at Piccadilly, and saw the carriages driving down to St. James's, I regretted not having postponed my return until the following day: I so thoroughly enjoyed seeing the company pass to the drawing-room through the King's presence chamber. Thus pleasure allures; but I was only twenty-two, and had led a restricted life at home. Besides, I was anxious to keep up and improve in my acquired accomplishments, and to retain my well-bred manner. Nor was Mr. Papendick less so, observing that as we could derive no consequence from money or appointment, we could only be received into good society by these means; and to form connections or acquaintance below our walk in life, that he would never consent to.

I found my babies well. I loved my children, and it was a trial to me when I had to leave them; but as Mr. Papendick was during the winter season more in town than at home, he naturally wished me to go up to him sometimes, and we could not afford to move our whole family. I always tried to make such regulations that when I was away from my babies they should miss nothing but my personal care, and, thank God for His merciful providence, no harm ever did happen to these sweet beings. If I erred in the conduct I pursued, I sincerely repent, and humbly trust for forgiveness.

I went to London once more to attend a musical night of these pleasant subscription meetings. This time I wore the puce satin again, with puce straps instead of white, and my watch and bracelets made the difference from dancing attire, and looked equally well. Mr. Duberly was there, but not his lady, who seemed to be no longer inquired after. She had not from the first made herself agreeable to her husband's friends, and now her desire appeared to be to show that she did not wish for their society. We met no more, and within a few years she intrigued with old General Gunning.

On Mr. Duberly taking her to her mother she said, 'You must approve my daughter having made choice of a gentleman, for really those friends to whom you introduced her, as well as your own family, move in a very different society from what she has been accustomed to, and she was not happy.' To this he answered, 'My family are worthy, friendly people, and my wealth that you looked after for your daughter has been appropriated to her advantage, both present and future.' They were soon divorced, but Duberly remained in Soho Square, and our friendship continued unbroken.

Early this year Höppner commenced the portrait of my little Charlotte which Augusta now has. On March 1 Mr. Papendiek was going as usual to fetch her, after a sitting, from Höppner's house in Charles Street, when he was surrounded by a mob in St. James's Square and robbed of his pocket-book containing notes amounting to about 10*l.*, which he had just taken from Ransome's & Co. This, of course, caused a little delay and some confusion, and upon entering, Mrs. Höppner, who evidently felt aggrieved, said, ' You can spare yourself the trouble in future to fetch your little girl, for she is more than I can manage. I have tried to whip her, but could not.' Mr. Papendiek said, · She is not much accustomed to that;' and when he lifted her up to kiss them, she said to Mr. Höppner, ' You are good to me, and I like the painting room ;' but to Mrs. Höppner she said, · You are not good to me, and I only wished to look out of the window.'

Mr. Papendiek called afterwards to know what the result would be, and Höppner told him that, much as he regretted it, as the portrait had been greatly admired for its sweet simplicity and the remarkably beautiful eyes, he could not finish it for this year's exhibition. Mr. Papendiek then begged to have it sent home at the end of the season, which was done, in the unfinished state in which it now hangs in my daughter's drawing-room.[1]

This spring, 1788, the King began to show signs of serious illness. Dr. Baker alone attended him, and gave it as his opinion that the bile did not flow properly, and as his Majesty would not consent to take any medicine likely to be beneficial to him, he was up and down in his condition—better and worse, but did not rally. All eyes were upon him, and party feeling ran high.

Among others observed, Mrs. Magnolley came under the lash of the Queen for receiving at her house such men as Fox, Sheridan, Whitbread, &c. When her Majesty spoke to the husband about it he answered spiritedly for his wife, but added that as the lease of her house was up, and her sister on the point of being married, she intended to leave Kensington Gore and retire with her mother to Camberwell.

My sister, who was now between twelve and thirteen, was by this change thrown out of her education. For the present she went home, and I hoped my mother would fit up the unused room at St. James's for her. But no—this was to remain a lumber and store-room, and a bed was put up for my sister in the maid's room.

At Easter the Royal Family were at Windsor as

---

[1] The picture is now in my possession.—ED.

usual.  Dr. Heberden, as physician to the King, was
ordered down, and as his house was in Church Lane,
and the garden wall adjoined the King's premises, a
door was now opened through, so that he could have
access to his Majesty at any moment.  Dr. Heberden
highly disapproved of Dr. Baker having so long
ventured to attend alone, and at once summoned Dr.
Monro.  He considered the case alarming, and this
peculiar practitioner said, ' there was quite enough for
him to do, but there must be a regular consultation.'

The great desire was to keep the circumstance
secret as much as possible from the public, to hasten
the session, and direct their hopes to the ease of
summer business, to change of air, and other restora-
tives.  The King was aware of the probability of his
malady, but was unconscious of its having already
made great strides.  Dr. Monro retired, and was not
again called in.

In this reign, when most things were regulated
with something like order and justice, it was the rule
that all palaces, houses, and apartments furnished by
the Lord Chamberlain's office, were every seven years
either newly fitted up, replenished, or put to rights ;
and on removing the old furniture, it was always
asked if one attached to the household wished to purchase any part of it.

This Easter a person came down to take the
Princess Royal's commands with reference to refur-

nishing her two rooms and closet at the Upper Lodge, and Mr. Papendick sent over a man to measure how the whole of the old would suit our drawing room. There was a sofa which fitted into the end of the room as if it had been made for the place, twelve chairs, two pier card-tables, a pembroke table to match, the curtains (four), as if they had been planned to the windows, the pattern something like my high bed, of a warm dark red damask, lined with white. The whole to be cleaned, finished, and put up for 25*l.*, ready money—a very fair-priced bargain. But where the sum came from I can only guess. Old Delavaux, I imagine, as he was always ready to advance money on heavy interest.

There was no carpet, but this we did not mind, for, as Mr. Papendick observed, our little entertainments were always music, when the carpet, if we had one, would be taken up. The Princess sent, in addition, a work-table as a present from herself.

The recess ended, all returned to town, but I remained stationary at Windsor. Dr. Herschel now married the Widow Pitt. Mr. Baldwin gave her away, her son was present, and Sir Joseph Banks acted as the friend of the Doctor. Miss Herschel received them at Slough, which was the honoured house for the reception of the newly-married pair, and where they spent their honeymoon. About six weeks after, cards were sent round dated Upton, so there, of course, the congratulatory visits were to be paid.

Not feeling inclined to take a carriage, I walked over with nurse and baby one fine afternoon in May, resting for a few minutes under the yew-tree in the Upton churchyard, where I put on my white gloves before going on to the house. Dr. Herschel and his bride received me warmly, and I was ushered into the well-known tent, where cake and wine were presented. I hoped for some assistance home, but none was offered, so we walked back again, and I was not so fatigued as might have been expected.

Some time after my father called, when he was down at Windsor during his wait, and told me that things were not going on well at St. James's, just as I dreaded would be the case. I entreated him not to disturb the arrangements of my brother, which were proceeding so satisfactorily, but to send my sister to school, her education being far from completed. He wished me to take her, but that was an anxiety far too great under any circumstances, and I proposed Streatham or Mrs. Roach's. The latter was fixed upon, and my sister placed there. I assisted my mother in making the arrangements, and in preparing her dress. Poor mamma thanked me, and again all was right.

About this time Ramberg, a son of the King's physician at Hanover, came over, highly recommended for genius and talent as a draughtsman. The Queen gave permission for the six Princesses to sit to him, and asked us to accommodate him while at Windsor. We gave him the two small rooms at the end of the drawing-room, and he mealed at the Lodge. In town he had a room at the Queen's House. He expressed himself as being extremely pleased at our attention to him, which was upon German principles—his pipe, the garden, a little English beer, and his coffee.

A few weeks finished his work for the Queen, and as a remembrance to us he left us the drawing of our sweet children which now hangs in the Arbuthnot's parlour.[1]  Although a performance not generally appreciated, yet it is a pleasurable recollection to me.

My father at this time took a house in Kensington, thinking that the air would be better for my brother than at St. James's, during the fine summer months, and less confined for a boy who had always lived in the country. The Kensington stages were then only sixpence all the way to the Bank, and my brother used to go daily by them to his work.

I was invited, according to his wish, to spend a few days with him, which I gladly did, and of an evening we sat or walked in those sweet gardens of

---

[1] This picture is now in the possession of Colonel H. T. Arbuthnot, Royal Artillery, second son of the late Mr. Arbuthnot, of the Treasury.

Kensington.  Forsyth was the gardener ; a clever man, who received from Government a large premium for the care of diseased trees.  He had a sweet, interesting daughter, and a considerable degree of intercourse was kept up between our families during the time that my father had this most pleasant little house.  My visit was all too short, and we said adieu in tears.

On my way home I called upon Mrs. Zoffany and invited her to stay with me, with her two little girls, Theresa and Cecilia, then, I should say, about eleven and eight years old.  In a few days she arrived, and at once consulted me about sending her daughters to school, for they were now evidently losing time.  I strenuously recommended Streatham, but again Mrs. Roach's establishment found favour on account of its more accessible position, and with her they were placed in due course.  They were to be my little pets, and I begged Mrs. Roach to lose no opportunity of bringing them forward in all points of elegance. They appeared to be amiable, but, poor dears, they preferred joining in all the domestic arrangements, and cared little for accomplishments.

My little Charlotte was pleased now to go to Mrs. Roach's too, but as she was not yet five we did not make it a daily rule.  I paid the quarter's fee, one guinea, and the days that she did not go to school she read at home, so that the classes were not disturbed, and Mrs. Roach said she even in that way got on too rapidly for the others.

Thus matters stood when the order for Cheltenham arrived. Privately it had been long known who were to be in attendance, and now the order came out.

Earl Fauconberg lent his house to the Royal party, which had now been got ready by the different offices for their reception.

The King was no better. Wine had been recommended in very small quantities to assist digestion, but as his Majesty had never taken it he doubted its efficacy. The Prince of Wales sent a few bottles of the finest Madeira, so he said, that the island had ever produced, and proposed tasting it with the King when the family dined at four o'clock. The King thanked his Royal Highness, but said that he hoped for the credit of his gentleman of the wine cellar, and for the pleasure of those who partook of such indulgences, that the best was always provided. For himself it would be his last trial, as he was sure it did him more harm than good.

An occurrence took place this spring which made another change in the Royal household. Miss Laverocke, who with her sister had been appointed assistant dressers to the Queen on her first coming to England, was suddenly taken seriously ill, and after a few weeks died.

Her sister had married Mr. Lockley, the Prince of Wales's first page at the time of the appointment of Miss Pascal to the Queen, on the demise of the Princess Dowager of Wales, to whom she had been dresser. The King had a great respect and regard for her, on account of her having been most dutifully and affectionately attached to his mother, but probably from her having held this situation the Queen never liked her, though she was well qualified for it. She dressed hair well, was active and very punctual; one of those lively, pretty German women, without the artificial affectation of excess of feeling.

No doubt the King intended to do a kindness to this faithful adherent by placing her with the Queen. Yet I fear that the emoluments of the place were less than in her previous situation, and I am sure the comforts were considerably so, as also her rank or position, for now she was under the commands of the Misses Schwellenberg and Hagedorn.

About seven or eight years previous to the time of which I am writing, Miss Pascal had married Mr. Theilcke, a friend of her brother's, and had now two sons and a daughter. The first step after Miss Laverocke's death was to place Mrs. Theilcke in her apartments at the Queen's House, which was very gratifying to her, who had patiently borne much persecution.

I must mention *en passant* one anecdote of her

spirited feeling of duty. When she was expecting her confinement the first time, she determined to remain at her post till the last possible moment. When this moment had come, she put the Queen to bed as usual at Windsor, at twelve o'clock or later, then went off alone in a postchaise to her rooms at St. James's, and by changing horses at Hounslow, the same conveyance took her sister back to Windsor in time for the Queen's rising at seven o'clock. Early in the morning she was safely delivered of a son.

When the sister died, no one applied for the vacant appointment; no one was proposed. The Ladies of the Bedchamber would not give up their own 'ladies' woman,' then the term, and had no one to recommend. At last a farmer's daughter, named Sandys, servant to Miss Waldegrave, was engaged. She was a pretty-looking, prepossessing young woman, but she was not fit for the post, as she could neither dress hair nor make new apparel. Mrs. Theilcke, however, endeavoured to train her to the duties of her new situation, and to initiate her into the etiquette of her higher station.

The party for Cheltenham was thus formed. Their Majesties, the three elder Princesses, one Lady of the Queen's Bedchamber, and one of the Princesses'; Lady Elizabeth Waldegrave, Misses Burney, Planta, Sandys, Mackenthum, Turner, and Willes; three equerries, that two might always be in attendance upon the King, an arrangement now for the first time instituted; Messrs. Kamus and Ernst, my father, and Mr. Papendiek.

The new hairdresser, Sonardi, was ordered to attend—his first command, but he wished to find his own way thither and be independent. When the Queen heard this she remarked, 'Then we shall have that woman there—his woman, for it is said she is not his wife.' She was a pretty woman, but large, and quite an Italian in appearance.

Poor Mr. Papendiek was in great anxiety at leaving me, as I was very near my confinement, but Mrs. Zoffany promised she would remain with me, and very kindly did. She brought me the silver tags to lace my gown ornamentally, which Augusta now has in her amateur theatrical wardrobe.

# CHAPTER XII.

The organ-loft—The organist at Windsor—Birth of Mrs. Papendiek's
fourth child, George—The Royal party return from Cheltenham—
Influenza—Salomon—Christening of the child—Presents—Music—
The Queen's illness—Some account of the Cheltenham visit—Dr.
Hurd—The china manufactory at Worcester—The glove manufactory
—Fashions in gloves—Mrs. Papendiek's visit to the Queen—Visits
to various ladies—Evening parties—New music of the day—The
Misses Stowe—The Cheshires—Terrible poisoning catastrophe—Lady
Fauconberg—The last of the Cheshire family—Mrs. Jervois—The
Misses Stowe play before the Queen—Dreary performance—Mr.
Papendiek relates to the Queen the Stowes' history—The Queen's
approval of Mrs. Stowe—Mrs. Jervois gives a grand drum—
Refreshments.

FROM Easter this year, we had been given two seats
in St. George's Chapel, and having friends ' at Court'
we also got access to the organ-loft, and as we constantly availed ourselves of this indulgence, we every
quarter gave certain *douceurs*, which, however, we
did not grudge.

The organist at this time was old Webb, a man
between sixty and seventy years of age. He had a
wen which hung from the nostril ; small at first, but
it increased so rapidly as to be a great inconvenience
to the poor man, besides being very distressing to
behold. He was in good health, and was therefore

encouraged to have it removed, as the operation could but last a second. Messrs. Aylett and Thomas accordingly proceeded to do it. It was said that they were not provided with proper styptics and sponges. Be that as it may, in less than a week poor old Webb died from extreme loss of blood. The Queen, not wishing the King to be troubled with anything that could be avoided, advised that Sexton, the deputy organist and teacher of the choir boys, should go on for the present alone, recommending the Prebends to consider him for his additional responsibility, but to hold out no promise of his ultimately succeeding to the situation.

On July 22, 1788, my son George was born, a day less than three weeks after my own birthday, when I was twenty-three. All went well, but I was still barely convalescent when the Royal party returned from Cheltenham.

Mr. Papendiek greeted us with joy, but most unfortunately he communicated to us an influenza, from which many of the party had been, and still were suffering. He was not aware that he was affected by it, but scarcely was he home before it showed itself.

He was soon in his bed at the Lodge, and baby and myself were objects of real pity. The fever ran so high that the milk curdled on his lips, which were blistered. Dr. Mingay gave medicine every hour, and at last said, 'If there is no change in twenty-four hours a physician must come from the Lodge. No one else in Windsor can assist me.' Providence, ever merciful, now blessed us with recovery, but what we suffered those three days I shudder even now to think of. My husband also recovered well and quickly, thank God.

Mr. Salomon called to introduce Mrs. and the Misses Stowe, whom we had long expected at Windsor. He was sensibly affected when he saw the state I was in, lying on the sofa in the drawing-room, and said he would call again on his return from Sir William Younges, whom he was going to visit at Formosa, near Maidenhead.

This formidable epidemic now began to give way. Princess Elizabeth had it badly, and one of the equerries and several others more or less seriously.

Mr. Papendiek returned home on recovery, and we settled together about the christening. On the Sunday within the month I went in a sedan to our parish church to be churched, and settled with the curate, Mr. Grape, to come down on the Tuesday following at six o'clock to christen baby. This was done, and he received the names of George Ernest. Mr. Ernst and my father stood as proxies for the King and Prince Ernest, and brought me ten guineas. Miss Planta stood for the Queen, with ten guineas more. She brought with her my ever dear Miss Burney, who still loved me.

We invited Madame de Lafitte and her daughter, and the Delucs, who brought with them Mrs. Kennicott, the wife of the editor of the Hebrew Bible, a work in which she assisted him. She was a most agreeable, though a plain woman.

We also had Salmon, Sale, and Gore, glee singers, with Rodgers to accompany them, as I was still too weak to do anything. Tea was made in the room at the extreme end, to show the new silver teapot, a present from Cheltenham.

The visit to Cheltenham did not prove the success that was hoped for, and a few days after the arrival of the Royal party the Queen fell ill and kept her room. The severe affliction and constant anxiety she was in was probably the cause, and from this time her Majesty's health was less uniformly good. The dropsy, which had been floating in her constitution since the birth of Prince Alfred, now made its deposit, and caused her at times much suffering. All anecdotes connected with Cheltenham are too well known for me to repeat them here, especially as I was not there myself, and could only give them at second hand.

From Cheltenham a visit was made to Worcester, where their Majesties, the Princesses, and the attendants were to be received at the Bishop's palace. On their arrival, this venerable man was led by two clergymen to meet his Sovereign in the accustomed manner, but so overcome was he on seeing and hearing the King that, as soon as it could be managed, he was conducted back to his study.

Through the communication of the Queen's lady, the Bishop submitted to her Majesty his earnest wish that she would command everything for her own and the King's comfort and convenience. Everyone in his household were ready to do their best with duty and respect; the clergymen were at their posts to receive and to attend to every command that their Majesties would permit them to execute.

The Bishop himself found that he was quite unequal to doing much himself, as he so ardently wished, but the duty of reading prayers night and morning the dear old man did go through.

The Queen, with her usual consideration and kind discernment, often sat with the Bishop, and her Majesty always allowed the clergymen to attend when their Prelate was present. In short, Mr. Papendiek told me that the magnificence, the respect, and the attention shown to them all could not possibly have been surpassed.

The Bishop had all those brought to him that he had known when he lived at Kew as tutor to the four elder Princes. The pages and Miss Planta were the only five, and the latter introduced Miss

Burney, to whom he was particularly attentive, extolled her publications, and urged her to continue setting virtue in the most amiable light before the notice of the young. Oh, Dr. Hurd, how have we all profited by your kind admonitions while at Kew, and from the many sermons delivered by you in our chapel there? This pattern of goodness was indefatigable in duty while he had the power, and I trust we did in some measure benefit by his judicious and affectionate lessons. I think he was never married ; certainly he had no family.

The assistant dressers took their meals in the steward's room, to the extreme delight of Miss Sandys, and to the great distress of Miss Mackenthum, who was an educated young woman, and daughter of the Controller of the Household in Hanover—a proper person to attend a Princess ; and she certainly never expected to meet the associates she now had to mix with.

The Cathedral had been beautified for this visit, and the Royal pew most appropriately and elegantly fitted up. The Bishop conducted their Majesties to it, while the clergymen showed the ladies to their seats on one side, and the equerries on the other side, and the household to their respective places. The public were allowed to fill up any seats yet remaining vacant.

No stranger was engaged to sing, but every per-

son, in whatever capacity, receiving emolument from
the Cathedral, was to be present on this Sunday
unless prevented by illness. Another Bishop was
asked over to preach. I am ashamed to say I
cannot recollect which ; indeed, I think and hope I
never heard. The Bishop of Worcester himself read
the Communion Service, and gave the Blessing. The
service was imposing, and the impression it made
was long remembered by many.

Mr. Papendiek was of a very affectionate and
tender-hearted nature, and the parting scene from
this palace was almost too much for him. He had
known Dr. Hurd from his early days, and was next
door to him when with Prince Ernest of Mecklenburgh. The Bishop remained at Kew until the Prince
of Wales was of age, and the three other Princes
went abroad. He then retired to his diocese, and
there remained.

While at Worcester the Royalties visited the
china manufactory sufficiently often to see the different modes of process by which the delicate finish
was then attained. Now they make their china
stronger and more durable, and the patterns are still
elegant. Purchases were of course made to some
extent.

The glove manufactory also engaged their attention, and to receive commands for present supplies
and for future accommodation, the head of the firm

was commanded to wait upon the Queen. He was a Quaker, and said that if her Majesty would just see him in his beaver, he would then consent to its being removed. Accordingly he was announced. The Queen even rose to receive him, and having advanced some paces, he then said, 'Gentlemen or Friends, unloose my temples and lift my beaver off.' The order was then given for the beautiful light grey gloves with smooth white insides, and also for the brown York tan, also to be smooth inside, but of the same colour. These latter I always had for myself and children. They wore them tied high over the elbow, to preserve the arm in beauty for womanhood. This Quaker despaired of success in preparing the white kid to make up the smooth side inward, so as to produce the rough side wearable. He did partly fail, but Hill, the glover in Pall Mall, and now of Regent Street, succeeded in all three. The Quaker took an affectionate leave, and spoke in the highest praise of the Queen's humility, judgment, and kindness.

Upon the return of the Royal Family to Windsor, the Queen appointed a day immediately after our christening for us to go and see her. Her Majesty received us kindly, and said she feared from the very pale look of the little boy, that he would be delicate. She was sorry that Papendick had given us the influenza, and then added, 'My dear Mrs. Papendick, we have all been far from well. The weather was too warm for Cheltenham.' Poor Queen! she looked broken-hearted.

I then called upon Miss Planta, who said I must call upon Miss Sandys too; the Queen expected it. This I did, and went to Miss Mackenthum also, but we had received her from her first coming to England. Miss Burney's rooms were at the corner of that story, so to her I went last. She was all politeness as usual, and said she would soon call to tell me of all the new regulations which were then being formed. After these visits I went to Mrs. Stowe, and found her in a two-roomed lodging, dark and dreary beyond description.

She returned my visit the same evening, and we found them a most agreeable, intelligent family. We mutually expressed our pleasure at this beginning of acquaintance, which we hoped would ripen into friendship ultimately. She wished her girls to have the opportunity of sometimes playing upon our grand pianoforte that they might keep up their touch, their own instrument being only a small one. This I readily granted, and told her that I was always at dinner with my children from half-past one to three o'clock, and it was important that I should take this uninterruptedly; that I drank tea at six, and in the evening took a trifle; so they would always know when to find me at leisure.

My mother and brother came down one day to see baby, and went back the same evening. None of my family were at the christening except my father, and no old friends but Mrs. Zoffany, who, in bringing her little girls to school, again stayed a few days. A few Cheltenham medals struck in honour of the visit were all that Mr. Papendiek had to offer. Mamma had, however, already had a pretty and useful needlebook.

We now organised two evening parties to introduce the Stowes. Mrs. Roach and our three satellites came to both, also the Herschels, and Charles Bostock, a brother of the minister of Windsor, and son of the Prebend.

He was a handsome, delightful man, and an excellent divine, benevolent and universally kind. He took lessons on the violoncello from Crosdill whenever opportunity offered, and every day from Henry Griesbach, and he really was an excellent player. With Forrest's flute, and Salomon, who had just returned, we were complete without any of the band. However, those who begged we allowed to come—four Griesbachs, Pick, and Kellner, so we had quite a grand concert; and the second night more of the band would come, Miller and the second horn, besides those already mentioned, and Rodgers to accompany and tune.

The new music of the day was that of Dussek, Kozebuch, Mozart, Haydn, and Hulmandel. Scarlatti and Handel's music was still most fashionable for solo performances. Not expecting such a band, and I may say not prepared for it, we did not know what was best to play, but the performances were principally trios or sonatas with obbligato accompaniments, in which the Miss Stowes took a part.

They were aged sixteen and fourteen. The elder girl took the leading portions, the younger sister those more *cantabile* and easier, and I must say their playing was exquisite. In those days amateurs had not risen to such a pitch of excellence—at least it was very rare, and this was really quite unusual, especially for such young girls.

It was the same Miss Stowe who sat on Bach's knee and played to the Queen when six years old.

Among our guests were some of the Prebends, Richard and William Roberts, sons of the Provost of Eton, Mr. Hopkins, and the Miss Guards and their younger sister Mrs. Graham of Turnham Green, the Lowrys, an Irish family who took the house at the corner of Hart Street to educate their sons at Eton, the young men being very prepossessing, and the family fairly agreeable, and some others.

The Stowes were soon sought after, as they took their entertainment with them. They chiefly played at parties Hulmandel's lessons—the fine octave one and others, and several sonatas that were very interesting, where the accompaniment was not obbligato. Mr. Papendiek often played with them, taking the violin parts on the flute, and the Rev. C. Bostock would join in trios with his violoncello.

So we were proceeding, when a message came from the Queen to ask if the Miss Stowes would play to the King during the evening concerts. Mrs. Stowe answered that she would bring her daughters at any time that the Queen would command, but requested that they might have a few days' notice.

About Michaelmas a most agreeable family of the name of Jervois took the house near Windsor Bridge, lately occupied by the Cheshire family. On the death of Mr. Cheshire, the barge master and coal merchant, More, had purchased the premises. Joining to the dwelling house, he built a neat and appropriate house for himself, his wife and daughter, intending to let the large one, which was now taken by Mr. Jervois. He (More) opened a handsome gateway which led to the wharf by the river, where he erected stabling for all his horses. Having a part of the King's coal business, he raised over the gates the Royal arms, handsomely emblazoned. Much to his credit, he did not, by repair, spoil the elegant suite of rooms in the house now let, nor destroy its conveniences. The drive to the door also remained unaltered, with the same double gates, only now there was a crown upon the lamps instead of Mr. Cheshire's crest. The principal rooms, two large drawing-rooms and a billiard-room, opened upon a lawn which ran down to the river's edge, encircled by shrubbed walks. On the Eton side of the river, just opposite, were the extensive premises of Piper, the boat builder, who, for the accommodation of the Etonians, combined every business and pleasure that related to water.

The Cheshires had been people of immense wealth, and Mr. and Mrs. Cheshire were considered one of the finest couples of their day. According to the habits of the leading gentry of that time, they drove their coach and six; four in hand, and a postboy on the leaders. They had one son and four daughters, fine and very pleasing women. The Earl Fauconberg, while at Eton, became enamoured of Jane, the eldest, and when of age made her an offer of marriage, to which her father incautiously gave his consent, and received the young earl at his house. As soon as the family on his side were apprised of this, they immediately broke off the match, and married the young man to another lady. The title came to him while still a minor.

Mr. Cheshire was of strong government principles, and took a lead and an interest in county business, and in all meetings, committees, and other occasions where he might be useful.

In those days the Guards never left London, but for the officers of any other regiments who were quartered at Windsor, there was always a seat at

Mr. Cheshire's table, and access to his billiard-room. The establishment was one of gaiety and hospitality.

Alas! the second daughter, Penelope, fell a victim to this somewhat imprudent open-heartedness and feeling of confidential kindness. The Lothario disappeared, and the poor victim never after joined the most private society, nor scarcely even her own family. The child died in infancy, and the young mother then devoted herself to constant employment, both ornamental and useful. She took the air only in the shrubbed walks, with her attendant, either early in the morning or at dusk.

When we came to Windsor in 1785, the splendour had already ceased with the Cheshire family; no longer any carriage, few servants, no company. The Miss Cheshires were nevertheless to be seen at given hours, on the walks and at the lounge in Delavaux's shop, showily dressed, but I should conclude in very different style to heretofore.

When I asked Miss Delavaux where the fourth daughter was, that I had never by any chance seen, she told me in her very shop the whole story as I have narrated it, adding that when Captain Grant found how matters were, he of course retired.

I also heard from Miss Delavaux the particulars of a terrible poisoning catastrophe that had occurred several years before, by which Mr. Cheshire nearly lost his life.

At a county meeting held at the 'Castle Inn,' Salt Hill, he was one of the three-and-twenty saved from the poison taken at the dinner which was always given on that occasion. Nineteen died, many of them even before they could reach their homes, and the cause could not be ascertained.

One circumstance that they endeavoured to impress, was that one of the victims, a commissioner of roads, had, upon delivering up his accounts, taken two glasses of wine with the other gentlemen, but had not dined with them or eaten in the house. After long investigation, therefore, it was concluded that the cause of this most appalling catastrophe must have been from drawing the Madeira too near the finings, as they could not trace it to anything else.

Of course the house was done for, and the landlord dying soon after, they could scarcely find buyers for his goods, stock, &c. Mrs. Partridge, the widow, and her three daughters took a house at Hammersmith, on the high road, and opened a school for young ladies, which was very prosperous.

The widow, on her death-bed, said that as she considered it right to disclose the secret of the poisoning now that it could no longer hurt any individual, and was at the time purely accidental, she would confess that it arose from the turtle having been left

in the stewpans cold, and then heated afresh for the
dinner. The cook, renowned for the dressing of this
favourite luxury, came down from London late the
evening before, expressly for this purpose. He said
that as the turtle was better for long stewing, he
should do it through the night, during which time he
would be preparing various other dainties. He did
not keep to his word. He slept, let the fire out, and
heated the turtle soup up again without removing it
from the pan.

On the alarm of illness being given, the husband
flew to the cellar, the wife to the kitchen, where she
at one glance perceived the cause. From the acids
used in dressing the turtle, the pan was covered with
verdigris. When she showed it to the cook, he said
he was not aware of harm, so she screened him.
One or two other dishes were impregnated with the
same deadly gris or poison, but I did not hear
whether the pans were of bell-metal, or of copper
tinned and worn. Such risks do we run !

I cannot quite reconcile to my mind Mrs. Partridge not having exposed the fellow at the time, for
the good of the living, and as some satisfaction to
the relatives and friends of the deceased, whose sufferings, and the manner of the death of many of
them, were horrible, baffling all description. The
commissioner, who was supposed not to have eaten
in the house, had, Mrs. Partridge acknowledged,

dined freely, before he went in with his accounts, upon the dishes as they came out from the dining-room.

It was undoubtedly a terrible calamity, and many were still living, at the time of which I am writing, who had been connected by ties of relationship or of friendship with those who were so suddenly, and in such an awful manner, removed from all who held them dear.

After the death of Mr. Cheshire, the family took a house in the suburbs with a good garden, and although they lived in complete retirement, there was in the establishment the appearance of a dis-tinguished family. Earl Fauconberg's regiment was at length ordered to take the Windsor duty. The lady he had married had died within two or three years, and on his arrival at Windsor he asked if the Cheshires would receive him. They did, and the offer of marriage to the daughter was again made, and accepted. Whether Mrs. Cheshire lived long enough to witness the wedding, I do not recollect, but at any rate she had the assurance that it really would take place this time.

When Lady Fauconberg was presented at Court, I was in the King's presence chamber, especially to see her pass. I had an interest in her from their having been so long opposite neighbours, and always friendly in their way of speaking to me and my children. The two younger sisters were in the presence chamber too, and we got together. As my lady passed, I received a gracious bow and smile from her—always a gratification for the bystanders to see—so silly are we on these points!

Lord Fauconberg now had hope of an heir, having by his previous marriage had only two daughters, the Ladies Charlotte and Elizabeth Bellasyse, but this hope was not fulfilled.

On the marriage of Lady Elizabeth Waldegrave with the Earl of Cardigan, Lady Charlotte Bellasyse was appointed lady of the bedchamber to the elder Princesses in her place, and Lady Elizabeth Bellasyse married Sir George Wombwell. He was brought up at Eton, and was intimate with the Cheshires, and Maria was invited to spend the summer with them. She lengthened her visit over Lady Wombwell's confinement, when it was discovered that she had taken her ladyship's place more than fully. She was then, of course, hurled from the house, and sent back to her own in a manner to carry distress with it, as may be imagined.

After these events the family seemed to fall back into retirement. The Fauconbergs were occasionally seen at Court, and heard of in the Royal mansion by polite abuse. Penelope Cheshire died soon after her mother, and about a year since (I am writing in 1837), I read in the newspaper of Margaret's death, with the observation attached, that ' she was the last member of that once distinguished family.'

The Jervois's engaged the house for three years on their arrival from Armagh in Ireland, for the purpose of educating their son at Eton, after which he was to go to one of the universities, to study for the Established Protestant Church, as it was the mutual wish of all concerned that he should be a clergyman. The two daughters were interesting, clever young women, and the mother all that was amiable. Mr. Jervois was perfectly a gentleman, and a musical amateur.

He soon found us out, and calling by chance, took me over to the ladies to introduce us to each other. The house was charmingly fitted up, and with taste. The drawing and dining-rooms remained as before, but the billiard-room was now appropriated to music, and was delightful.

Mrs. Jervois expressed a desire to be on friendly terms with us as neighbours, and said she would feel grateful to anyone who would indulge the musical follies of her husband, who having been thrown out of his employment by the arrangements for their son, now made music his chief amusement, and almost occupation. She told me all her household arrangements, and hours of meals, &c., to induce me to feel that we should give them greater pleasure by coming than by staying away. We proposed another party to introduce to them the King's band, particularly the Griesbachs, whose quartett playing was a treat seldom to be heard.

Soon after this, the Jervois's gave a party in return, and then followed a concert at the Gibbons's, where all the performers were to be amateurs. The Miss Stowes played, and a daughter of Widow Foster. She was a fine girl about eighteen, but stiffish. She played the first part of the first movement of Hulmandel's octave lesson with great confidence, then got up and said 'she was accustomed to a harpsichord.' The fact was, the concluding part was too difficult. There was also some good singing, both solos and glees. Ices were not in those days given in our rank, but refreshments of cakes and beverages, and these in profusion.

The next thing was the grand summons to the Lodge for the Stowes to play at the King's concert. I thought their muslin frocks would do—but no, they were to be new gauze, cheap of course, but were to be neatly made and a good fit. Easy, *juste* bodies, with a satin cord to mark the bib shape in front, and so arranged as not to cut the stuff, for letting out or fashioning the next spring. They looked very genteel and smart. Under the frocks they wore gauze handkerchiefs laid quite across in front, small bustles, and a few well placed bows.

Mr. Papendiek asked the Queen's permission for

our pianoforte to be sent, as the girls made such a point of it. Her Majesty consented, and also that Rodgers should be permitted to tune; his first introduction at Court.

The evening arrived. The Queen spoke to the mother in the music-room with her usual affability. After the first overture, the equerry, Major Price, handed Miss Stowe to the instrument. The Queen had a chair placed to her right, and spoke encouragingly to her.

Then Miss Stowe, without thinking, although we had endeavoured so thoroughly to instruct her, sat down before she was commanded to do so, to the horror of her mother, who wisely stood still. The Major quickly rushed up, but the Queen feelingly said, 'Let her sit; they are ready to begin.'

We had fixed upon the lovely lesson of Kozebuch in G. Every movement is so perfect. George and Henry Griesbach did justice to their sweet accompaniment, but Miss Stowe they thought rather flippant, and she did not make the impression expected. The younger sister, Bell, in the first act, played that enchanting lesson of Mozart with only a violin accompaniment, and this performance, too, was rather tedious, though well executed by the mild player.

In the second act Miss Stowe played the second

concerto of Handel. The King proposed her playing it upon the harpsichord, as Mr. Papendiek had previously so entreated her to do, as being more suitable to that ancient music, but she begged to be allowed to use the pianoforte, and so it was determined.

The King kept repeating, ' Not so fast.' George Griesbach pulled in, but the young lady rushed on. Again no great pleasure expressed.

Bell was now to make the finish, and played a very favourite sonata of Pleyell's, with an obbligato accompaniment for the flute. Mr. Papendiek being at leisure, as tea was over and the card parties formed, took the part himself. Now so pleased was the Queen that she laid down her cards, had a chair brought, and desired the variation movement to be repeated. Poor things, this brightened up the scene, which had gone off despairingly heavy. The Queen being very partial to Pleyell's music, gave rise to his composing that fine set of sonatas with flute accompaniment, dedicated to her Majesty.

At supper the Queen asked Mr. Papendiek some particulars about the Stowes, and he told her the whole history of their family, with which she was much struck, and said, ' Thank you for this very interesting account. The girls are fine, prepossessing young people, and the mother has the greatest merit for what she has already done, and for her future intentions.' This conversation was balm to the mind of Mrs. Stowe when Mr. Papendick repeated it to her. Miss Planta also, who had been permitted by the Queen to stand by Mrs. Stowe in the music-room, with Miss Burney, extolled the young ladies, so the accounts spread were highly in their favour, and the visit therefore proved most gratifying.

Mrs. Jervois now proposed giving the large entertainment that she had talked of, and I suggested that our instrument had better go direct to their house from the Lodge. She asked me to go over and dine, which I did, and found cards ready to go out for a general invitation—the invitation specifying no entertainment, merely to a grand drum. The night arrived; everybody came. Mrs. Batty and Susan Canon, meeting me in the cloak-room, said, ' My dear, what a pity you do not play cards; we should wish to visit you.' I answered, ' My trumps are at home; we may name them as we please.'

I went through the parties with my muslin, varying the capes. This night they were purple, with a bandeau in my hair of that becoming colour. In the large drawing-room, adjoining the dining-parlour, there were eight card-tables; middle room for company unoccupied; music-room, of course, for music. Miss Stowe opened the concert; her sister also played, and all the performances were excellent, both instrumental and vocal, professional and amateur.

The Griesbachs' quartett playing was exquisite, and Miss Stowe durst not be flippant. Among other pretty things Dr. Herschel asked me to take a part in a catch of his, which went off excellently well.

Tea was handed when we first arrived, and refreshments two or three times during the evening. A tray with compartments of cakes, home made; a tray with compartments of sandwiches; a tray with every sort and size of glasses; a tray with the beverages, in pint decanters labelled, and cold water, and also hot water in a handsome pitcher, with real silver top, hinged, pounded and lump sugar, &c. A good supper for the performers, professional and amateur, which Mr. Papendiek joined on returning from the Lodge, finished this complete evening's entertainment, with which I believe everyone was pleased and gratified. I made a good supper of sandwiches and a glass of wine, and then ' sedaned ' home to my little nursling.

Salomon, during the autumn, came down once or twice to meet Dr. Shepherd, his patron, and with Charles Bostock he was always as a brother. He slept at our house to enjoy his coffee breakfast, to have his shoes buckled and his cravat tied. No one in our rank then travelled with a servant. It necessitated vails, certainly, to those who waited on one, but these served as an encouragement to civility, and when we received guests, we were spared the trouble of accommodating and endeavouring to please that unconscionable race of people.

Thus ended our pleasures and amusements for some time.

END OF THE FIRST VOLUME.

S & H

PRINTED BY
SPOTTISWOODE AND CO., NEW-STREET SQUARE
LONDON